PRAISE FOR LAST PLACE CALLED H

"Betsy Hartmann's novel is a beau
a setting that feels like a character
—READERS' FAV

"This is a novel about the complexities of love and loyalty, and the heart-wrenching choices people are sometimes forced to make. . . . While *Last Place Called Home* offers fresh insights into the tragedies of the drug crisis, it also celebrates the restorative power of nature and the surprising resilience people find within themselves."

—CORINNE DEMAS, author of *The Road Towards Home* and *The Writing Circle*

"Hartmann masterfully brings home the national opioid crisis to a declining town where loyalty is a dangerous concept and no one—even the law—can be trusted. The heartbreaking desperation of its mothers, lovers, and friends will shake your conscience and keep you guessing until the very last page."

—MARISA LABOZZETTA, author of *A Day in June*

"The emotional grip never lets go, and the plot is as believable as it is intricate and dramatic. . . . *Last Place Called Home* brings to life the truth of a community in all its human aspects, and delivers a visceral understanding important to our divided times."

—ROGER KING, author of *Love and Fatigue in America* and *A Girl from Zanzibar*

"Filled with characters whose fate you will long ponder, *Last Place Called Home* is both a compelling read and a plea for community engagement in countering the opioid crisis."

—MICHAEL KLARE, defense correspondent for *The Nation*

"An intimate page-turner that reveals the relation between drug policy and the economy of despair. . . . a nail-biting drama of loss and redemption."

—BILL FRIED, drug policy activist and former staff member at Law Enforcement Action Partnership

PRAISE FOR OTHER BOOKS BY BETSY HARTMANN

The Truth about Fire

"Two unlikely heroines who converge to expose a bioterrorist plot inspired by neo-Nazis and implemented by cultists on Michigan's Upper Peninsula are the protagonists of this absorbing first novel. . . . Hartmann proves herself an able storyteller, creating fearless, idealistic, knowledgeable, and opinionated female characters who make difficult choices and reluctantly get involved in dangerous enterprises to protect themselves, their families, and their communities."

—*PUBLISHERS WEEKLY*

"This politically charged thriller unfolds through the perspectives of two very different women enmeshed in the same terrifying situation. . . . These well-drawn women lend real drama to a tense, multilayered story."

—*BOOKLIST*

Deadly Election

"Betsy Hartmann has written an elegant mystery story, a political thriller that confronts the darkest imponderables of our post-9/11 world. *Deadly Election* is that rare thing: a thoughtful page-turner."

—KAI BIRD, coauthor of Pulitzer Prize winner *American Prometheus: The Triumph and Tragedy of J. Robert Oppenheimer*

"Betsy Hartmann has done something extraordinary: created a virtual-reality version of the Bush administration that is both utterly convincing and even more bone-chillingly scary than the real thing."

—ANTHONY GIARDINA, author of *White Guys* and *Recent History*

The America Syndrome: Apocalypse, War, and Our Call to Greatness

"In an insightful, crisply written blend of memoir, social history, and political theory, Hartmann shows how the prospect of the imminent end of days has been used for centuries to justify almost any American action—and feed the destructive conviction that this country has a special mission of salvation."

—CHARLES MANN, author of *1491* and *The Wizard and the Prophet*

". . . a desperately needed, incisive analysis of dystopian beliefs that undergird white supremacy in the US."

—LORETTA ROSS, author of *Radical Reproductive Justice*

LAST PLACE CALLED HOME

A NOVEL

Betsy Hartmann

SHE WRITES PRESS

Published 2024
Printed in the United States of America
Print ISBN: 978-1-64742-642-2
E-ISBN: 978-1-64742-643-9
Library of Congress Control Number: 2024901818

For information, address:
She Writes Press
1569 Solano Ave #546
Berkeley, CA 94707

Interior Design by Tabitha Lahr

She Writes Press is a division of SparkPoint Studio, LLC.

To those we have lost and
those who are trying to make a difference

PART ONE

Diamond River

I

ON AN EVENING IN LATE APRIL, Laura Everett drives straight from her job at the *Stanton Gazette* to the old elementary school a few miles away. She pulls into the deserted parking lot, turns off the ignition, and reaches for her cell to check messages. After giving up smoking, she needs something to do with her nervous energy, but unlike cigarettes, the phone doesn't give her any pleasure. Nine times out of ten, the message is from her son, Donnie, and he's in trouble again.

No messages. Good. She reaches for the bag of almonds she keeps in the glove compartment. Dinner will be late tonight, and she's already hungry. As she pops a nut into her mouth, she glances up at the abandoned three-story school with its boarded-up windows and sagging roof. Except for one freshly painted, yellow F-word, the graffiti on the sides has faded into indistinguishable marks. Like a grandparent's slow death, the school's decline saddens her. She can remember walking up and down the stairs, the wood on the banisters worn so smooth it felt like touching mother-of-pearl. The classrooms had high ceilings and big windows, drafty but full of light. The new elementary school is charmless, a concrete box surrounded by bald playing fields. Stanton hardly has enough tax revenue to pay the teachers, much less keep up the turf.

She checks her watch: 6:25 p.m.. The other birders will arrive in a few minutes. These outings are the one thing she looks forward to every week. It's the art of waiting she appreciates—the way their guide, Nate Waterman, has them stand quietly in forests and fields, gazing up, ears keen, binoculars at the ready, patience rewarded by a sudden bird call or fluttering of wings. And if she's honest with herself, she just likes being in Nate's presence. Maybe something's growing between them—she can't quite tell.

A steel-gray Volvo turns into the lot. Like her, its occupants, Keith and Emily Addison, are always a few minutes early. The couple moved to the area after Keith retired from teaching high school biology in Worcester. He now puts his energy into leading a battle over a large tract of forest land on the edge of town that Sullivan Lumber Supply is threatening to sell to a Boston developer. Laura's working on a story about it for the newspaper.

The Volvo pulls up next to her, and Keith rolls down his window. He looks agitated, rushed, as if he drove through heavy traffic instead of country roads to get here. "Is this the right place?" he asks. "Where are the others?"

"We're early," Laura says calmly.

"Right on time by my watch."

"Then they're late."

He seems perplexed by the reply. "Doesn't really matter," he says. "Sunset's not till seven thirty. We're going to be standing out in the cold for too long as it is."

Laura nods, and he rolls up the window and says something to his wife, who smiles furtively at her.

By the time Nate arrives in his truck, six cars have assembled. He's wearing his typical uniform of an old bomber jacket, flannel shirt, and corduroy pants with ridges worn down at the knees. He isn't classically handsome—his torso is too long for his short legs, and his face is scarred from adolescent acne—but he has fine blue eyes. He used to be much talked about and pursued by the area's single women, but as far as Laura knows, no one succeeded in getting him to bed. A rumor once circulated that he was gay, but there was no proof of it. A closet priest was the ultimate conclusion, and her friend Megan dubbed him St. No Fucking Francis of Assisi. Laura suspects depression by the worry lines etched around his eyes. Often his smile is forced, but lately not with her.

To those in the birding group, he's simply the best naturalist around, world-class really. It's a mystery why he moved all the way to the middle of Massachusetts from southern Texas, where his work at a wildlife refuge helped bring the whooping crane back from the brink of extinction. He wrote a book about it but nothing more after that. Although she's curious about why he stopped writing, Laura has never had the nerve to ask him.

Leaning against the side of the truck, he begins describing the purpose of the evening's trip, to see the dance of the American woodcock. He explains how at dusk in mating season, the male woodcock calls repeatedly and then rises in circles high into the air, still whistling, until it flies suddenly back to earth. He reads a long passage from what he says is his favorite book, Edward Forbush's *A Natural History of American Birds*. His copy is old, the cover frayed and water-stained. He admires the late ornithologist who by the age of sixteen was already the curator of birds at the natural history museum in Worcester.

As usual Nate reads spiritedly like a storyteller who takes pleasure in each turn of phrase, each anticipatory pause. His voice has the precise diction of the private-school elite, modulated by a slight trace of Texas drawl. Everyone is quiet, even seven-year-old Jeff, the only child in the group, who seems mesmerized. "It sounds more dramatic than what you'll actually be able to see with your naked eye," Nate advises as he closes the book. "Unfortunately, it will be getting dark, so you'll have to use your imaginations as well as your binoculars. Anyone want to sit up front with me in the cab? It's getting chilly. Cora?"

Cora, the oldest birder, walks with a cane but hates to be singled out. "No, no, I'm fine."

"C'mon now. I don't want to sit all alone."

"If you insist."

The rest of them bundle into the back of the truck, which is outfitted with benches along the sides. It's probably illegal to transport people this way, but the local cops have worse things to worry about, and Nate largely sticks to the back roads. The wind is cold, so Laura zips up her jacket and wraps her scarf around her neck. Even at the end of April, New England spring is a daytime affair, and winter returns each evening with a vengeance. Nate drives west out of town where a few box stores—Walmart, Stop & Shop, Family Dollar—look less than splendid in their isolation. There isn't enough economic activity in Stanton for a proper mall. The town hangs by the single thread of the Diamond Tool and Die factory, and the only growth industry is drugs.

Past the stores and the last stoplight, Nate accelerates on the empty road. The wind is fierce now, and Laura pulls her scarf tighter. After a few miles, he turns onto a dirt road and follows it until it comes to Hawkins Meadow, gateway to a wetland ideal for birding. Nate offers his hand as they climb out of the truck.

The group crosses the meadow and then enters a path into the brush. A few mosquitoes buzz around Laura's head, but it's too cold for them to bite. The sun has just sunk below the horizon, and pink light suffuses the evening mist. The glow is so thick and rich the figures in front of her seem to encounter resistance as they move through it. That's what she would capture if she still painted: the resistance, as if some force were pushing them back. It would require the boldness of oil paints, not watercolors.

They reach a clearing where they stand in a semicircle, all except for Cora, who sits in a collapsible chair Nate always carries for her. She once confessed to Laura that she has bad eyes but comes along to hear the bird calls. The ground is damp, and there are a few complaints about cold feet. Jeff's already bored, so his father, Bill, tries to placate him with the offer of snacks. "We have some time yet," Nate says preemptively. "I got you out here a little too early. Take a few minutes to wander around—see if you find anything interesting."

Laura peels off from the group, walking toward a vernal pond where she once collected frog eggs with Donnie. The pond is much smaller than she remembered, maybe because back then, she viewed it through her young son's eyes. She did that a lot—tried to see the world like a child. She magnified everything. Ponds became lakes, hills grew into mountains. The paintings she produced then were among her best. She used large canvases, loose brushstrokes. Portrait of the artist as a young mother, or the paradoxical freedom of constraint.

The pond is now brown and murky, foul smelling. An empty beer can floats on the muck. "So what have you discovered here?" Nate's voice startles her. He's never approached her alone before.

She points at the can. "Tell me, is that a native or alien species?"

He chuckles and then grabs a long stick and prods the can toward shore. He picks it out of the water and, after shaking it dry, sticks it in his jacket pocket. He gives her a mischievous grin as if trying to implicate her in a secret game.

"People will think you snuck off to have a drink," she says.

"Wish I could have."

"Does it get tiring taking us on these outings?"

"No, of course not," he replies almost too quickly. "I wouldn't do it if I didn't like it." He looks hard at her as if trying to bring home the point, and then his face softens into an expression she's been hoping for. When she smiles back, he touches her arm. "I guess we should be getting back," he says.

The group's eyes are on them as they walk back together. Nate's attention is coveted, she knows. "Any minute now," he announces, resuming his position in the center of the group.

"It's so dark, how will we be able to see the bird?" Emily asks.

"Like I said, you'll have to use both your eyes and your imagination." He tilts his head and raises a finger. "Hear that?" From about thirty feet away in the brush comes the nasal *peent* of a woodcock. "It'll take off soon," Nate whispers. In the dusky sky, the bird appears as a dark speck, a piece of leaf defying gravity and spinning upward higher and higher. Laura catches it in her vision, then loses it, then catches it again on its descent as it chirps melodically before it plummets to the ground.

A few people complain they couldn't see or hear it. "Wait a minute and you'll have another chance," Nate tells the group. "Now listen. . . ."

What they hear instead is the ring of Laura's cell, canned salsa music to signal calls from Donnie. How stupid, she thinks—she forgot to mute it, a major strike against her. She walks away from the group, fumbling in her purse until she finds the phone. "What do you want, Donnie?" she asks irritably.

"Mrs. Everett?" a woman says.

"Yes," she replies cautiously.

"I'm calling from the hospital on your son's phone. Don't worry—he's going to be all right. The doctors are just stitching up a minor wound in his side."

"What happened?" she asks, barely able to control the shaking in her voice.

"He was stabbed superficially in a fight. The boy he was with is in worse shape."

"Is it Ricky Gillen?"

"We're not at liberty to give out his name."

"Please tell Donnie I'll be there in about twenty minutes."

Returning to the group, she lets the birders know her son is in the hospital, and they gather around to comfort her.

She's grateful for their sympathy but surprised by it too—she doesn't know any of them very well. Nate insists that they leave immediately. On the ride to the elementary school lot, she sits up front with him and Cora. They try to engage her, but by this point she's feeling stunned and unresponsive. She musters a quick thank-you as she departs the truck for her car.

Adrenaline finally hits as she drives to the hospital. Parked by the emergency entrance is a police car that looks like Uncle Jack's. Sure enough, he's waiting in the lobby for her, feeding coins into the soda machine. After a Diet Coke rolls out with a bang, he grabs it and pops the top. The chief wanted to send Tommy, Jack says, but he insisted on coming instead. She thanks him—Tommy is mean, combative, and on the make, the opposite of a good neighborhood cop like Jack. "Donnie's okay," he assures her. "Go see him, and then I want to talk to you."

"Is Ricky okay? It is Ricky, isn't it?"

He nods jadedly. "Of course it's Ricky. They transferred him to Worcester by ambulance. He needs some surgery, but he's not in critical condition."

She finds Donnie in a cubicle off the emergency room, hooked to an IV and so drowsy from painkillers he's barely aware of her presence. The young woman doctor on duty pulls down the sheet to show Laura the bandage on his side. "He received several puncture wounds," she explains, "but fortunately, none of them are very deep. We gave him a tetanus shot and stitched them up, and he's receiving an intravenous antibiotic now. Our only worry is infection. We'd like to keep him in the hospital overnight, but by tomorrow afternoon he should be ready to go home. At home you'll need to dress his wounds and make sure he takes his antibiotics. You can do that?" She looks straight at Laura then as if to judge her competence. Laura's used to that now. People in authority tend to assume you're a screwup if you have a screwed-up kid.

"Yes, I can do that," she states with an edge to her voice.

"Good."

"When can he go back to school?"

"A week of rest should be enough."

After the doctor leaves, Laura sits for a while with Donnie, stroking his forehead, which is damp but not feverish. How little I get to touch him now, she thinks—it takes something bad like this. In the dimple at the center of his chin is a dark shadow of facial hair. He just turned seventeen, and his face is changing from boy to man. He looks more like his father every day: the same firm jaw, aquiline nose, even the start of a furrow between the brows. His eyes are the hazel color of hers though. "I'm sorry, Mom," he murmurs, opening them slightly. "I was just trying to help Ricky. Is he dead?"

"No, no."

"Are you sure?"

"They've taken him to Worcester."

"But maybe they're lying—they don't want me to know he's dead."

"Jack saw him leave in the ambulance."

There's no look of relief on Donnie's face. She wonders about that afterward, wonders if subconsciously he wishes Ricky had died. Or is it she who wishes that?

She stays with him until he falls back to sleep, and then returns to the lobby. Jack accompanies her to her car, where they sit inside in the streetlight's sallow glow. "I don't know how much you know about the fight," he begins.

"Nothing," she says, holding her hands on the steering wheel as if she's driving.

"It's beyond what we've seen before."

"Because of the knives?"

"We've seen knives before."

"Then what do you mean?"

"We think Ricky's being recruited by a gang."

"You're kidding."

"Afraid not. Some members of a Boston gang have been checking out Stanton, looking to move some of their operations outside the city to escape the heat. First step is to recruit young kids like Ricky. That's trouble enough, but there's a rival gang in Springfield that doesn't like them intruding on their territory. That's what the fight was about—who controls the drug corridors up to the New Hampshire and Vermont borders. The battle starts by culling the weak. Ricky would be dead if Donnie hadn't been there to provide some diversion."

"What happens now?"

"Maybe make an arrest or two, but only if the Springfield police feel like cooperating. They've got bigger fish to fry than a knife fight forty miles away in Stanton."

"And the gang members here?"

"We're working on it—that's all I can say."

"What should I do about Donnie, Jack?"

"I want to talk to him—I'll come around to the house tomorrow after he gets out of the hospital."

"No charges?"

"Not this time. He didn't do anything except try to protect his friend. That's not a crime, but he's marked now on their radar screen. Do you understand that, Laura? We've just entered a whole new ball game, and it's a lot more dangerous. Tell him that for me, will you?" He opens the door to get out but sits for a moment more as if contemplating his exit strategy. Approaching sixty, he's overweight, short of breath, at risk of heart disease. He grasps the doorframe to pull himself up.

"Thanks, Jack," she says, wishing she could give him a hug, but in uniform he's never physically affectionate.

"Thanks for what? For the bad news?"

"For caring about Donnie."

He leans back into the car. "I promised your dad I'd look after him, but frankly, I don't know how much more I can do.

I'm retiring in six months—I'm a lame duck, Laura. Tommy's taking over the kid beat."

On the ride home she turns on the radio but switches it off after only a moment or two. She needs silence. She needs the meadow again, the crazy flight of a besotted bird. Fear will overwhelm her soon, she knows. No matter how high she turns up the heat or piles on the covers, she'll shiver all night. At least Donnie's safe for the moment. How safe is she?

Before pulling into the driveway, she checks the street for strange cars. The neighborhood is in the western part of town, a 1960s suburban development with most of the houses set close together. Theirs is the original farmhouse that Mike's parents made a down payment on as a wedding present. Mike's been dead for seven years now, but she still thinks of it as theirs together. It's at the end of the block, where a half acre of lawn and a tall evergreen hedge seclude it from the neighbors. Normally she appreciates the privacy, but not tonight.

She unlocks the front door and disarms the alarm system. It's relatively new, installed after a rash of break-ins in the area. Loneliness hits her as she enters the empty living room. Donnie's bedroom is located just off it—he recently colonized the den to put a staircase between him and her. She's come to depend on his presence there, irritating as it often is. Tonight there's no light leaking from his room, no blasting music, no aroma of pot smoke. She knows she should call her mom and sister, Nina, in Florida but can't bring herself to do it—they'll be too upset to be helpful. Instead she checks her voice mail. Two messages. The first is from Ricky's older brother, Justin, who just reached the Worcester hospital. His mom wants Laura to know Ricky's in serious but stable condition after several blood transfusions. They'll update her tomorrow. The second is from Nate. He asks how Donnie is and tells her to call back if she needs any help.

She forces herself to eat a sandwich, washing it down with a cup of tea. The couch beckons—it would be so easy to collapse there, put her head in her hands, and cry. But what use would that be? Instead she sits down at the desk, where she googles gangs and Massachusetts on the internet. For over two hours she's rooted there until she can't keep her eyes open anymore and gives herself permission to go to bed.

DONNIE OPENS HIS EYES. His mom's gone. She must have left when he fell asleep. Blue lights blink, the IV machine clicks, but they make him feel even more alone. He stretches his left leg just a little bit. The wound is on the right and he doesn't want to feel it. He wants it to be outside his body, not inside. He never wants to see his own blood again or touch it. Touching it was the worst thing. His shirt was soaked with it.

He wants to forget but can't. Every time he wakes up, the scene plays in his head like he shot a video of it. Ricky taunts the guy threatening him with a knife. Donnie just wants to run, so he shouts for Ricky to follow. But then Ricky's down on the ground bleeding and the guy goes to stab him again. Donnie rushes over and lands a punch, but not hard enough. The guy still has the knife in his hand. He slashes at Donnie while the other two punks yell something like "Let's get the fuck out of here!" After they leave, Donnie crawls over to Ricky and dials 911. And then the screen goes dark. They say he was passed out when the ambulance came.

Let's get the fuck out of here.

But what if they're still around? What if they come looking for him? Talk their way into the hospital?

Why did his mom leave? She never gets when he needs her and when he doesn't. His dad would have known to stay all night.

2

THE BUZZER RINGS AT THE *Gazette* as Laura puts the finishing touches on the layout of the weekly edition. Not expecting any visitors, she doesn't feel like walking three flights down to unlock the front door. She's no believer in ghosts, yet the old mill building where she works spooks her with its labyrinth of dark narrow halls and back staircases. Last year she saw a rat in the bathroom.

When the weekly was a proper daily, it had its own small brick building across from the fire station. The sign outside, written in a big, chunky, reassuring cursive, gave it a certain retro charm. She misses it, misses her coworkers too. After the downsizing five years ago, everyone was laid off except for the editor, Frank Amato, and herself. Frank bought the paper for a pittance and stopped working except for soliciting ads from Rotary Club buddies and covering high school sports. With a few stringers and volunteers to help, she acts as chief reporter, designer, and editor while paid the same low salary she made before. And she has no real power either—Frank takes a perverse pleasure in ordering her around, inventing lines he forbids her to cross. She's sick of it but not sick enough to leave a steady job with benefits.

Maybe that's him at the door. He always forgets his keys.

The buzzer rings again, followed a few seconds later by the ding of an incoming text on her cell. She hopes it's not from Donnie—it's his first day back at school. With relief she sees the message is from Ricky's brother, Justin: Are you in the office? I see your car.

She hurries downstairs to let him in and gives him a hug in the lobby. Justin's an ice hockey star, the town's best in years, and that along with good grades won him a full scholarship to prestigious Williams College a couple of hours west of Stanton. Three years there have smoothed the last of his rough edges, and he could just as well come from a rich Boston suburb rather than an old factory workers' duplex in Stanton. She notices his preppy outfit of tan suede jacket, button-down shirt, and khakis. "We just brought Ricky home from the hospital," he tells her. "I'm driving back to college, but I wanted to talk to you first—if that's okay?"

"Of course it's okay. Does your mom know you're here?"

He shakes his head. "I wanted to speak to you alone."

"All right, we can go upstairs—no one's there."

In the office she clears a pile of papers off the couch and gestures for him to sit. Nervously he clasps and unclasps his hands, though his gaze is steady. In high school the right side of his face was slashed by a skate blade and the scar's still there, though less prominent than before. She's struck again by the unassuming kindness in his face. It's as if he expends all his meanness on the ice, slashing at the puck, slamming players into the boards, so that outside the rink he has the liberty to be gentle. "How are you?" she asks.

"Ricky's much better," he replies.

"No, how are *you*?"

He takes a moment to answer, as if it's a trick question. "Worried," he says at last. "That's why I came to see you."

"I'm worried too."

"I think Ricky's getting involved with a gang," he blurts. "A cop told me that might be the case."

"Ricky denies it, and Mom refuses to believe it. What does Donnie say?"

"He says he doesn't know, which is probably a lie. I can tell he's scared."

Justin removes his jacket and drapes it carefully on the arm of the couch. His neck is thicker and his shoulders broader than she remembers. There's the slightest gleam of sweat on his forehead. "Do you think I should stay in Stanton this summer?" he asks. "The semester ends in a couple of weeks, so I could come home then. But my biology professor wants me to go to Peru with him for the summer. He comes from there and is doing research on traditional medicines in the Andes. Did my mom tell you I switched majors? I got sick of computer science and am doing premed. I want to be a doctor."

Angie hasn't said a word about it, but then Laura and she rarely speak anymore. Laura's called her a couple of times in the last week to ask about Ricky's recovery, but their conversations have been short, to the point, awkwardly polite. "That's great, Justin," she says.

He blushes slightly. "My professor will be upset if I don't go to Peru. He already bought the plane tickets—we're supposed to leave right after classes end. But I could stay here to keep an eye on Ricky. Coach would be happy—he wants me to work at his hockey camp, and he's afraid I'm going to get sick or something in Peru and miss out on the season."

"Does your mom want you to stay?"

"I don't know. I didn't ask her."

"So you're asking me?"

"I guess."

Laura played the mentor role with Justin once before when she encouraged him to accept the Williams offer and play hockey at the Division III level, rather than be a walk-on at Division I UMass. He was intimidated by the prospect of the hard academics and privileged kids at Williams, so she gave him a lot of pep talks about how this was the opportunity of a lifetime. Is Peru such an opportunity? She doesn't know, but she wants him to get out of Stanton and stay safe, so she advises him to go. The look of relief on his face tells her it's what he wants to hear. "Don't worry, I'll keep an eye out while you're away," she reassures him, "and let you know if anything happens."

"I will worry."

"Leave that to me and your mom."

His laugh is bitter. "My mom lives in la-la land when it comes to Ricky. She thinks he was knifed because he beat some kids from Springfield in a pickup basketball game. That's what he told her, and what he says is always the truth. He's always the victim, you know. She doesn't want to see how he's screwing up. She turns everything around to make Ricky look good." He pauses for a second. "Did you know he's been going out for a while with Rebecca Sullivan?"

"Mimi Sullivan's daughter?" she asks in disbelief. Rebecca's a beautiful girl, smart too, and belongs to an entirely different social class than Ricky—or Donnie for that matter.

"Yeah. Kids call her 'Royalty' behind her back. Mom despises her."

"Why? You'd think she'd be pleased."

"She thinks Ricky's playing the tough guy to impress her."

"Is that what you think?"

He shakes his head. "You know, my brother started getting into trouble way before Rebecca Sullivan. He's got a talent for it."

He leaves a few minutes later, promising to stop by in a couple of weeks when the semester is over. She hopes he'll go to Peru and resist the impulse to rescue his brother—he's done enough of that already. She'd like to know what Angie thinks, torn as she probably is between letting Justin leave town and wanting him to stay, but Angie no longer asks for her advice. They carefully measure the words between them like they're following a recipe for ending a friendship. Less butter, less sugar, less love.

After turning off the computer, Laura packs up her things, planning to get home early to make a nice dinner for Donnie. Maybe he's ready to turn over a new leaf. Yeah, right, she catches herself, wishful thinking again.

As Laura drives home, a memory comes of her own mom. She's sitting next to her in church, staring up at a painted crucifix and the blood dripping from Jesus's wounds. "Why can't he just get down?" Laura asks. She's only five or six, not yet schooled in the virtues of suffering.

"Because of the nails," her mom replies matter-of-factly.

"But if he's God, why can't he take out the nails?"

"He's the son of God, Laura, God made flesh."

"You mean he's still alive?"

"He's watching over us."

"From the cross?" she asks, horrified that no one has taken him down yet.

"No, no, that's just a statue. He's up there"—her mom points toward the ceiling—"in Heaven." Laura looks up, but all she sees is a dusty light fixture.

From that point on, she began to reject her mom's Irish Catholicism in favor of her dad's thinly disguised atheism. When she finally called her mom in Florida last night to tell her about Donnie getting stabbed, "I'll pray for him" was her response. And then as an afterthought: "I'll pray for you too, honey."

At home she makes ravioli and garlic bread, Donnie's favorite meal, but he doesn't have much appetite. He's still weak—his cheeks are colorless, and the dark circles under his eyes suggest he hasn't slept for days, though that's all he's been doing. "How was school?" she asks as he picks at his salad.

"Okay."

"Kids talk much about the fight?"

He pushes a green pepper slice to the edge of his plate. "Most people don't even know about it, Mom, and if they did, they wouldn't care."

"Why?"

"Because people mind their own business."

"It wasn't like that when I went to Stanton High. The place was a rumor mill."

"Things have changed."

"Apparently. Got much homework?" He shakes his head. "Don't you have work to make up?"

"I did it in study hall."

She knows he's lying, but doesn't feel like a fight. She slides the garlic bread toward him. "Here, have another piece."

He mumbles, "No thanks," and pushes back his chair, then tells her he's going over to see Ricky.

"I wish you wouldn't. . . ."

"Jesus, he just came home from the hospital, Mom."

"You didn't let me finish my sentence."

His chair scrapes the floor as he pushes back farther from the table. "Finish it then."

"I don't think you should be seeing so much of Ricky, Donnie. You know what Uncle Jack told you."

"Uncle Jack doesn't know shit."

"Don't talk about him that way. He's trying to help, you know."

"He doesn't know shit," Donnie repeats.

"You just don't want to believe Ricky might be involved with a gang."

"A few guys come into town and the cops call them a gang. They were just looking to have some fun, start a fight with the local boys."

"You call that fun? Ricky and you are lucky to be alive."

Donnie mutters an epithet under his breath, then gets up, grabs a sweatshirt, and heads toward the door. Summoning what little's left of her parental authority, she tells him she wants him back in an hour.

The first time she tried to separate him from Ricky was the year their grades sank and detentions soared. Angie and she were on the same page—no more movies or sleepovers or trips to the mall. But the more they tried to force the boys apart, the more time they spent communicating on social media. And then came the pandemic lockdown. To avoid being stuck in the house day after day with their sullen and fractious sons, Angie and she formed a pod, and the boys got even closer.

But there's more to it than that, she reflects now. They're like brothers or cousins, the ties that bind them are so tight. From time to time those ties may fray around the edges but not enough to snap. Is it because they're both fatherless? Both different in their own ways? As little boys, their imaginations were so lively and compatible—they loved to build things outside, not just forts but roads and tunnels for their toy trucks and rocky landscapes for their plastic dinosaurs. They took longer than other boys to be seduced by video games, preferring outside in nature to inside in front of a screen. Neither took to team sports. Each of them displayed a stubborn nonconformity she alternately admired and worried about. That same quality is still there, but it was cuter, and much safer, back then.

She starts washing the dishes, squeamish at the sight of the tomato sauce on Donnie's uneaten ravioli. The smell of garlic, usually welcome, turns her stomach. She thinks of her husband, Mike, and their early negotiations over who was going to do the dishes, take out the trash, change Donnie's diaper. He had to be talked into things, patiently, logically, but once convinced, he carried through. He was a model husband and dad, but that made it even harder when her love wore thin. She cheated on him once with a graduate student, Peter from

Brooklyn, who taught her studio art at UMass. He used to linger by her sketches of nudes, giving too much advice. In the afternoons, while Donnie was still at daycare, he advised her in bed too, instructing her on how to touch him in far too much detail. She ended the affair well before Mike got diagnosed with bone cancer, but she always associated one with the other until a therapist finally convinced her that cheating on your partner doesn't cause cancer. If it did, the human race would be close to extinction.

But she never got over the guilt, not really. She never had the nerve to tell Mike about Peter, so there was no apology, no forgiveness, no reckoning. Or maybe the guilt was really about something else—her failures as a mom. Parenthood came more easily to Mike. When Donnie was a baby, Mike could make him stop crying when she couldn't. And his silly rhymes and songs made Donnie giggle. Though she was envious of it, she loved listening to their laughter.

She wishes Mike were here now so she could share her worries about Donnie. He'd take out his guitar afterward and strum a few tunes to calm her down. Then he'd massage her shoulders, and she'd lean into him. Instead she leans against the sink, finally allowing herself a few weary tears.

Later as she waits up for Donnie, she falls asleep watching TV, waking with a jolt when the phone rings. It's Nate. He asks how Donnie is and then invites her to go kayaking Saturday morning on Lake Amity. Before she can think of a reason not to, she agrees.

DONNIE FINDS RICKY LYING on the couch, wearing pajama bottoms and an old white T-shirt, scrolling through channels on the TV. "Sox aren't playing tonight," Ricky says. Donnie nods and then just stands there waiting for a signal, but a signal of what? "My mom's working the late shift. Bring a joint?"

Donnie nods again. "Open the windows. If she smells it, I'll blame it on you."

"Thanks a lot," Donnie replies. After dealing with the windows, he sits down in the armchair next to the couch, lights the joint, and hands it to Ricky, who takes a couple of hits before giving it back to him.

"Better than the painkillers," Ricky says. "I don't know why people are into that shit. Makes you feel fucking weird."

"You feeling any better?"

"I guess so." Ricky's eyes settle back on the TV, a Jeep commercial with snow-capped mountains in the distance. He mutes the volume. "How was school?"

"Sucked. Tuna Melt called me into his office."

"What did he say?"

"Sorry to hear about the fight, welcome back, stay out of trouble. And then he handed me the underachiever bullshit again." Donnie takes a hit and then stubs out the joint, recalling the guidance counselor's words: *You're hurting your chances, young man. Mr. Robinson says you have an A on all your math tests, but you don't do your homework, so he'll have to give you a C on your report card. Don't you want to go to college? You're college material, Donald.* What Tuna Melt really wanted to say, Donnie figures, is *don't hang with that stupid fuckup, Ricky.*

"See Royalty?"

"In English class."

"She's still pissed off at me. Won't answer my texts."

Of course she won't, Donnie thinks. Ricky doesn't deserve her. He had sex with her a couple of times, then dumped her, and she started cutting herself again. Before the fight, he told Donnie he wanted a girl with bigger tits. No one should treat her that way. With Royalty you take the whole package. Donnie would take her any day, even with tiny tits and sliced-up arms. Even if her crown were busted into a thousand pieces. She deserves red carpet treatment, not getting screwed in the back of a car. His own car as it turns out. Ricky borrowed it without telling him what for. "You want to get back together?" Donnie asks.

"I don't know. Maybe. Tell her I say hi."

On the TV, another commercial comes on about pills to make your cock big. Donnie has the opposite problem. Too many hard-ons. He wishes he could laugh about it with Ricky, but his friend's eyes are closed now, and he's breathing slowly, falling asleep. There's so much more Donnie wants to talk to him about. For a start, why they got jumped, why Uncle Jack is talking all this trash about gangs. And he wants to know if Ricky's as scared as he is. Every time he goes out, he worries he could be jumped again. Sometimes he shakes so hard he makes excuses that he's cold. But he sweats too. His body temperature's never right anymore.

He and Ricky never used to keep secrets from each other, but something changed even before the fight, even before Royalty came into the picture. He gets up and gently lays a hand on his friend's forehead, which is cool to the touch. Ricky opens his eyes for a second and then closes them again. "Bye," Donnie whispers.

At home before he goes to bed, he works on a poem due tomorrow in English class. Ordinarily, he wouldn't care whether it was finished or not, but the teacher, Mr. H, likes his poems and encourages him to read them aloud in class. And Royalty praises them. This time the assignment's hard. Mr. H showed them a picture of a bombed-out building and some bodies trapped in the rubble. "Write something about war," he said. The dude is obsessed with war, tried to get the army recruiters removed from the cafeteria.

"For or against?" some kid asked.

"Whatever you want," Mr. H replied. "I won't judge the poem on your politics."

No words come to Donnie's mind. Maybe that's what he should write about. The silence of it, like snow falling. No ground underneath. Just falling and falling. The same feeling he had after he was stabbed.

3

THE TRUCK WINDOWS ARE wide open, letting in the first truly hot air of the season. Last night as the wind shifted to the south, Laura woke up sweating and kicked off her comforter. "Did you pack a bathing suit?" Nate asked when he swung by at ten to pick her up.

"Bathing suit? You must be kidding."

"It's almost the middle of May. Time to take the first plunge of the year—why not?"

And so she packs a suit and towel, though it seems ridiculous. Even the shorts she's wearing seem ridiculous. Her legs are alabaster white. Arms too. Nate's already tan from working outside, or maybe his skin is just darker than hers. When he lifts her kayak into the truck, she notices the taut muscles in his calves. She's noticing too much, too fast. Slow down, she warns herself. One warm day, and sex is on her brain. She hasn't slept with anyone since Martin, and that relationship ended almost two years ago. Who says she's going to sleep with St. No Fucking Francis of Assisi? But he noticed her too, didn't he? She made it easy for him, wearing a tight V-neck T-shirt that shows some cleavage.

She gazes out the window as Nate drives north out of town. The blur of red buds in the woods is turning a fuzzy green, and already the maples have sprouted tiny leaves. The time has come to go in search of trillium, her favorite wildflower, before its bloom passes. She likes the elegance of its three distinct maroon petals that turn shyly downward. Sometimes she stoops and bends the flower toward her as if forcing it to show its face.

"I saw two yellow warblers and a scarlet tanager in my yard yesterday." Nate breaks her reverie. "They're all coming back."

"I know," she responds. "This morning the wrens chattering outside my window woke me up."

"Better than an alarm clock."

"Much better."

They talk birds the rest of the way to Lake Amity, or rather he talks, and she listens. He's already asked about Donnie, and she's told him enough but not too much. Even if he likes kids—all the men she's dated claim to—a troubled teenager is a turnoff. Only Martin gave it a real shot. He tried hard with Donnie, and in the end it was his obsessiveness, not her insolent son, that doomed the relationship.

At the boat launch, Nate helps push her off into the water. She starts to paddle, but the motion feels awkward, and her shoulders strain. The last time she kayaked was when she scattered half her dad's ashes in the lake. The other half went to Florida with her mom. She's been wary of going to the lake ever since, worried that grief might overcome her.

Her dad loved Lake Amity. In the summer when her mother went to church, he went fishing, sometimes managing to spring Laura from Sunday school. Her older sister, Nina, refused to come—she was squeamish about worms on hooks and fish eyes. Unlike her, Laura felt an obligation to accompany him. She was the daughter who was supposed to be a son. Her dad never said that, of course, but she sensed it. And over time she came to like those canoe trips, not so much for the fishing but for the long comfortable silences that evolved between them. "Give the fishing rods to Donnie when he's old enough to want them," he told her before he died. When will that ever be?

Within a few minutes, Nate's way ahead of her. Trying to catch up only makes her stroke worse. Less effort is better, she reminds herself. Don't pull, push. Rhythm is everything. Don't think about your dad. Or Mike. Or Donnie. Don't think about anything.

Nate turns to look for her. She waves, and he waits for her to catch up. "Am I going too fast?" he asks as he pulls abreast.

"I'm just out of shape."

"No problem, I'll slow down." He gestures toward the ridge. "Just think, if Mimi Sullivan gets away with it, there'll be a bunch of ugly condos up there looking down on us."

Laura's heard that the developer plans to build a high-end retirement community of a hundred units or more. "Maybe Mimi won't sell," she remarks. "You never know with her—she's complicated. I'm interviewing her next week."

"I'm curious what you'll find out."

"Me too."

Passing a few small electric fishing boats, they traverse the length of the lake and enter the river that leads to the more deserted Birch Pond upstream. Theirs are the only boats on the river, so they kayak side by side, gliding over the reflections of young marsh grasses, iridescent in the morning light. For the first time in a long time, Laura feels far away from town and troubles as if they traveled miles to get here. No doubt more boaters are on their way, and the pristine view will soon be spoiled by the brightly colored plastics of their watercraft. But why anticipate? Enjoy the moment, silly girl. Her stroke gains force, the paddle cuts and scoops in tandem with Nate's. He points out two eastern painted turtles sunning on a rock.

The entrance to Birch Pond is cluttered with debris from a beaver dam, so they paddle shallow but hard in order to cut through. The pond's surface is so still that only the water bugs make a mark on it. Searching for elusive waterfowl, they do the circuit, Nate now paddling more slowly than her as he trains his binoculars along the shore. He's so intent on looking down that it's she who first spots the bald eagle perched on top of a tall pine. "Good work," he praises her. "I've never seen eagles here before." He points ahead to a rock. "That's where I usually do lunch." They disembark in a sandy patch, tying the kayaks to a sapling.

"Doing lunch" turns out to be a euphemism for a minor feast. Now she realizes he is truly courting her, for why else the French baguette, expensive cheeses, a nice bottle of red wine, and dark chocolate? He must have gone elsewhere to get the food—no stores in Stanton stock such items. The giddier she gets from the wine, the more she likes watching even the slightest of his movements, like the way his hands break the thick chocolate into two pieces. He gives her the biggest one and she eats it all.

When she's done, she leans against a tree, one hand resting on the knob of an exposed root. He leans against another, his gaze more intense now as if he's studying her. "I hear you're a painter as well as a reporter," he begins.

"Once upon a time," she replies. "In college I majored in journalism and minored in art, but Donnie was a toddler, so I didn't learn either particularly well. Or maybe I'm just using him as an excuse."

"I saw a painting of yours in the library. Interesting ice formations on the mill pond." He brushes a fly from his arm. "You've got talent. So why'd you give it up?"

She hates that question. How can she possibly explain that painting gave her up, not the other way around? After Mike's death, her muse departed for greener pastures, more eager hands. Her focus turned inward, her eyes no longer drawn to the colors, shapes, and patterns of things. She mutters something about not having enough time and not being very good anyway, and then asks if he still writes.

"Ah, you know about my book on the whooping crane."

"Everybody knows about your book, or at least every birder around here."

"I still write a little, but only for myself. I keep a nature journal—maybe someday I'll turn it into something, I don't know."

"So how do you make a living? Sorry," she adds quickly, "I didn't mean to be so blunt."

"No, it's a legitimate question," he replies and then tells her he hasn't had a proper job for a long time. He explains that the book still brings in royalties since the whooping crane continues to make a comeback on the Gulf Coast, and there's a big tourist industry around it operating out of Rockport, Texas. When his parents retired, they moved there from Houston, bought a boat, and set up a tour company that his sister, Alana, and he inherited when they died. "Everything was destroyed in the hurricane," he continues, "and it was a really hard time, especially for Alana, who lived through it. Eventually, the insurance money came through, and we're doing pretty well at the moment. She manages the day-to-day operations, while I do the taxes and accounts from here. Between my share of income from the business, book royalties, and living simply, I get by." And then, his face coloring slightly, he admits he also has a small trust fund from his grandparents.

When she asks why he moved here, he reaches for his water bottle and takes a swig. "I'm not a true Texan, you know," he explains. "Both my parents were born in New England. My grandfather and father went to Amherst College and they were hell-bent on sending me there. I hated it, really, full of preppies back then. But I studied with a great ornithologist and became his research assistant. He took me all over the state—we even came here once.

"When I left Texas—long story for another day—I decided to come up here and buy some land. This county's about as cheap as it comes, or at least it was ten years ago when I moved here. My goal was to live the simple life, and I've succeeded, but now I'm growing tired of it. Not that I want more things, but the hubris it takes to think you can live so differently from other people, that you're purer than them, the next reincarnation of Henry David Thoreau—for me, that's getting in shorter supply. I guess you could say I'm fed up with my own arrogance." He pauses, waiting for her to say something, but she doesn't know how to respond. *Arrogance* isn't a word she associates with him. *Aloofness*, maybe, but that's different. Finally she asks how old he is.

"Forty-one. And you?"

"Thirty-five."

Silence again. She guesses he's doing the math, subtracting Donnie's age from hers: seventeen-year-old son, eighteen-year old mother. Teen pregnancy probably turns him off; there's still such a prejudice against "irresponsible" young moms. People think that if you were a bad girl then, chances are you're still a loser now. But maybe she's wrong about Nate because he suddenly smiles shyly and asks if she wants to go for a swim.

Behind a clump of mountain laurel, she changes into her bathing suit, feeling exposed and self-conscious as she joins him on the rock. They dive in together, emerging quickly for gasps of breath. The water is too cold to immerse her head, so she swims the breaststroke, watching her arms turn eerily brown in the tannic-colored water. He does four or five brisk crawl strokes and then heads back with her to shore. Bodies shivering and teeth chattering, they make a confederacy of the cold as they wrap themselves in beach towels. He looks boyish with his wet hair slicked back from his forehead. "Let's lie down on the rock," he suggests. "Maybe the sun will warm us up like those turtles we saw."

They stretch out chastely with over a foot between them, but she says yes to his offer to put sunscreen on her back. He takes his time, massaging it in slowly, introducing her to the pleasure of his strong fingertips. She reciprocates, tracing the outline of his shoulder blades. It's the first excursion, a faint erotic line on a map of uncharted territory.

Kayaking back, the current is with them, so the trip is shorter, too short. Time accelerates even more on the road and they reach her house by midafternoon. She considers inviting him in, but Donnie's due home from work soon, and she isn't ready for Nate to meet him yet. He carries her kayak into the garage, where she thanks him for the outing. He thanks her back. And then they just stand there, neither quite ready to take leave. "I want to ask you a favor," he finally says.

"What's that?"

"I invited the Addisons over for dinner next Saturday. They're going on a tour of Costa Rica for a couple of weeks, and he wants to discuss tropical birds."

"I don't think they like me."

"They give that impression to everyone. They're just shy."

"They clearly like you."

"It's taken some time, believe me." He pauses. "Please, Laura."

The intimate way he says her name makes her blush, and she's grateful that it's too dark in the garage for him to notice. He draws closer, lifting her chin with his hand, and kisses her more hello than goodbye.

DONNIE EASES OUT THE DRIVEWAY in his grandma's old Chrysler, a low-riding clunker from the Stone Age that easily scrapes bottom. He lights up a joint, but about a mile from Stop & Shop, he notices a cop car tailing him. Another glance in the rearview mirror confirms the driver is Tommy. Donnie puts out the joint and stuffs it into a hole in the upholstery—pot may be legal now, but if you're under twenty-one, you can still get in trouble for possession. Why take chances with that asshole? He's always harassing Ricky and him.

At the light he pulls into the left turn lane, and Tommy follows. Follows him into the parking lot too, pulling up next to him. Donnie gets out and starts walking toward the store until Tommy lowers his window. "Hey, come over here," he commands.

"What do you want?"

"For you to come over here. You deaf or something?"

Reluctantly, Donnie obeys. Tommy likes to play games, and if you don't play, you pay. He's got his arm stretched leisurely along the window edge. Shiny new watch, Donnie observes. Oakley shades too. Showing off as usual. "I got a question for you, Donnie," Tommy says. "Is it true you're gay?"

"What?"

"Your friend Ricky's telling people he ended up in the hospital because you're gay, and those punks were giving you a hard time about it."

"That's not what happened."

"Maybe so." Tommy pauses, drumming his fingers on the car door. "But that's what Ricky claims. I thought you'd like to know." As Donnie turns away, Tommy calls after him, "Aren't you going to thank me for keeping you informed?" Donnie shakes his head and keeps walking. Tommy's bluffing as usual, he reckons. He's not gay, but in ninth grade when he stood up for Drew Larsen, who is, he got bullied by a couple of jocks until Ricky told Justin, and Justin took care of them. Still, what Tommy said about Ricky makes Donnie feel uneasy, and his stomach churns.

Bagging groceries helps steady him. He's fast and efficient, so cashiers like him. Today Patty's at the register. She's short with graying hair and horn-rimmed glasses that make her look like an owl. In a lull between customers, she tells him that someone overdosed in the men's restroom this morning. A cleaner found him with a needle hanging out of his arm, but the manager gave him Narcan, so he got lucky. "I'm scared to go into the bathroom now," she says. "You never know what you'll find." Donnie's afraid too but doesn't admit it to her. He knows a kid who died of an overdose in the fall. He was in Justin's class in high school and worked construction. "At least you men can pee in the bushes out back."

"Yeah," he replies, embarrassed that maybe she's seen him there on his break.

A couple of carts roll up. Second in line is Royalty's best friend, Michelle, who thinks she's hot shit because she rides horses. When she reaches the head of the line, she unloads a carton of soda and some bags of chips from her cart. "Hi, Donnie," she greets him in a friendly voice. He's surprised—she's a snob who never speaks to him. "When are you getting off work?"

None of your business, he wants to respond but mumbles instead that he'll be off in an hour.

"It's so warm out, Rebecca and I are having a party at the swimming hole. It starts at four. She wants to know if you can come."

Is this for real or is she putting him on? "I'll try," he answers noncommittally.

"Try hard. She'll be disappointed if you don't come."

As she walks away, Patty nudges him and winks. "Girls interested in you now, eh, Donnie?" He feels his face flush. Maybe Royalty does want to see him. She liked his war poem and kept looking at him all through English class on Friday as if to figure something out. Whether he's gay or not? he wonders. What if Ricky *is* spreading that rumor?

He arrives at the swimming hole on the Diamond River about a half hour late, but no one's there. So it was all a hoax, he thinks. He lies down on the grass and stares up at the sky. There are a few high clouds, too thin and wispy to imagine many shapes. He liked doing that as a kid, still does when he's high, but what he sees is different now. Fewer faces, more patterns. The cloud just passing under the sun could just about be a fern or feather. . . .

He closes his eyes. He doesn't want to go home yet because maybe he'll run into his mom's date. It's been a while since she had a boyfriend. Last one was so uptight, cleaned the kitchen counters all the time. Ricky and he called him Mr. Clean behind his back. He had an annoying laugh too. What will he call this one if he sticks around—Birdman? He's seen the weird dude around town, always wearing baggy pants with binoculars hanging around his neck.

Where to go? Can't hang with Ricky because then he'll have to ask him about the gay thing, and what if the answer's yes?

He dozes off for a few minutes, waking up to the miraculous sight of a bunch of giggling girls in bikinis staring down at him. Except for Royalty; she's on the side, still in her clothes. And then the girls are all over him, pulling and pushing and shoving, and somehow he gets his wallet and keys and bag of weed out of his pockets before they throw him into the freezing water. They throw Royalty in too, and she comes up for air right next to him. Michelle swings out over the river on a rope and jumps in screaming. Everyone's screaming and laughing, including him. Royalty tells him she wants to go down the river to the waterfall, so he follows. She makes her way to the spot where there's a butt-size scoop in the rocks, and you can sit right under the falls and let the rushing water pound you. "Put your head under it, Donnie," she says. "It clears your brain."

A machine gun fires ice at his skull, but he pretends to like it because she's Royalty, and he'll do anything she wants.

She grabs his hands and they spin around like little kids. The water pushes up her sleeves, revealing the cuts on her arms. She notices him looking but doesn't say anything. He's suddenly conscious of his knife wounds, even though they're numb now like the rest of him.

After they get out of the water, she asks for a ride home so she can put on some dry clothes. In the car he turns up the heat so high that the windows steam up, and he has to turn on the defroster. She asks him to drop her off a couple of blocks away from her house. "My parents don't trust me," she confides. "They didn't like me going out with Ricky." She cracks open the car door but doesn't get out, turning back toward him. "I have a question for you, Donnie. Are you gay?"

"Where did you hear that?"

She shrugs. "It's going around. I just want you to know I don't care if you're gay. I don't have a problem with it."

"Thanks," he replies, "but I'm not."

She smiles. "I didn't think so. Will you show me where they stabbed you?" After he lifts his shirt, she bends down to kiss the scars. "I'll text you," she says as she leaves.

4

SUNDAY MORNING, STOPPED AT a traffic light, Laura reads the placard in front of the Unitarian Church, a quaint wooden building that's folksy looking like the people who go there. This week the quote is from writer Anne Lamott:

I DO NOT AT ALL UNDERSTAND
THE MYSTERY OF GRACE—
ONLY THAT IT MEETS US WHERE WE ARE BUT
DOES NOT LEAVE US WHERE IT FOUND US.

On the opposite corner by the bowling alley, a homeless young man and woman she recognizes are setting up to panhandle, their sleeping bags rolled up beside them. At least the nights are getting warmer now, Laura thinks. If she were walking by, she'd say hello and give them some cash. In the old days, Angie and she used to take the boys to the bowling alley on the weekend. She wishes that were her destination now instead of this obligatory trip to welcome Ricky back.

When the light turns green, she takes a right on Clinton and, after a few blocks, a left on Jefferson, entering Stanton's wealthiest neighborhood. A speed bump forces her to slow down near Mimi Sullivan's house, a Victorian antique painted a bright yellow that to her eye is only one shade shy of garish.

On the wide wraparound porch are pots of multicolored pansies, hardy enough to withstand a frost. She thinks about what Justin told her—that Ricky's dating Mimi's daughter, Rebecca. Such an unlikely match since Rebecca has everything going for her. No wonder the kids call her Royalty.

Like Rebecca, Laura too was once a perfect girl. In grade school, it branded her as teacher's pet, but by high school, it was a source of almost mystical power. The trouble was she couldn't escape the spell she cast. A perfect girl can never break free of her perfect image; it trails along beside her like a hungry dog that's never satisfied. While she starts off giving it a few scraps, it soon demands everything on her plate until she's the one who goes hungry.

When the perfect girl finally breaks the spell—*sex* is the magic word—she breaks more than she bargained for. Rebecca's trying out Ricky the bad boy, while Laura went for Mike, who was good, way too good, so good that when he got her pregnant, he married her. Her mother played the Catholic card to prevent her having an abortion, but her real motive had more to do with faith in the American Dream. At that time Mike's dad was chief engineer of Diamond Tool and Die, and no doubt his clever son would follow in his footsteps. Her mother reckoned that in one fell swoop, Laura's marriage to Mike would propel her into the upper middle class. Never mind that her pregnant daughter was just turning eighteen.

And so the perfect girl gave up her full scholarship to the university and watched her husband go instead. Even though, in the end, she graduated from UMass, it was by the circuitous route of community college, which wasn't the same.

But Rebecca isn't me, she reminds herself as she drives slowly over another speed bump. Rebecca has other choices. For one, her family has money—otherwise they wouldn't be living on Jefferson in the heart of Stanton's historic preservation district. A century ago, wealthy merchants and mill owners lived here, and in addition to their houses, they left behind a stately legacy of trees—huge white oaks, hemlocks, and horse chestnuts that will soon break out in full, heady blossom. The quality of shade is different here, protective, as if nothing can harm you if you stand underneath. But of course that's an illusion, just like it's an illusion to think the thick brocade drapes that hang from the bay windows of the houses can somehow ward off evil. When it comes to safety, the rich have an unfair advantage, Laura reflects, but it's not foolproof. After all, the only son of Charles Diamond, the factory's founder, survived the invasion of Normandy, only to turn into an alcoholic and die in a bar brawl in Brockton.

No tragedy of that magnitude is associated with the Sullivan family, though Laura's heard Mimi's marriage isn't exactly idyllic. Martin told her Mimi's husband, David, is a drinker with a gambling habit who came close to draining the family coffers a couple of years ago. Mimi re-mortgaged the house to save the business. Martin knew because he arranged the deal. Maybe having such a deadbeat for a husband is why Mimi kept her own last name and passed it on to Rebecca, Laura muses.

Nothing marks the divide between Stanton's gold coast and the washed-up neighborhood she enters now. In the space of a few blocks, one historic district gives way to another, but the poorer one doesn't rate an official designation. No plaque here commemorating the clapboard duplexes that once housed a bustling mill worker community. No preservation grants to restore the neighborhood's former glory. Many of the houses are deserted and boarded up, forlorn victims of the latest wave of foreclosures.

Swerving around a couple of kids riding bikes, Laura turns onto Lawson Street and parks outside Angie's house. This block, mainly inhabited by factory workers, isn't as bleak as the rest. You can tell most of the houses are owner-occupied by the care that has gone into fixing them up. She knows people here live in fear that the factory will close—Chinese competition is driving profits down—and they won't be able to find skilled manufacturing jobs elsewhere. In these parts, Diamond Tool and Die is the last big plant left standing.

Angie's house has been recently renovated with a new roof and paint job. Laura walks up the steps and rings the bell, a box of chocolates under her arm. When Angie opens the door, she glances at Laura coldly as if she's a religious proselytizer or traveling salesman. A few seconds later, she manages a smile and gestures for her to come in, but the distance remains. No hug. No kiss on the cheek. "A little something for you," Laura says, offering the chocolates.

"Thanks," she replies, "but you'd better give them to Ricky—I'm on a diet."

"Why? You look great." Angie's tall and stocky but not fat, though she thinks she is. Laura's always admired the way she carries herself, projecting toughness when she needs to, softness when she's ready to cut you some slack. She's one of the few female machinists employed at the factory, and men know better now than to give her any shit. By her early twenties, she'd had enough for a lifetime, she once confided to Laura. She forced changes at the plant and was recently promoted to forewoman.

Laura follows her into the living room, where Ricky's lying on the couch, watching a ball game. When she asks how he's doing, he turns from the TV long enough to flash his winning grin. He's always been a handsome kid, shorter and lankier than his brother, Justin, but with big lips, dark eyes, and long lashes made for the camera. The problem is he's the spitting image of his no-good dead dad, and people won't forgive him for it. Pushing a lock of hair from his forehead, he tells her he's better and can start going out again.

"Not for very long though," Angie quickly interjects. "He still needs a lot of rest."

"I brought you some chocolates," Laura says, handing the box to him.

"Thanks."

"How are the Sox doing?"

"The Sox are on later. I'm watching the Yankees and Blue Jays."

"Who's winning?"

"Second inning. No score."

"Going back to school soon?"

"He's not going back to the high school," Angie cuts in. "He's going to take courses at community college next session and finish up there."

"A lot of kids like that," Laura replies, trying to hide her relief that he'll be in a different school than Donnie. As Ricky reaches for a glass on the table, he stretches his arm very slowly, grimacing with pain. She has a flashback of the time he broke his arm falling out of the apple tree in her backyard. He was only seven or eight, and she comforted him until Angie arrived. She remembers the feel of his head on her shoulder and how she loved him like a second child. That affection isn't there anymore, neither in her nor in him, and it makes her sad.

"Let's go in the kitchen so Ricky can rest," Angie suggests. "Want a cup of coffee?"

"No thanks, drank too much at breakfast."

Angie pours herself a cup and sits down at the kitchen table across from Laura. She zips up her sweatshirt—a Williams College one, Laura notices. Angie usually wears contacts but has glasses on today. Her blond hair is pulled tightly off her high forehead and pinned back in a twist. The effect is to make her look sterner and more intimidating, like a teacher preparing to hand out a punishment. No pleasantries pass between them. Instead Angie cuts to the chase: "You and I need to talk. We can still be honest with each other—right?"

"Right," Laura repeats but without conviction.

"Last night I told Ricky I don't want Donnie over here anymore."

"That's fine," Laura replies, her back tensing. She sits up straighter in the chair.

"Look, I don't know how to say this. . . ."

"You've said it before. I've said it before. We need to separate the boys. COVID got in the way, but we need to try again."

"The stakes are higher this time, Laura. The police are targeting Ricky. They say he's in a gang. It's nuts. Your friends in the police don't say Donnie's in a gang, do they? It's because Ricky's dad killed a cop and died before he did prison time for it. After all these years, they still want revenge. Being a hockey star saved Justin—otherwise they'd have gone after him too."

"But maybe there is a gang around here," Laura ventures. "I mean, what was the fight about?"

"The fight was about Donnie. He hasn't told you?"

"Told me what?"

"That he's gay. You need to face up to it, Laura. That's why those kids attacked them. They called Donnie names so Ricky tried to protect him. . . ."

"Ricky told you this?" Angie nods. "And you believe him?"

"I believe my son, yes."

Which one? Laura wants to ask. Why do you believe Ricky and not Justin about the gang? But she can't betray Justin's confidence, at least not yet. "I don't think Donnie's gay," she begins, "but even if he is, it doesn't matter."

"It does matter to you, Laura. That's why you won't admit it to yourself. I'm sorry I'm the one to tell you. I'm sorry you're in denial."

The patronizing way Angie says "denial" is too much to take. "Everything I've heard suggests it was the other way around," Laura shoots back. "Donnie intervened to protect Ricky. What if Ricky is in a gang, Angie? What are you going to do about it?"

"So you're taking the cops' side?" Angie says angrily.

"I'm not taking anybody's side. I just want the boys to be safe."

"That's what you always used to say, and I listened to you." Angie pauses, her expression turning to pity. "I try not to blame you," she says in a more measured tone. "You fooled yourself, so you fooled me. Maybe you had to. It was so hard on you when Mike was dying. I remember once when you were at the hospital and Donnie stayed here overnight, I checked on the boys before I went to bed. They were sleeping all cuddled together. I didn't think anything about it—I just thought Donnie was sad and scared. But maybe that was the start. . . ."

"Mike's death has nothing to do with this," Laura responds indignantly.

"It's affected Donnie—you know that. How many times did you talk to me about it?" As their eyes meet, there's an old flicker of recognition, but it doesn't last. "At least we both agree that the boys shouldn't be together," Angie proceeds.

"Of course, but there's not much we can do about it."

"I've made Ricky promise. . . ."

Laura pushes back her chair, making a loud scraping noise. "You're the one who's in denial, Angie. We lost control of their friendship a long time ago."

"This time's different. Ricky doesn't want to see Donnie anymore."

"That's fine with me."

Laura makes her own way out, fighting the urge to slam the door behind her. She starts the car but stays put, not sure where to head. She wants to go home, crawl back in bed and beat her pillow, but she can't face Donnie. Suppose he is gay, she thinks, what should she do about it? Be supportive, but how, when he so closely guards all his secrets? And it doesn't ring true somehow. Too many times she's caught him looking at girls the way teenage boys do. Who knows, maybe he's bisexual. But whatever her son's sexual proclivities, Ricky is spinning a tall tale about the fight. That she's confident about, but she wants to know more.

If there's anyone who can help, it's Uncle Jack. And so she drives to his house, hoping to find him alone since her aunt Nancy faithfully attends church. When she pulls into the driveway, he's riding his tractor mower and doesn't see her at first. Finally, after she shouts a couple of times, he kills the motor and disembarks, hobbling toward her on stiff legs. His unshaven face makes him look older too. "Hi," she greets him, "sorry to interrupt you."

"Trying to beat the rain," he replies.

"Your grass doesn't look very long."

"Well, it's too long for Nancy," he says with a sigh, and Laura nods sympathetically. Her aunt is a taskmaster. "C'mon, let's sit on the porch. I could use a rest."

The three-season porch is on the south side of the house, its glass sliders opening onto a stone patio he laid by hand. Her dad and Mike helped with the project, getting the rock from a quarry in the Berkshires. She takes the love seat, leaving him his favorite wicker rocker. Roxie the black Lab soon joins them—she's over ten, and her hips are arthritic. She passes by Laura for a quick scratch behind the ear before lying down at her master's feet and closing her eyes. "I should offer you something to drink," Jack says. "There's iced tea in the fridge."

"Don't worry about it."

"So what's up?" He sits back and stretches his legs.

As she describes her difficult conversation with Angie, Jack scowls and shakes his head. He tells her what Ricky's saying about the fight is nonsense and that Angie needs to wake up and get over her grudge about the cops. It's ancient history now. "Ricky wasn't even a year old when her husband shot Bruce Baxter."

"Memories are long in this town."

"Maybe, but it doesn't mean the police are out to get Ricky. I'm surprised you're taking Angie's side on this."

"I'm not, but I do wonder about Tommy. Bruce was his cousin."

"Tommy has it out for everyone. He doesn't discriminate."

Ah, but he does, she thinks. Angie's not making it all up. Laura's seen how he glares at Angie when their paths cross. "He'll never let me forget," she once told Laura, "as if it was all my fault. I didn't know my idiot husband, Evan, was going to rob that convenience store. I didn't even know he owned a gun. He was high as a kite—if that Baxter cop had only talked him down, they'd both be alive today. Baxter shot first, you know. The worst thing is I literally prayed for Evan to die in the hospital so the boys wouldn't grow up having their dad in prison for life." Angie asked her never to tell anyone about that prayer, and she hasn't. She drops the subject of Tommy and instead inquires whether Jack has learned anything new about the fight.

He eyes her warily. "There are limits to what I can tell you. In case you forgot, you're a reporter."

"I'm also your niece."

"Everything's off the record then." He pauses. "I mean it this time—everything. Not a word in print or in conversation or anything until I tell you it's okay."

"You know I'm good at keeping my word."

"Yes, but this time is different. Even the slightest little slip from you, and I'm toast." He draws a finger across his throat. "The department's keeping a close watch on me because I'm the only one willing to ask tough questions. I figure, I'm retiring at the end of the year, so what the hell."

"What kind of questions?"

"About why we're sucking up to the bastards at the top, I mean the very top."

"Federal law enforcement?" He nods. "But the fight Ricky and Donnie were involved in was hardly bigtime."

"Tip of the iceberg, at least according to them."

"I did a little research," she says. "The Springfield gang's called the Jags, isn't it? And the gang Ricky's in here—is it the Blades?"

"Yeah. We don't know if Ricky's a member or just being courted. Courtship's an elaborate ritual with the Blades. If it was up to me, I'd intervene right now and defuse the situation. But we've been given other instructions."

"Such as?"

"Oh shit, Laura. I really shouldn't tell you this." He glances outside. A tall wooden fence separates the patio from his neighbor's driveway, but he seems nervous, as if someone might be watching. Leaning toward her, he lowers his voice to almost a whisper as he explains how the new administration in Washington is reloading the war on drugs to make good on its campaign promises of wiping out the drug lords and sealing up our borders. Most of the new operations target the southern border, but the northern one is in play too. "If you ask me, the primary goal is to beef up border control, not to stop the flow of fentanyl and other drugs, most of which are smuggled in by US citizens, not immigrants. And yes, some drugs come to us from Canada, but not enough to warrant a big operation in this region. And people are manufacturing counterfeit pills right here with blenders and pill presses they buy off the internet. Just last week a couple of guys got busted in New Hampshire with thousands of pills they made that look like prescription Xanax or Percocet but are really fentanyl mixed with a little powdered sugar or baby powder."

He goes on to describe how the Fed's operation in this region is called Snakehead. Presumably the name comes from the eastern snakehead invasive fish, though ironically only a few have been found in Massachusetts ponds. At this point, or at least as far as he knows, Snakehead consists mainly of a joint task force with multiple members, including the DEA—Drug Enforcement Agency—FBI in Worcester, ICE, and Border Patrol. Then there's the state police and local departments, whose job is to keep their mouths shut and follow task force orders. "That includes the Stanton department," he says.

When she asks what this has to do with the knife fight, he responds that he's not certain yet but has some theories. "Cities like Lawrence in the eastern part of the state used to be the key hub for fentanyl," he explains, "but it's gotten too hot there, and the traffickers are moving out to the suburbs and rural areas farther north and west. The Blades could be a link in the chain, so the Feds want to know why the gang's setting up here. Their goal is a grand bust of the entire fentanyl network, with gold stars for DEA and border control that will translate into good publicity and bigger budgets. I may be too cynical, but I also wonder if it's a strategy to undermine the sanctuary movement here—maybe by having tighter control over state and local police, they hope they'll have better luck in getting them to cooperate with ICE in arrests of undocumented immigrants. Or maybe they just want to stop the police reforms that have been happening.

"Don't get me wrong," he adds. "I want to see the big traffickers busted as much as anyone. But I'm not willing to see kids like Donnie and Ricky sacrificed in the process. If it was up to me, the Blades would be quietly pushed out of Stanton tomorrow. But our orders are to watch and wait and take notes for the bosses. Oh sure, the Feds ask us what we think, but they don't really give a crap. And they're playing favorites so they can divide and conquer. The chief started off resisting, but the pressure got to him and he's caving, even after all he's done lately to keep people with addiction problems out of jail and get them treatment. Tommy wants the glory of a major bust, so he's already in their pocket. The chief uses the excuse that I'm retiring to keep me out of the loop. But tell me, who knows more about the kids in this town? Tommy? Are you fucking kidding me?" He stops and sits forward in the rocker, planting his feet firmly on the ground. When Roxie wakes with a start, he bends down to pet her. "I'll tell you one thing, Laura. You have to send Donnie away this summer. Find a camp or something. I'll give you the money if you need it."

"He won't go to camp, Jack—you know that. I can hardly get him to go to school."

"Then send him down to your sister Nina's in Florida. I'll pay the airfare."

"Thanks for the offer, but money's not the problem. I can scrape together enough for a ticket, but he'll probably refuse to go. And even if he agrees, I'm not sure Nina will take him. She's got her hands full with her own family plus dealing with Mom. It's asking a lot, you know."

"That's what families are for." It sounds trite, but Laura knows he means it. As a kid, Jack was passed from one South Boston foster family to another until the system finally spit him out into Stanton, where he ended up with her grandparents, who later adopted him. The family saved him, he always claims, especially her dad, who assumed the role of elder brother and mentor. "Ask Nina, Laura," Jack urges. "Beg if you have to. I know you don't like asking favors, but sometimes there's no choice. Channel Mike—he'd back you up, you know that."

"And what about Ricky?"

"He's Angie's responsibility, not yours. And I'll do what I can to help him."

"Talk to her, please."

"I've tried more than once," he says, sighing, "but I'll try again." The sound of the garage door opening gets Roxie to her feet and she walks slowly out of the room. "If I know Nancy, she's going to ask you to stay for lunch."

"I can't, Jack. I have to make sure Donnie gets off to work, and then. . . ."

"No excuses. You need to have more fun in your life, Laura, cut yourself a little slack. That's another reason to get Donnie out of town—for your own health. Nancy and I worry about you. You hardly ever smile anymore."

"There's not much to smile about."

"Really?" he asks coyly. "I heard you're going out with Nate Waterman."

"Where did you hear that?"

"It's a small town, my dear. A fishing buddy of mine saw you together at the lake."

"It's not serious," she says too quickly.

"I'm not saying it is. But he's a nice guy, Laura. Kind of odd, but what the hell. Give it a shot." He rises from his chair and stands in front of her. "Now, you are staying for lunch, aren't you?"

DONNIE WATCHES FROM THE car as Ricky grips the handrail and climbs down the front steps like an old man. "Get me out of here," he pleads as soon as he gets in, wincing as he puts on the seatbelt. "Feels like I'm in prison or something. My mom's driving me nuts. Your mom was over this morning, by the way." When Donnie asks what for, Ricky tells him he couldn't hear what they were talking about in the kitchen.

"Probably the same old shit."

"Yeah, they don't want us to see each other. You're a bad influence, did you know that?"

"My mom says the same thing about you."

Ricky laughs. "Yeah, but in her case she's right."

"Oh, I don't know—I turned you on to weed. Where do you want to go? We could hang out somewhere, get high, whatever. I don't have to show up for work until two."

"Just drop me at Walmart—I need to get a couple of things." When Donnie offers to wait for him, Ricky says not to worry, he has a ride home.

Who with? Donnie wonders but doesn't ask. Maybe Ricky's back with Royalty already; maybe yesterday at the river didn't mean anything. Before he can lose courage, he asks Ricky about what Tommy said in the Stop & Shop lot.

"He's bullshitting you," Ricky responds quickly. "You know he's a liar."

"That's what I thought, but then someone else told me they heard I was gay. The rumor's going around." He pauses a moment. "Those guys who attacked us—do you know who they are?"

"Losers from Springfield. Don't worry—they won't be coming back."

Donnie wants to know more but lets the subject drop. The rest of the way they hardly speak, and it feels like Ricky's head is off somewhere else. If only they could get stoned and drive around like they used to, maybe hang at the secret place, but instead Donnie follows orders and drops Ricky at the Walmart entrance. As he pulls away, he checks in the rearview mirror to see if his friend made it inside okay. He spots him standing by the curb, lifting his arm to wave at someone. A second later a white van pulls up, the side door slides open, and Ricky gets inside. So much for going shopping, Donnie thinks. Something else is going down.

At work Donnie gets a text from Royalty, who wants to see him. During his break they message back and forth, arranging to meet in front of the town library. When he swings by at six, she's sitting on the steps outside, reading a book. "I don't want to go home," she says as soon as she gets in the car, then bursts into tears. She tells him her parents had a huge fight that morning and asks if she can go to his house.

And so he takes her home to his astonished mother, who sets another place for dinner. Royalty acts super polite, even offers to help with the dishes. He's embarrassed to show her his messy room, so after dinner they sit on the couch in the living room, watching TV until she says she's finally ready to go back.

This time she instructs him to drop her off at the playground a few blocks from her house. It's dark and empty, and she asks if he wants to hang out for a while. They sit on the swings passing a joint back and forth. "Push me, Donnie," she says, and he walks around behind her, picks up the back of her swing, and lets it fly. Soon she's laughing and pumping so hard he's afraid she'll go over the bar. When she gets off, she dizzily grabs hold of him. "Thanks for being there for me, Donnie," she says. "You can kiss me." As he does, his hand moves underneath her shirt, but she pulls away, telling him it's past her curfew.

5

MIMI SULLIVAN SHUTS THE front door firmly behind her and then watches from the window. David's already too drunk to drive, so they're going out in her cousin Gary's van. She hopes whatever restaurant they've chosen is far away. To get rid of them, she pleaded a migraine coming on, which isn't far from the truth. The sight of Gary turns her stomach. She told David she didn't want her cousin to set foot in the house again, but he went ahead and invited him over for a drink. "He's your cousin, Mimi, and he wants to see Rebecca," he argued at breakfast.

"All the more reason for him not to come over," she countered. "I don't want him having anything to do with her. He's a lowlife punk."

"If you want to cut a deal with him, you're going to have to be nicer."

"Is that why you invited him here? So I could butter him up?"

"Yes, actually."

She studied his face to see if he was lying. Maybe, maybe not. As usual, his pre-caffeine pout was impenetrable. "Well, he's not allowed in my house, David."

"It's my house too, dear."

"Not any longer. Have you forgotten I'm the sole owner now?"

That set him off. He shouted she was a bitch, triggering her to call him a useless failure. Back and forth they vented, avoiding worse slurs only because Rebecca was upstairs. Hopefully, she slept through the fight, but as soon as she got up, she hurried out of the house and then texted at six o'clock that a friend had invited her over for dinner. Which friend? Mimi texted back. Donnie, Rebecca replied. Mimi let it go at that. Whoever this Donnie is, better that she was with him than here with Gary.

After closing the curtains, Mimi sits on the couch, opening her book though she doesn't feel like reading. After a restless sleep last night, she's too worn out to concentrate. The words blur; it's a medieval palace intrigue, and she can't remember the storyline or the characters' names. Historical fiction isn't her thing, but Cindy Mitchell, who convenes the book club, was keen to read this one. Mimi never finishes the books, but it doesn't matter—the other women don't expect her to. She'd stop going except that the gossip's useful. The name Donnie suddenly rings a bell. Cindy's husband is a guidance counselor at the high school, and he told Cindy about Ricky and the knife fight. The other boy involved is Laura Everett's son, Donnie. Is that where Rebecca is tonight? Should she be worried?

When isn't she worried? She has layer upon layer of worries, and now Gary is the icing on the cake. "I was expecting to see Rebecca," he remarked pointedly to her as he left. "I'll just have to come back another time." She glared at him, but he pretended not to notice. He's good at that; he knows it drives her nuts. Then he just stood there in front of her, taking an inordinately long time to zip up his tight black jacket. Coyly, he stretched it down over his narrow waist. "Sorry your head hurts," he said.

She closes the book. Maybe she's hungry. She has no appetite anymore, just eats to keep going and to provide some semblance of normality for Rebecca. That's what the psychologist advised: regular sit-down meals, scheduled family time. But David's hardly home for dinner anymore, and when he is, he drinks too much. Yesterday he washed down macaroni and cheese with two glasses of bourbon. No wonder Rebecca disappears upstairs.

Once again Mimi runs through the reasons she hasn't yet filed for a divorce. The list is getting shorter. The main reason is she wants to pack Rebecca off to college first so she won't be here to witness the nastiness. But college won't happen for more than a year, and in the meantime, things are getting worse, and not just at home. Business is slow. The glut of houses on the market means contractors aren't building. She's still hurting from David's gambling debts—any money she gets from the Lake Amity land deal will go half to Rebecca's depleted college fund and half to reducing her home equity loan. She wishes she had the cash flow to send her off to boarding school next year because then she'd kill two birds with one stone: remove her daughter from all the trouble in Stanton and divorce David a year earlier. But she barely has enough in the account to pay Steve, her private investigator, whom she's seeing at the end of the week.

It's past eight when she finally heats up some leftover soup. Rebecca's supposed to be home by nine thirty, but Mimi feels too tired to stay up waiting for her. So far Rebecca hasn't violated her curfew. Not staying up is a sign Mimi trusts her. Give her some signs, the psychologist said, reward her good behavior whenever you can.

Upstairs Mimi rewards herself with an Ambien. She got through another day, survived Gary's visit. In the kitchen as she was getting him a beer, he placed a hand proprietarily on her shoulder, laughing when she shook it off. "You always were wound tight, Mimi," he told her. Of course she's wound tight. Who wouldn't be in her circumstances? If she takes a sleeping pill now and then, who can blame her?

REBECCA TIPTOES UP THE STAIRS. Her mom left a note on the dining room table that she has a headache and went to bed early. Her dad's out. The trick is to get ready for bed and turn off the lights before he returns so she won't have to face him. She'll never forgive him for what he said to Ricky the night he caught him in her bedroom: *Get your hands off my daughter, you fucking loser, or I'll call the police. You're scum just like your no-good father.*

She stares at herself in the bedroom mirror, pushing a long lock of hair behind her ear. Donnie is way into her; it would be so much easier if she were way into him. She doesn't mind him touching her, but it doesn't turn her on, not like with Ricky. Donnie's sweet, though, and cuddling with him would be nice. He's her protection right now, new boyfriend. A game she needs to play, but she'll try not to hurt him.

It's all about not hurting. She smiles at herself in the mirror, then pulls her lips up to make a clown face, down to make a frowning one. Happy, pretty Royalty—how she hates that nickname; she'll have to tell Donnie to stop using it—or sad, ugly Rebecca, which one is she? Neither, she thinks. The faces belong to someone else, the shadow she's sick of, that follows her around endlessly, whispering to do this, do that, echoing her mom. The real her needs to escape the shadow, but where can she flee? Maybe the trick is to dissolve and then re-form like the experiments in chemistry class when you melt things and they cool down and turn into crystals.

She wants to melt. She's past cutting now. It didn't help, and it drew too much attention. Too many people watch her already. She can understand how some women choose to wear the veil, but when she said that in current events class, everyone jumped all over her like she supported women's oppression. If she had a veil now, she'd wear it. It would free her because the shadow couldn't find her.

Across the hall is the master bathroom with a second door into her parents' room. She sneaks in there sometimes to steal an Ambien—her mom hasn't noticed so far. She wonders if there's anything stronger like the Percocet the doctor prescribed when she had her tonsils removed. There were only a few pills, but her mom wouldn't let her take them and gave her Tylenol instead. Knowing her mom, she probably hid the Percocet somewhere for her own use. She's always hoarding medicines.

The night-light casts just enough of a glow for Rebecca to see her way in the bathroom. She's already searched through the medicine cabinet once, so she tries the drawers in the vanity. Tucked at the back of the lowest one, behind a plastic bag of nail polishes, she finds a Kleenex box. Between layers of tissues are two bottles of prescription painkillers. She takes a Percocet tablet back to her room and swallows it after brushing her teeth. In bed she lies flat on her back, pulls up the covers, and then crosses her arms close to her chest as if to make sure her body will still be there when she returns.

6

SHIVERING, LAURA BUTTONS HER sweater, then zips up her fleece. The warm spell is over, and the cappuccino she's nursing on the deck of the French café in Petersham is cooling quickly in the wind. The blooms on the azalea bushes are limp and lifeless from last night's heavy rain. She wishes she could sit inside, but Mimi's instructions were explicit: meet me on the deck at ten o'clock. Oh well, all the tables inside are taken anyway. She glances at her cell. Mimi's already fifteen minutes late, which pisses her off.

She didn't want to come here. Petersham is too preserved and quaint for her taste. The architectural gems ringing the common—from the turreted stone library to the gracious Greek Revival houses and country store—look like a movie set. When the Quabbin Reservoir was built in the 1930s to provide water for the thirsty citizens of Boston, it drowned four towns in the vicinity, including Enfield, where her great-grandmother grew up. Petersham survived. There's old money here, lots of it, and it rubs her the wrong way. If only some of it would flow upstream to Stanton.

She takes another sip of the tepid coffee, hoping Mimi will be forthcoming enough that she'll at least get one good news story for this week's *Gazette*. She'd prefer to write about what Jack told her, but he swore her to secrecy. "Don't even write notes on your laptop about it," he warned on Sunday when he walked her out to the car. Maybe he's being paranoid, maybe not.

A few minutes later, Mimi arrives and sits down at the table with a quick hello and no apology for being late. Her leather jacket looks as soft as baby skin, and she's wearing tailored slacks and suede boots. Once she was beautiful like Rebecca, and her accomplishments were the pride of the town: captain of the champion field hockey team, class president, honors student to boot. Even though Laura was five years behind her in school, Mimi was her idol.

Now she looks older than her age, her skin prematurely wrinkled from too many cigarettes, her hair streaked an unbecoming gold to hide an even more unbecoming gray. Her shoulders curve slightly forward. "Can I get you something?" Laura offers politely. "Coffee? A croissant? They're fresh from the oven."

Mimi shakes her head. "No thanks."

"Really? It's on the *Gazette*," Laura says, though in truth she doesn't have an expense account.

"Really. I don't want anything."

Laura starts off the interview with prepared questions. Is Mimi close to a deal with Glendale Properties, the senior housing developer? Or is she still open to exploring the conservation option? What would it take to strike a deal with the town and state? Would they need to match Glendale's offer?

When Mimi places her hands on the table, it rocks slightly, rattling Laura's cup and saucer. "I'm carefully weighing all the options," she begins, "and I haven't ruled out the conservation route—you can put that in the paper. But I don't appreciate the attitude of people like Keith Addison. Frankly, dealing with him and his cronies on the conservation commission has been a total nightmare. They treat me like I'm the devil, and they're all saints. *Sanctimonious* is the word. But don't put that in, please. Just say something like 'Going forward,

Ms. Sullivan would appreciate a more respectful dialogue with the conservation commission.'"

Laura jots down the sentence. She feels sympathetic to Mimi on that score—Keith's crusader behavior puts her off as well. "Can you tell me anything more?" she presses. "Like what's the final deal-maker or breaker—whoever offers the highest bid?"

Mimi sighs. "Ah, if only it was that simple, just a matter of dollar signs. But the situation's a lot more complicated than that."

"Can you tell me why?"

"Off the record I can."

"That's all right with me."

They lock eyes. "Can I trust you?" Mimi asks.

"Of course."

"Not all reporters are trustworthy, you know. Your boss, Frank, is a good friend of ours. I wouldn't want you to give me a reason to call him."

Laura tries hard not to show her anger. Sometimes rich people like Mimi mess with her, alternating between leading her on and threatening her. Like taunting a dog, the sport gives them a perverse sort of pleasure.

Mimi rocks the table again, apologizing this time round. "You see, Laura," she explains, "I'm not a lone actor. People like to think I am—they love to have a scapegoat, especially an uppity female one. But I'm not the only owner of the property. I have a cousin Gary who inherited a quarter share. He's the problem, not me. I've been trying for years to buy him out, but he won't budge, no matter how much I offer. He's delusional—thinks we can push Glendale into accepting a much higher price. Last month he moved to Stanton from Vermont just so he can breathe down my neck." Reaching into her purse, she retrieves a pack of cigarettes and a lighter. "You'll soon have the delightful experience of meeting him personally," she resumes. "He's setting up a ceramics studio in your building. When he's not busy harassing me, he plays at being a potter. I'm trying to work around him, but it's going to take time. So just let your readers know that Mimi Sullivan hasn't said yes to the conservation commission, but she hasn't said no either. She likes nature too, she really does. Just buy me some time—I'd be very grateful."

"Why not go public about your cousin?"

"Because he's a jerk; because if I cross him, a deal with the conservation commission will be out of the question. You have to take my word on this."

You have to take my word on this. A request or an order? Laura wonders.

Mimi taps a cigarette from the pack. "Mind if I smoke?" Laura tells her to go ahead, even though it will be painful to watch her since almost every minute of every day she still yearns for a smoke. Mimi cups her palm around the lighter flame flickering in the wind. When the cigarette finally catches, she leans back and takes a deep drag, then exhales off to the side. "I have something else I want to talk to you about," she says, "something personal. My daughter, Rebecca, tells me she's been having dinner at your house the last few nights. Is that true?"

"Yes, my son, Donnie, and she are friends."

"How long have they been seeing each other?"

"I don't know, but Sunday was the first time she came over."

"Do you think they're sleeping together?"

Her directness takes Laura by surprise. She replies that she doubts it but really has no idea.

"You see, Rebecca's going through a slut phase." The word *slut* falls harshly on Laura's ears. After she got pregnant in high school, people called her that, and she still resents it. "She's had her share of boyfriends," Mimi continues, "but it started in earnest with Ricky Gillen. My husband found them together in bed one night. She let him in after she thought we'd gone to sleep. But David heard them and chased him out."

"That doesn't make her a slut. Things like that happen in high school."

"I know, but it's her choice of boys that's the real problem."

"Because Ricky's working-class?"

"I'm not prejudiced, if that's what you mean," Mimi snaps. "His older brother, Justin, came out fine, but not Ricky. He's bad news. Rebecca not only likes to sleep with bad boys, she thinks she can save them. But she's much more fragile than she seems. We're only trying to protect her. We've forbidden her from seeing Ricky."

"Will you forbid her from seeing Donnie too?"

"That depends, doesn't it?"

"On what?"

Mimi takes another long drag, this time exhaling in her direction. "On how much control you have over him. I hear he's a friend of Ricky's and that both of them were involved in a fight a couple of weeks ago."

"Another bad boy then?"

"You tell me. I also hear Donnie's very bright. I'm not inclined to crack down on the friendship just yet, but I will if I have to."

"What exactly are you asking of me?"

"To keep an eye out. Like I said, Rebecca's fragile." Mimi looks away in the direction of the parking lot. In profile her face is haggard, and Laura wonders if she's fragile too. "Rebecca cuts her arms," Mimi reveals as she turns back to face her.

"I'm so sorry to hear that."

"They say it's not as serious as an eating disorder, but it has us concerned."

"Of course."

"Just be glad you don't have a girl."

"Believe me, raising a teenage boy is no picnic either." The rueful expression each gives the other makes for a fleeting fellowship, but then Mimi consults her watch and announces she needs to leave for an important meeting. She drops the remains of her cigarette on the deck and grinds it out with her boot heel. "I look forward to reading your article," she remarks tersely in parting.

Laura buys a croissant for the ride back to Stanton, convincing herself she's earned every single buttery calorie sitting out in the cold. In the office she mulls over her conversation with Mimi. How far should she trust her? Buying time with the local press could be a ploy to drive up Glendale's offer. And then when the deal's done, Mimi can blame her cousin for sabotaging negotiations with the conservation commission. She could be stringing Laura along, on and off the record both. Even her confidences about Rebecca could be part of the plan. Or is that too cynical a take? Maybe Mimi is reaching out to her. And if truth be told, they're united in wanting to keep their kids away from Ricky.

At five o'clock as she's climbing down the stairs, she notices the front door of the mill building is ajar, even though she made sure to shut it tightly when she came in. A few moments later, a man enters carrying a large cardboard box that he balances on the banister when their paths cross. He has blue eyes, white-blond hair, and pale skin, and the New England Patriots sweatshirt he's wearing hangs loosely on his tall, bony frame. Something about him bothers her—maybe it's his pointed little chin that brings his long face to an abrupt conclusion.

"I'm renting the studio on the third floor," he announces in a flat voice. "I'm a potter—used to live in Vermont." Laura doesn't let on that she knows he's Mimi's cousin. He gives his first name, Gary, but not his last. He doesn't crack a smile, so neither does she.

"Be sure to keep the door locked at all times," she advises. "We've had a couple of break-ins."

Nodding noncommittally, he turns to continue up the stairs. Whether or not he's a jerk, he's certainly a man of few words. Outside, his white van is parked next to her Subaru, the only two vehicles in the lot. She peers in but can't see anything through the tinted windows.

At the hairdressers, her stylist, Debbie, is waiting alone at the front desk—everyone else has gone home. She's in her late twenties and hoping one day to own her own beauty parlor. Her station is decorated with cute photos of nieces and nephews. She's unmarried and says she wants to keep it that way.

With a nylon cape draped around her shoulders, Laura gazes critically at herself in the mirror. Her hair is unruly, a wild mop of dark brown Orphan Annie curls. She wants to look good for Saturday dinner at Nate's. Debbie studies Laura's image in the mirror too, cocking her head one way, then the other. She lifts the back of Laura's hair. "I have a new idea for you," she says. "I think you should grow it out longer. Your hair's so beautiful and thick—it would look great around your shoulders."

"But it looks awful now."

"I'll shape it so it falls better—you'll see. And I'll keep shaping it while it grows out."

"I guess so," Laura reluctantly agrees.

Debbie laughs. "You're so conservative. It's time for a change."

At the sink she feels herself relaxing as Debbie massages shampoo into her scalp. It's such a relief to be passive, if only for an hour. A spray of deliciously warm water rinses her hair. During the haircut, her cell rings but she doesn't pick up, not wanting to spoil the mood. Debbie's right that the new style suits her, and she gives her a generous tip.

She doesn't check her messages until she's halfway through cooking dinner. There's a voice mail from Frank, curt as always. "Got a tip from a cop I know in Orange," he says. "Another batch of bad pills. Two high school kids overdosed. One didn't make it. Leave space for a brief article and another obituary."

THURSDAY MORNING DONNIE SITS with Rebecca and her friends toward the back of the high school auditorium. English class was canceled for a special assembly. It's strange being with this group of girls; he's not their type, but Rebecca holds his hand as if to show him and them that he belongs. Her fingers are cool, cold almost. His are embarrassingly sweaty.

The principal, Mrs. Dumble—Dumbbell to the students—gets up on stage. Special assemblies are usually for chewing them out. Last time it was sexist graffiti in the girls' locker room, before that a protest against the army recruiters. She used the word *violence* to describe the way a couple of kids from Mr. H's class swept all the promo shit off the recruiters' table and stomped on it. They got suspended for a week. Mr. H almost got fired.

Dumbbell's so short she can barely see over the podium. She bends the microphone down toward her mouth and in a high, scratchy voice announces they have several guests today who want to share some very serious news. Donnie watches as two men rise from the front row and make their way to the stage, where they sit behind a table. One's Uncle Jack, dressed in his cop uniform, and the other she introduces as Dr. Goldin, chair of the Opioid Response Coalition. He seems familiar to Donnie—maybe he went to him once when he was a little kid. In a tracksuit and running shoes, Goldin doesn't look like a typical doctor. His legs are jittery like he's aching to go out for a jog.

Rebecca squeezes Donnie's hand and then drops it, reaching in her backpack for her cell. As she bends over to look at it, her hair spills forward. He wants to touch it, to feel it brush his face the way it did last night when they were making out in the car. Uncle Jack clears his throat and starts to speak: "I'm sorry I have to be here this morning to give you some sad news." He pauses, looking out over the audience, and Donnie wonders if Jack can see him. "Yesterday a high school student in Orange died of a drug overdose. I'm not at liberty yet to give her name. Her friend survived. Both received Narcan after the police found them passed out in a car parked near the Diamond River. The pills they took appear to have been mixed with fentanyl. Dr. Goldin will tell you more about that. Emergency personnel tried hard to save the girl's life, but it was too late.

"We have reports from other towns in the region that this isn't an isolated incident. A man died in Brattleboro two days ago from what looks like the same batch of pills. In response, the Stanton police have set up a new Facebook page where you can get all the latest information and warnings about what drugs are out there. These pills look like real prescription ones, but they're not. There's also a lot of fentanyl-laced heroin on the streets." A blowup of the page and the URL appears above him on a screen. "We need your help getting the word out. You could save someone's life. And remember the Good Samaritan Law allows you to report an overdose without getting in trouble with the police. Just dial 911. We're here to protect you."

No one claps, but no one laughs or catcalls either. The room is eerily quiet. A couple of rows ahead of Donnie, a girl starts crying. Bowing her head, she stands up and makes her way to the aisle, followed by a friend, and they leave the auditorium. The door swings shut. Rebecca puts her hand on his arm as if to steady him.

He needs steadying. Death is real to him. He was there when his father died. An image of the dead girl comes into his mind, though he doesn't know what she looks like. It's her eyes he sees. Empty, but wanting to be filled with one last look. He feels nauseous like he might throw up. He wishes he could leave too, but if he gets up, everyone will wonder why.

When Dr. Goldin starts his talk, Donnie tries to focus but finds the accompanying PowerPoint too upsetting to look at, especially the closeup photos of young people who have overdosed. A fentanyl overdose causes your body to go rigid, the doctor says, and you look like a statue with eyes open, jaw and fists clenched. The doctor describes the signs that someone is using and where to get help for them or yourself. Another Facebook page is projected on the screen. Everyone wants to protect them, it seems.

They don't get that there's no protection. Because we're all just floating around, and whether or not you make it back to shore isn't about knowing how to swim. It's about luck. His dad died, so he's unlucky. But the weed helps keep him floating. Heroin and fentanyl sink you, that's what the doctor should say. Kids could understand that. Because as long as you're floating around, you just might make it. A wave could wash you in. Or a girl like Rebecca. Your luck can turn. You can float together for a while.

7

MIMI HEADS SOUTH ON 91, her foot heavy on the gas. Despite being a fast driver, she never gets ticketed because of a sixth sense about radar and cops. She exits onto Route 5, a stretch of Anywhere, America, with Golden Arches, Dunkin Donuts, mega-stores, and packed parking lots. With its look-alike raised ranches, she finds the West Springfield neighborhood where Steve Kowalski lives cookie-cutter charmless too.

She pulls into his driveway, parks in the space reserved for clients, and then gets out and presses the back doorbell hard. His wife and kids live upstairs, and the noisy chaos of family life—baby crying, toddler shrieking, dog yapping—often drowns out the bell. Steve always greets her looking slightly disheveled, as if he's thrown on his suit jacket running downstairs. One time he forgot to take the burp cloth off his shoulder. Never mind. He's worth waiting for—a smart and trustworthy private investigator is hard to come by.

He offers his usual apologies when he finally opens the door. She follows him into the musty office with its fraying red shag carpet and fake-wood paneling. By contrast the desk is new and sleek, and he keeps it neat, the one place he can impose a little order. He doesn't offer her tea or coffee—they're past that now. She's known him since he first started his business eight years ago. He's good at numbers as well as tracking people. She first hired him to find out which employee in accounts was siphoning off cash. Then she put him on retainer to monitor David's gambling habits.

Steve sits across the desk from her, his thick-lensed glasses making his eyes seem extra large. His brown hair is cut military-style—he served in army counterintelligence in Afghanistan. Son of a local farmer, he's straight-up with his clients. A framed picture of his parents' tobacco barn hangs on the wall, its plank siding swung open to dry the large leaves hanging inside. He asks how she's doing. "Well, David's not draining our bank account anymore," she begins. "He claims he stopped gambling. Has he?"

"What do you think?"

"Well, he's drinking more, and his temper's terrible. Sometimes that means he's off gambling, the price I have to pay. Lately he's been picking fights with me all the time. It's not good for Rebecca."

"Or for you."

"I'm used to it," she says with a sigh.

He casts a disapproving look. She expects it—having done his share of domestic abuse cases, he doesn't like to see victims giving in to get by. He's the only person she knows who sees her as a victim. Sometimes she wishes he were a therapist, not a PI. He slides a file toward her. "This is why I wanted to see you."

Her hand trembles a little as she opens it. On top clipped together are a couple of photos of David at a blackjack table. "When were these taken?"

"A few days ago. At the casino in Springfield." He slides another file. "These were taken yesterday at another one in Connecticut. He's making the rounds."

"He's such a liar," she pronounces, but the words sound stale, past their shelf life. "Is he winning or losing?"

"A bit of both. That's what I want to talk to you about. It's a new pattern."

"How so?"

"Well, according to my sources, at both places he bought chips with about ninety-five hundred dollars in cash, gambled for a little while—no wins, but no major losses either—and then cashed them in. It's unlike him. In the past with that kind of money he'd go for higher stakes, blow it off all at once. Do you know where he got the cash?"

"Well, not from our joint account. I only keep enough in it for groceries and paying bills. And he's blocked from my personal account and all the company ones."

"Maybe somebody made him a loan?"

"I don't know who that would be. Nobody trusts him anymore—friends or family—and I've made sure there's nothing he can use for collateral for a bank loan. I own the house now. But I'll check with my banker just in case."

"I'll continue to keep an eye on him too. Maybe it was a one-off, or rather two-off."

A loud thud on the floor above momentarily halts the conversation. When it's quiet again, he leans forward, placing both his elbows on the desk. "There's something else I want to talk to you about, Mimi," he starts. "I followed David after he left the casino here at about nine in the evening. He pulled into a truck stop off the highway where sex workers hang around to service the drivers. He drove to the back of the lot where it's dark and parked there for about half an hour. If you want, I can arrange to take some photos if he goes there again." He hesitates, then adds, "For when you decide to file for divorce."

"I'm not quite ready to do that yet."

"I know you're not, but it wouldn't hurt to have more dirt on him. Like it or not, we still live in a puritan state and David's sleazy sex life will be to your advantage."

"How much more will it cost for you to take the photos?"

"Nothing. Consider it part of the package."

"You're getting too nice, Steve."

"I've known you for a long time, Mimi."

What he knows, she thinks, is that she's barely holding the business together. Last month she was late paying him and had to sell a sapphire ring to cover the check. She's kept him and her banker Martin in the dark about selling the family jewels. She's ashamed of it. If things continue this way, there will be no jewelry left for Rebecca to inherit.

Another loud thud upstairs interrupts her reverie. It's followed by more shouting and barking. "Enjoy them while they're young," she advises Steve as she rises to leave.

On the drive back, she calls Martin, who tells her no banker in their right mind would give David a loan. In the office she looks through the company accounts—no apparent discrepancies there. How can he be gambling with money he doesn't have? she wonders. Maybe Steve will dig up something. The thought that David's having truck-stop sex sickens her. What if Rebecca finds out somehow?

REBECCA FEELS WEIRD BEING AT the stables, like she's performing in a play she was in a long time ago and has forgotten all her lines. The set's the same—she remembers where the props are, but not what to do, how to act. She gave up riding three years ago when it got too competitive and stopped being fun. Michelle continued, obsessed. For her, horses come first, friends second. You get dragged along.

Like today. Rebecca didn't want to come, but Michelle pleaded with her in the cafeteria. "Ruggles is sick," she said. "Maybe he'll perk up when he sees you. Of all my friends he likes you the best." Ruggles is Michelle's first horse. Rebecca used to ride him sometimes, groom him too. He's sweet but cranky.

It was weird in the car too. Driving over, Michelle asked a lot of questions about Donnie and Ricky, but Rebecca's forgotten that script too—how to talk to your girlfriend about boys and sex like it's a game of giggles and tears instead of the lasting taste of sperm in your mouth, the heavy need in their eyes, their wanting too much of you like you're the cure for all their problems. She wished she could talk instead about how depressed she is, about taking Percocet, about what to do when the pills run out. But she can't trust her friend to keep a secret anymore. Michelle told her mom about Rebecca's cutting, and then Michelle's mom called hers. The same thing could happen again.

"Ruggles, look who I've brought to see you—your old friend Rebecca," Michelle says as they approach the stall. "She has a carrot for you!"

Dutifully, Rebecca feeds the carrot to the horse and then strokes his head, trying to recover her old feelings for him, to soothe him with a kind word or two. Something's wrong with him, she can see that. He's much thinner and mangier. "Do you know what's the matter?" she asks.

Michelle shakes her head. "Not yet. They're doing some tests."

Rebecca strokes him again, going through the motions but without emotion, watching herself from afar. There's nothing coming from inside her. Being so empty is kind of a relief, but you can't let people notice. She gets that now. If she can fool her best friend, she can fool anyone. Just pretend that you care.

8

THERE'S A TOUCH OF SUMMER in the evening light, a fiery hue, as Laura drives west out of Stanton. The wayside grass is slick and shiny from a late afternoon thunderstorm, the air still charged with negative ions. She turns onto Ridge Road and begins a steep ascent around winding curves. On top she pulls over at a lookout point, wanting to calm her nerves. All day long she's been in a state of high excitement about the dinner at Nate's. It's silly, she knows, but she can't help it. She preens herself in the little mirror on the sun visor and then scolds herself for being vain. But it's not vanity exactly, more like recalling what she used to do, how she used to be before she started treating her body as a utilitarian vehicle to carry her brain around.

She looks out the window. Nothing but state forest lies on either side except for a slight peek at the Quabbin Reservoir to the south. She fixes her eye there, inhales deeply. As much as she's prepared herself for a good time, she needs to brace herself for disappointment. Suppose Nate and she don't get along the second time around. How will the drive home feel?

Stop! she orders herself. Don't foresee what can't be foreseen. She surprises herself with a laugh. She hardly ever laughs at herself anymore, and it feels mildly transgressive.

The rest of the way to Nate's she manages to keep a smile on her face. The road turns to gravel before ending at his mailbox. In the driveway she parks next to the Addisons' Volvo. She imagined Nate's place as funkier, a kind of back-to-the-land rustic retreat, but instead the house is a tidy saltbox with cedar shingles and dark green trim, more like a summer cottage on Cape Cod. He comes down the stone walk to greet her, and as his lips graze her cheek, he whispers, "Thank god you're here." He studies the label of the wine bottle she gives him, but whether he approves or not, she can't tell.

Keith and Emily are standing in the kitchen, where they shake hands formally as if they've never met her before. Nate pours them all a glass of wine and suggests they relax in the living room while he finishes cooking. Reluctantly, Laura follows the couple down the hall. The living room has a low ceiling, wide pine flooring, and a woodstove that's churning out too much heat. On top a pot of water is steaming.

Keith and Emily take the couch while she faces them in an armchair. Like elderly models in an L.L.Bean catalog, they both wear khaki pants, hers topped with a turtleneck, his with a plaid flannel shirt. Emily has her hair pulled back in a bun, and Laura notices for the first time a certain elegance in the plainness of her face, a kind of noble resistance to adornment. Keith would look better if he lightened up, she thinks. Scorn, or is it worry, has left deep tracks on his forehead and around his mouth. He tells her he read her interview with Mimi Sullivan in the paper this morning. "So you're hopeful?" he asks skeptically.

"I'm not sure. I just reported what she said."

"You can't believe anything that woman says, that's my experience. She lies through her teeth."

"She has a lot of respect around here."

"Because she's rich," he scoffs.

"No, it's more than that. After Diamond Tool and Die, Sullivan Lumber does the most for the town."

"Well, let her put her money where her mouth is then."

"If I can offer some advice," Laura suggests diplomatically, "take her at her word right now. Negotiate in good faith. She's a proud woman, and you don't want to get on her wrong side."

"That's what I've been telling him," Emily chimes in, "but he won't listen to me."

"I'd love to hear about your trip to Costa Rica," Laura says, quickly changing the subject. As they describe their itinerary, her eyes survey the room. The decor is too dark, she concludes. The pine flooring should be stripped and restored to its original color, the burgundy upholstery switched to beige or gold. And more pictures on the wall. Bright pictures. The prints of Audubon birds have seen better days.

On top of the bookshelf is a classic family photograph of father, mother, two sons, and a daughter, all in their Sunday best. When Nate calls them into the kitchen, she stops for a moment to examine it. She recognizes him even though he's only about twelve, sporting a crew cut with a little lick in front. He's told her about his sister, Alana, but nothing about a brother. The brother is much younger—three or four, she guesses—an impish sparkle in his eye. The sister is between the boys in age, chubby with straight brown hair and bangs and a tight smile that probably means a missing front tooth. The mother looks startled, caught out by the flashbulb; the father wears nerdy glasses and has a paunch and slumped shoulders.

In the kitchen they sit around a thick oak table with only candles for lighting. Nate sets about carving a roast chicken surrounded by potatoes, carrots, and greens. It's one of his own chickens, he tells them, just slaughtered this morning. "I'm not sentimental about chickens," he says without apology, serving up hefty slices of the bird and spooning the juices over the potatoes. He then offers a toast to Keith and Emily: "To Costa Rica. May you see the elusive quetzal and add many new birds to your life list."

All through dinner he pours wine liberally. Flushed by the end of the second glass, Laura begs off a third, but Emily keeps going, and her words start to slur. Though the men are intent on talking tropical birds, every so often Nate steals a glance at Laura. Over dessert—Emily has brought an apple pie—the subject changes to Stanton, with the usual complaints of how the town is going downhill. "Have you driven down Pine Street lately?" Keith asks. "It looks like the apocalypse hit. Abandoned houses, trash blowing around, the only people you see hanging around are people using drugs. . . ."

"That's why I live out here," Nate says. "Laura's the only one of us who has the courage to live in town. What do you think, Laura?"

She looks down at her plate. The pie is all gone except for a piece of burned crust in a puddle of melted ice cream. "It's complicated," she begins, buying time. How can she tell them that each time a factory closed, her parents fought because her father gave loans to friends who lost their jobs, loans that were rarely repaid? *This place is drying up like a desert*, he lamented once. *One more sandstorm, and it will be buried forever.*

What's happening to the town is nobody's fault, she finally tells them, at least nobody who lives in Stanton. Larger economic forces are to blame. That Diamond Tool and Die still exists is a miracle, and it will take more of that kind of loyalty, loyalty to place, for Stanton to survive.

"Is that why you stay in Stanton?" Keith asks. "Loyalty to your hometown?"

"That's part of it," she replies defensively. She readies herself for a challenge, but his response isn't what she expects.

"I envy you," he admits with a sigh. "I was a military brat—never lived long enough anywhere to call it home. I missed out on that kind of attachment. Emily moved around too, but she always had her grandmother's house to come back to, the one we're living in now."

"It's your house too, Keith," his wife says.

"I know, but it's not home yet, and I wonder if it ever will be. Sometimes I think it's the state of mind I missed out on more than anything."

Nate leans toward him with an earnest expression on his face. "I know what you mean. I never had a real home either." He tells them his father trained as a geologist and wanted to get an academic job, but the job market was tight, and so he moved from one visiting position to another. Finally, with a growing family to feed, he got a job with an oil company. "He always felt bitter about it," Nate says. "He wanted to do research, but they pushed him into management, which he hated."

"That must have been hard," Emily remarks.

"Yeah, it was—for all of us, but my mother took the brunt of it." Nate doesn't elaborate and instead reaches for Laura's plate, stacking it on top of his, and then stands up to gather the rest. "I'll put on the kettle," he says. "Tea or coffee?"

Keith glances at his watch. "I'm afraid it's time for us to go. We haven't finished packing, and we leave tomorrow at noon."

"I'd love some tea," Emily counters.

"No, we are going home now, dear." He articulates each word separately as if talking to a child or someone hard of hearing.

"Oh, Keith, we can stay a little while longer."

"We're going home now," he repeats, but more gently, almost sadly. Laura detects a slight twitch in his eye, a sign of vulnerability, and wonders how they will fare on the trip. Emily has difficulty standing up and accepts the offer of her husband's arm.

After they leave, Laura goes to the sink and starts scrubbing the silverware, which is real sterling, engraved with a *W*. "You don't have to do that," Nate says as he comes up behind her.

"I want to."

"No, really, I can clean up later." He's so close she can feel his breath on her neck. "I'm sorry I got talking about my dad. Not the happiest subject."

"Families rarely are. It's good to know something about him—something about you. You're considered very mysterious, you know."

"So are you."

"I don't think so," she says with a laugh.

"Oh, but you are. You're the most attractive eligible woman in town, but guys are scared of your intelligence."

"Thanks for the compliment, but what really scares them off is my son."

"I'm not scared of either." He puts his hands on her shoulders. "Come, let's take a walk. I want to show you around the place."

The night is chilly, so he lends her a jacket. The feel of it hanging off her shoulders reminds her of wearing Mike's letter jacket in high school and feeling owned but also protected. Nate's high-beam flashlight lights the path as he introduces her to the seven wonders of his world: the greenhouse, barn, chicken coop, woodshed, garden, spring-fed pond, and then, at the top of the hill, the viewpoint he loves the best. He turns off the flashlight so they can stare unencumbered at the sky. "The stars are never so clear from my house," she says.

"Then you should come here more often." He doesn't wait for a reply, just turns her face toward his like he did after the kayak trip, and they kiss again. Only this time they wrap their arms around each other, press into each other, their jackets standing in for an outer skin it's time to shed.

In the dim light of the bedroom they take off their clothes. She climbs into bed first. The sheets smell newly washed and hung out to dry, but the blankets still have the woodstove scent of winter. "I have a confession to make," he says as he nestles close to her. "I haven't done this in a long time."

"It's been a while for me too."

"I'm sure it's longer for me. I hope I remember how."

"It's like driving—you don't forget."

"Oh, I hope it's better than that." As his hand traces the contours of her breasts, she runs her fingers along the tip of his penis and then shifts and uses her lips. "Laura, Laura, Laura," he murmurs.

His knowledge does come back, but it's awkward at first. To her it feels like they're two musicians practicing together for the first time, searching for the right tempo and notes. Once inside her, he comes too fast. She tries to ward off her disappointment as she goes to have a pee. When she returns, he's standing naked by the dresser putting on some music. "Let's dance a little," he suggests. He stoked the woodstove before coming upstairs, and now the pipe running through the center of the room is throwing off enough heat to keep their naked bodies warm. The music is jazz piano, slow tunes Laura recognizes but can't put a name to. She rests her head on his shoulder and their feet hardly move. Slowly he dances her to the edge of the bed. "Lie down, Laura," he whispers. She complies, closing her eyes as he goes down on her. She focuses on the tempo of the music, nervous about his need to please her. What if she fails? Her back stiffens, she takes short breaths. Nate stops and asks if he's doing something wrong. "I think it might be better without the music," she says.

In the silence she can hear sparks crackling in the chimney pipe. She makes herself breathe more deeply. In her mind's eye is a forest of white birches, and then a line from a Robert Frost poem comes to her: *One could do worse than be a swinger of birches.* She's taught herself to expect so little. *One could do worse.*

His tongue and lips are insistent, and she gives in, gives herself over to the rush of pleasure. His hands cup her rear as he slides into her. They change position so she's on top, her hips locked on his, and she makes love hard, showing off her stamina. Unbearably hot, she tries to kick off the covers, but their feet get tangled in a sheet. They let it tie them down, knot them together. He comes again with a shout loud enough to reach the road, but there's no one listening but her. She likes that. She likes the way they roll off each other's sweaty bodies onto their backs with only their fingers touching.

And then it's cool again, and they pull up a blanket. Her head rests on his chest, rising and falling with the rhythm of his breathing. As she lies there, sleepy and sated, sadness gradually creeps closer and closer like a cat slyly making its way from the end of the bed to its owner's pillow. Mike. The curve of his shoulder when they snuggled. She starts to cry.

Nate strokes her hair. "It's okay," he whispers, "it's okay."

He wants her to stay the night, but she can't. There's Donnie, of course, but that isn't the whole reason. The memory of Mike threatens to linger, and she doesn't want it to drain away the raw joy of their lovemaking. She wants to take that joy home with her, keep it close, nurture it like a new plant on the windowsill. Nate escorts her downstairs in a robe and moccasins, waving from the front door as she leaves.

She floats back to Stanton on empty roads. The lights are out in Donnie's room, but when she goes to check on him, she finds him sitting in front of his laptop, screen-saver stars surging toward him. "Hi," she greets him.

"Where have you been?" His tone is accusatory.

"I told you I went out to dinner. Remember those people I go birding with—the Addisons, the ones who live in that beautiful old farmhouse on Sugar Hill Road? Well, they're going to Costa Rica tomorrow for two weeks, so a mutual friend had us all over for dinner. . . ."

"You mean the guy who keeps calling."

"Yes, Nate—we were at his house."

"It's one in the morning, Mom."

"The party went late."

"You never come home this late."

The exchange is such a reversal of roles that she almost laughs, but something in his voice warns her not to. She switches on the hall light so she can see him better. Sure enough, his eyes are red and swollen. "What's the matter, honey?" she asks. "Did something happen?"

"Nothing happened," he says too fast. "You don't need to worry."

"Are you sure?"

"Yes, I'm sure. I'm not in trouble."

"Okay, but if you need any help. . . ."

"I'll be all right."

She could press him more but knows he'll resent it. "Get some sleep" is all she says as she lightly touches his shoulder.

She can't fall asleep. Her body's tired, but her mind keeps asking questions that seek answers. Why has Donnie been crying? Is he angry or hurt about Nate? He always disapproves of her relationships—doesn't want his mother to have a sex life—but she doubts that would make him cry. Maybe something happened with Rebecca. Maybe they went out on a date. That would explain the new bottle of aftershave in his bathroom and the fact that in the afternoon he did his laundry for the first time in a month and vacuumed his car. She hopes the girl hasn't been mean to him; he's such a softie underneath all the bravado.

She dozes off at last but wakes shortly after to the sound of a car turning into the driveway. She pulls back the curtain and peers out the window next to her bed. As Donnie turns on the outside light, three girls emerge from the car; Rebecca is the only one she recognizes. They enter the house through the side door and go into the kitchen, which is directly under her bedroom. She hears the refrigerator open and close, the sound of water running. Their voices are agitated and one of the girls is sobbing. The kettle whistles, not a sound she associates with Donnie.

The girls don't stay long, maybe half an hour. She knows because she spies again from the window. Donnie hugs Rebecca before she gets into the car. No kiss, just a hug. After they leave, he stands in that spot for a few minutes as if rooted there. And then he comes back inside and turns off the light. Though the house is quiet, it takes her over an hour to fall back to sleep.

DONNIE BURIES HIS HEAD IN his arms on the cold tabletop, battling another urge to cry. He was going to make love tonight for the first time—Rebecca said she was ready. He's had sex before, but it's not the same.

He lost his virginity a year ago when Ricky and he picked up two girls from New Hampshire at the bowling alley, lying about their age. One of the girls had a car, and they all got high and went to his and Ricky's secret place, an abandoned fishing shack on the Diamond River. They had found it in fifth grade when they peeled off from the rest of the Boy Scout troop on a hike. In middle school they started cycling out there to smoke cigarettes, then pot.

Ricky had sex in the car with the driver, so Donnie and the other girl used the shack. Just after they finished fucking, the girl saw a mouse running along the rafters. She screamed, and when he put his hand over her mouth, she bit him. Even drew blood. He just didn't want them to get caught—there could be a canoe out on the river—but maybe she thought he was trying to suffocate her. He wished then that he were in the car and not that stinking shack, but he always gave the best to Ricky. Ricky got the best looking one too.

What Ricky did tonight is worse, though, so much worse.

Rebecca and he were parked outside the diner when Ricky strutted up, trying to look cool in his new black hoodie. He climbed into the back seat and told Rebecca he needed a few minutes alone with her. "I'll be right back, Donnie," she said. "Wait for me." Except she didn't come back, and when he heard a car take off, he knew Ricky was taking her away.

It's lucky her friends found her, talked her down, brought her over to his house because she was freaking out from whatever drug Ricky gave her. Her teeth were chattering, but not like the time they swam together in the river. No, not like that at all. "I'm so scared, I'm so cold, I'm so sorry," she repeated over and over. Michelle made her tea and Donnie held her until she stopped shivering. He hates Ricky for not even telling her what drug it was.

"After Ricky got her high, he had sex with her in the back of a van," Michelle whispered to him as they left. "She says she didn't want to, she wants to be with you. You have to do something, Donnie."

PART TWO

Where Grace Leaves Us

9

SHAKEN LOOSE BY EARLY MORNING rain, blossoms litter the streets like confetti tossed in a parade. Laura opens the car window to smell the spring and hear the waning notes of the invisible marching band. Being with Nate almost every night the past week has left her body sated, her senses keener than they've been in a long while. She wishes she could slow down and capture this moment in time. The symmetry is too good to be true, but what the hell. She's in love, and so, apparently, is Donnie. Rebecca and he are inseparable now. Maybe it's irresponsible of her to leave them alone when she goes over to Nate's, but they would be having sex somewhere, and it's safer at home.

As if to punish her for her good mood, a blast of heavy metal music accosts her when she enters the office. She can forgive Gary the occasional screech of power tools, but not this brazen assault on her ears. She's about to head upstairs to his studio to complain when a text comes in. Justin's waiting outside—she couldn't hear the buzzer. She texts him that she'll be right down.

In one hand he holds a cup of iced coffee, in the other a bag of donuts. "I brought you a cider one," he says. "I remembered you like them."

"I do," she replies, though she's not hungry.

He tells her he was just passing by and hoped she might have a few minutes to talk. She suggests they sit outside by the river where it's quieter. She leads him along the abandoned railroad tracks that once transported goods from the mills, and then veers left toward the river. At the entrance to a little waterfront park, a historical plaque commemorates Stanton's golden age of commerce. As usual the park's empty except for a nattering flock of Canada geese. Under the gazebo she finds a dry bench, where they take a seat. When Justin offers her the donuts, she tells him she'll save hers for later but to go ahead. He picks a glazed chocolate one, demolishes it in a couple of bites, and then washes it down with coffee. She asks what's up.

"I'm leaving for Peru tomorrow," he answers with a nervous smile.

"Wow, you must be excited."

"I am, but I'm also worried about leaving Ricky and my mom."

She nods sympathetically. "I haven't seen your brother in a while. How's he doing?"

"Physically he's much better." He pauses, wiping his chocolatey fingers with a napkin. "I know it's a terrible thing to say, but I wish he was in worse shape so he'd stay home. He's out all the time now and lies about where he is. Last night he said he was going to the new *Star Wars* movie, and some guys I didn't recognize picked him up. This morning he gave me a bunch of bullshit when I asked him how he liked the film. It was clear he hadn't seen it. Has he been over at your house at all?"

"I don't think so. Did you know Donnie and Rebecca are an item now? Donnie spends all his time with her. It seems serious. . . ."

"Don't count on it," he warns. "She's really screwed up."

"Well, at least your mom must be happy Ricky's not going out with her anymore."

"Oh, she is. But she still refuses to see what else is going down. At least she's finally bugging him to get a job."

When she asks if Ricky's found one, he tells her there's a part-time custodial position at Diamond Tool and Die, but Ricky considers it beneath him. "He claims he has other higher-paying opportunities."

"Such as?"

"Dealing drugs probably. That's why I shouldn't go away."

Placing a hand on his arm, Laura tells him he can't put his life on hold for Ricky. He sets his empty cup on the ground and gazes pensively toward the river, which is swollen from rain, rushing fast. She's touched he's seeking her advice and even remembered her favorite donut. She recalls how sometimes on weekend mornings when Angie had to work, she drove him to hockey practice, stopping at Dunkin Donuts beforehand to give the boys and herself a quick sugar fix. Angie and she helped each other out that way. The reciprocity came naturally with neither of them keeping score.

"I'm worried about my mom too," he confides as if reading her mind. "I know the two of you aren't getting along so well, but she needs support."

"If you want, I'll check in with her periodically."

"I'd appreciate that. I liked it when you were friends, you know. It felt more secure."

"I liked it too."

"Promise to email me if something happens, okay? And I'll let you know my emergency contact numbers in Peru. I'll come home if I have to."

"You won't need to," Laura assures him, hoping she's right.

They talk for another ten minutes about his work in Peru, and then she walks him back to his car, noticing with relief that Gary's van is gone from the lot. She hugs him goodbye and waves as he drives off. The promises she just made—will she be able to keep them? she wonders. How receptive will Angie be?

The office is blessedly quiet as she spends the next few hours laying out the paper. She reads over the Stanton police blog, which is always a strange mix. Among the entries are a rabid raccoon on Tremont Street, two bear cubs in a tree near the elementary school, a 911 caller who reported gunshots outside her house that check out to be tree debris hitting her roof during a windstorm. But then the more serious entries:

Caller reports man passed out in laundromat. Officer administers Narcan and subject taken into protective custody.

Attempt to serve summons, 14 Brook Ave. Apartment found to be vacated and vandalized.

Caller reports prescription medication missing from 73 Noble St. Officers investigate but make no arrest.

Hardest to read are the obituaries. A few elderly people have passed away peacefully, but two more drug-related obituaries have come in, the first for a thirty-five-year-old single woman in New Salem—the same age as herself, she reflects—the other for a homeless man in his fifties found dead on a park bench. At least they're both older than the high school girl in Orange. They've seen something of life.

But then again, what have they seen? What caused them to develop a substance use disorder in the first place? Neither of the obituaries provides a clue.

If journalists had a Hippocratic oath, she reasons, it would be to ask hard questions and seek clear answers. The past few years she's become so passive in her job, doing the minimal, that she's almost forgotten what she once expected of herself. Frank prefers she cover the opioid epidemic sparingly, claiming that people mainly want to read good news about their town. But the crisis is enveloping them like a toxic fog, and the paper's role should be to shine some light on or through that darkness. Whether Frank likes it or not, she needs to do some in-depth stories. Two weeks ago Dr. Goldin, head of the Opioid Response Coalition, wrote a letter to the editor decrying the *Gazette*'s lack of coverage. Frank was pissed off, but she convinced him to print it. Maybe the doctor will give her an interview—worth a try. She looks up his number and calls. To her surprise the receptionist puts her straight through, and he agrees to meet her later this afternoon after his last patient.

Dr. Goldin's family practice—he's one of the last solo practitioners around—is on the ground floor of a modest double-decker house a couple of blocks from the town center. Above him is a yoga studio where she used to come when Mike was ill, and everyone told her she needed to "manage her stress." She hates that phrase; it's like telling someone hanging from a cliff by their fingertips that they can control the situation.

The doctor's running late, so she takes a seat in the reception area and leafs through free handouts on family planning and substance abuse. She brought Donnie here once when their own pediatrician was on vacation. He was five or six and had a bad earache, one of many. She can still remember how he took to Dr. Goldin immediately, not even flinching when he inserted an otoscope into his ear. Afterward, the doctor gave him a couple of Batman stickers that he treasured for a long time.

Dr. Goldin comes to fetch her himself, informing her his nurse has just left for the day. In the office he takes off his white coat and hangs it on the door. He's dressed casually in a short-sleeve shirt, jeans, and running shoes. Though he has the physique of a younger athlete, she notices his well-trimmed beard has specks of gray. He sits down at his desk and twirls around to face her. "How's your boy?" he asks. "I saw him a long time ago, didn't I? What's his name?"

"Donnie."

"Donnie, that's right. Cute kid."

"It's amazing you remember him. He's a teenager now."

"How's he doing?"

"Not great, but I guess it could be a lot worse."

"Is that why you came?" he prods, scrutinizing her face for a reaction. "Do you need some help with him?"

His questioning throws her off guard, but she recovers enough to assure him her purpose is to learn about the coalition's work. "I really appreciate you taking the time, Dr. Goldin," she remarks.

"You can call me Alan."

"Likewise—please call me Laura."

"I just asked because a lot of people come to see me on some pretext or other when all they really want to talk about is how worried they are about their kids. I don't mind helping out. I was at Stanton High School last week after the tragic death of that girl in Orange. Did Donnie tell you about the assembly?"

She shakes her head. "He doesn't tell me much."

"Well, that's not so unusual at his age." As he studies her face again, she tries to strip it of all emotion so she's Laura, the reporter, not Laura, Donnie's mom.

The interview takes about half an hour. He explains how the coalition started out small with a few medical people, educators, concerned citizens, and law enforcement officials coming together to figure out what to do. Punitive approaches clearly weren't working—throwing people with an opioid addiction in jail for selling a few drugs on the side did nothing to help them get over their addiction. Things were improving elsewhere in the state, like Gloucester, where people with substance use disorders could go to the police without fear of arrest and get assigned to a treatment program. "But many local prosecutors pushed back," he recounts, "since their jobs depend on ratcheting up case numbers. Basically, more arrests mean more resources flowing into the criminal justice system, more inmates for the prisons and jails too. But the compassionate approach in Gloucester worked so well and got so much national attention that the model spread. There's been a lot of progress around here recently with decriminalizing addiction, but it's not enough. The next step is developing a more holistic approach toward treatment so that people can get help not only for getting off drugs, but for other co-occurring mental disorders that drove them to start using in the first place. The current district attorney is on our side—she even supports our current campaign for safe drug consumption sites—but there's always the risk she'll be replaced with a hard-liner."

He pauses to take a drink from his water bottle, then studies her face for a moment as if to gauge her reaction. She knows there's a lot of controversy around opening a site locally—perhaps he wonders which side she's on. "Our main worry right now is all the talk in Washington about escalating the drug war," he continues. "A lot of us worry that the treatment clock is going to be turned backward, and we'll lose funding for harm reduction even as overdose deaths continue to mount. It's crazy, but the people running the government are crazy, so what can you expect?" He pauses again. "Better not put that last comment in your article."

"Don't worry, I won't," she says. "I'll pass the draft by you if you want."

"I'd appreciate that."

She wishes she could tell him about Operation Snakehead and prepare him for the heavy hand descending on the area, but she can't, not yet. She's run out of questions but senses he wants to keep talking. If nothing else, her years working as a reporter have taught her to rest easy with silence, to wait patiently for the confidences that tend to come later in an interview once there's more personal rapport. On the wall is a poster of snow-covered peaks in Nepal. Perhaps he's been trekking there, she thinks but doesn't ask since it's not small talk she's after. He taps a foot, leans back and then forward. Finally, he tells her he wants to share his daughter Tracy's experience, but off the record. She agrees.

He begins by pointing to a photo of Tracy in a soccer uniform on his desk. She has big eyes, braces on her teeth, long hair in a ponytail. Middle school age, Laura guesses. "I keep that photo to remember what she was like when she was healthy," he says. Bending over, he pulls out a drawer and extracts the items inside, handing them to her one by one: a hat, a clock, a teddy bear, a golf ball, and a video cassette entitled *I Got My Life Back: Patients in Pain Tell Their Story*, all bearing the OxyContin logo. As she returns them, he sets them up in a neat line on the desk. "Show and tell," he remarks ironically. "I can't tell you how many times a Purdue Pharma salesman came through this office, showering me with this promotional shit—a teddy bear, for god's sake—and free samples of their miracle drug OxyContin. Primary care doctors were their main target, and unfortunately, I was one of them. Once they had you in their database, the pressure was relentless. I'm ashamed of it now, but I drank the Kool-Aid. I even went on one of their junkets—an all-expenses-paid pain management conference at a resort. I got a nice tan."

He laughs bitterly. "I was so naive. I was treating a lot of patients then with work-related injuries. When I first started practicing, opiate prescriptions were a no-no except for terminal cancer patients. But I had guys coming in—guys with factory and forestry jobs who had chronic back and joint pain that was ruining their lives. They had no medical leave or decent insurance, so they begged me for a quick fix. When OxyContin hit the market in the late nineties, I started prescribing it, and they were so grateful. A lot of them told me they got their life back, just like that video claims. I didn't worry about addiction, no one did at first. The company claimed, falsely we know now, that the risk of getting addicted was less than one percent of users. So I kept writing scripts and upping doses. People with chronic pain problems started flocking to see me. I wish the story stopped there. But I didn't just mess up these patients' lives, I messed up my own daughter."

Tracy was a shy kid, he reveals, a bit of a loner but a talented athlete. In high school the soccer team was her social anchor. She played midfield and was a fast runner, made varsity as a junior. Toward the end of the season, she twisted her back going up for a header. Nothing too serious, but it hurt a lot and she was dead set on being in the playoffs. He gave her some Oxy, and it worked—she played brilliantly. Afterward, her back kept hurting, so he let her take Oxy through the indoor season. Finally, after a couple of months, he stopped giving painkillers to her, but she had developed an addiction problem by then and found other ways to get them.

"What other ways?" Laura asks.

The usual at first, he replies. She rummaged through other people's medicine cabinets and used her savings from babysitting and summer jobs to pay for pills on the street. Then she stole one of his prescription pads and started forging his name. She stopped hanging with her soccer pals and took up with a group of troubled kids. One night when he was asleep, she stole his keys, and she and a guy broke into his office, where she knew he had a supply. The next day the cops showed him footage from the security camera. There was Tracy, unlocking the door.

"Of course I didn't press charges," he says. "They stole only from me, so the owners of the yoga studio were cool about it. Or *kind* is a better word. Exposés about Purdue and Oxy were just starting to appear at the time. Still, I had a hard time accepting Tracy had a substance use disorder. My wife saw it more clearly. She insisted we put her into treatment, and so we withdrew Tracy from school and found a rehab place in the Berkshires. After she came back, she was okay for a while. We got her admitted to Livingston Academy for the fall—they needed a good midfielder." He pauses, reaching for the water bottle again and taking a few long swallows. "It was a huge mistake."

The drug problem is actually worse at the academy than at public school, he explains, because a lot of the boarding students come from wealthy families and have easy access to cash. It wasn't long before Tracy started acting as a go-between with local dealers, and the kids paid her in kind. She played soccer for a couple of months until she stopped showing up at practice. She flunked out at the end of the first semester. "Crashed and burned," he puts it, "though it turned out she had a hell of a lot further to fall."

His cell rings, but he doesn't pick up. She steals a glance at the clock. Donnie will be home from work soon wondering where she is, but she doesn't want to bring the conversation to a close. "My wife and I go to a family support group where we hear these kinds of stories all the time," he continues. "I finally realized there's a point in your kid's struggle with addiction when they lose a lot of their individuality and the path they follow is horribly predictable. Tracy's story is not that much different from others we've heard. She became unbearable to live with. She stole her mother's jewelry and her sister's iPad. Some nights she never came home, and later we learned she was starting to sell sex for drugs. When pills got more expensive and harder to get, she switched to heroin. She left home and lived god knows where. We tried a few interventions, and she even cleaned up for a while and did a twelve-step program, but it didn't last. Before long, she was back on the streets, dealing small amounts of heroin to finance her habit. She got arrested and put in jail. That was six years ago, before the court system was reformed."

"Where's she now?"

"In Sacramento, where my brother lives," he responds. "My wife went back to work as a nurse so we could pull together the funds to send her to an expensive rehab place as far away from here as we could get her. It's not a twelve-step place; they use a medical model instead. She went on suboxone, which kills the craving for opiates, makes you feel sick if you use them. And they also started treating her for a mental disorder. It took a long time to diagnose, but a psychiatrist there finally figured it out, and she's on meds for that too. She's been clean for over a year and a half now. Graduated into a halfway house and then into what they call a sober house. These houses are a bit of a racket, but I'll save that for another interview.

"My brother keeps an eye out. She's completed her GED and is now taking courses at community college. We try not to get too hopeful, just take each day as it comes. But we feel so fortunate we have enough money for this kind of comprehensive treatment—you won't believe how much it costs. Insurance plans only cover a small fraction of the cost."

"That would make a good article too," she remarks.

"Yes, it would." He takes a deep breath. "Laura," he says, pronouncing her name like they're old friends, "I really hope you never have to go through anything like this with Donnie. But if you do, remember you can call me anytime."

Before leaving, she thanks him for his honesty and tells him she hopes Tracy continues to improve. "Let's stay in touch," she adds. "I'd like to cover the coalition's work more regularly."

On the way home she stops to buy pizza, enough for Rebecca too. There's something comforting about carrying the flat, warm box into the kitchen and setting it on the table. She rarely feels lucky, but she does this evening.

DONNIE FLOATS NAKED ON THE surface of Drake's Pond, languidly moving his arms and legs as he gazes up at the crescent moon. Even though the water's cold, the pond is the only place he can imagine being after being inside her. At last she let him make love to her, and afterward, they snuggled under the covers. He fell asleep, but a little past nine, she woke him so he could drive her home. Watching her get dressed turned him on again, though in a different way, like she was letting him in on a secret as she fastened her bra and pulled on her underwear. He wants to know all her secrets. Before, he assumed sex would automatically break down any walls between them, but now he understands that it's only the first step, the first real sharing.

Shivering, he climbs out and wraps himself in a towel. His dad used to take him fishing here when he was little. Once when it was muggy and mosquito-infested, his dad stripped off his clothes and told Donnie to strip too. Holding hands, they jumped into the water together. Donnie could hardly swim, but he wasn't scared because his dad held on to him. He can still hear his dad's laugh as he threw him high up into the air and caught him just as he hit the water. "Again! Again!" Donnie pleaded.

Before his dad died, his mom made some videos of them goofing off together. A couple are on his laptop. Maybe when he gets home, he'll watch the one where his dad pretends to be a bear and chases him around the room. Ricky's the only friend who's seen it; maybe he'll show it to Rebecca too.

10

MIMI WAITS IMPATIENTLY AT Steve's back door. Nobody's home, no cars parked in the driveway, no text message from him either. She looks at her watch. He's almost twenty minutes late, worse than usual. She's already smoked one cigarette and reaches in her purse for another. Her irritation is tinged with dread. This morning on the phone he said he had new information that couldn't wait. Steve doesn't like to send photos or documents over the internet—he's worried about being hacked—but the trip here is taking a big chunk out of her day. Her secretary thinks she's going to the doctor on these outings, that there must be something wrong with her, and she keeps it that way.

There *is* something wrong with her. Some days she aches all over and can hardly stand up when she gets out of bed. Maybe it's the legacy of the Lyme disease she got last fall or one of those even worse tick-borne diseases. She forgot to put on insect repellent when she worked in the garden over the weekend. Easy to get paranoid about ticks.

Probably it's just stress. She's worried sick, as her mom used to say. Though Rebecca's more compliant lately—perhaps this boy Donnie is good for her—Mimi knows the calm won't last. It never does. Every day David is more of an asshole. She banished him from the bedroom, so he sleeps in the den. She won't go in there anymore because it reeks of booze and his body odor.

Five minutes later Steve's black SUV finally pulls into the driveway. He parks next to her car, hops out, and practically runs to the door, keys jangling in his jacket pocket. "Sorry, sorry," he apologizes breathlessly, "I dropped my wife and kids off at the airport—they're going to visit her brother for a week." She considers complaining, but he's undercharging her, and she's dependent on his generosity.

In the office he lays out seven photographs on the desk. "From the truck stop," he explains, "yesterday evening. I have more, but these give you the picture." It's not what she expects to see. A sex worker or two she's prepared for, but as far as she can make out, the story the photos tell isn't about sex. It's about David's car and a white van parked side by side in the lot. It's about Gary getting out of the van, walking over to the car, and an exchange of manila envelopes through David's window. Afterward, David leaves, but Gary doesn't. "The other guy stuck around, hired a sex worker," Steve says. "I tried to get his license plate number, but the plate was smudged with mud, intentionally or not. All you can see is that it's from Vermont, Green Mountain State."

She tells him she knows who the driver is—her cousin Gary Plant. She asks if he has any idea of what's being exchanged.

"Well, the easiest explanation is that David's buying drugs from him."

"He doesn't do drugs. For an alcoholic, he's surprisingly moralistic about it."

"Sometimes guys like to do a little cocaine or another upper before they have sex," he says, blushing. "But David didn't wait around for any sex workers to appear. Of course, he could be going somewhere else higher-class. But maybe you're right and it's not about drugs. There are other possibilities."

"Such as?"

"Before he went to the truck stop, he was at the casino again, and it was the same deal. He bought around ninety-five hundred in chips, played for a while, then cashed out. Could be he's laundering money for your cousin, though that's just a hunch. Casinos don't have to file a report to the IRS if the currency transaction is under ten thousand. So someone can go in with dirty money as long as it's under that amount, win a little, lose a little, and cash in the chips for clean money." He stops, considers a moment. "What's your cousin do for a living?"

"He's a second-rate potter who has a small business distributing glazes he makes."

"Not an easy way to make a living. Does he distribute anything else?"

Gary has always occupied the sociopathic borderland between lawful and criminal. She strayed into it once with him, but she can't tell Steve—she's never told anyone—about that. "I don't know," she says, "but I wouldn't put it past him to be doing something illegal. I've always suspected the pottery business is a front. He just moved from Vermont and opened a studio in Stanton. We don't get along very well." She describes their land dispute to Steve, speculating that maybe Gary's bribing David to come over to his side. They could be plotting against her.

"I could do some research on your cousin too," Steve offers, "but I'm afraid that would cost extra. And there's the deeper question of how much you want to know. What if your cousin is involving David in something illegal? At what point would you or I feel compelled to report it to law enforcement? Perhaps we should keep it simple like before—I'll monitor David's gambling habits but nothing else. I'll tear up these pictures. Your choice."

She hears the dog barking plaintively upstairs. Lonely probably, missing all the commotion. "Let me think about it," she remarks.

All the way back to Stanton she ponders Steve's offer but comes to no conclusion. In the office she does an hour or so of work, then heads home early, feeling exhausted. As she enters the driveway, the sight of Gary sitting on the porch with Rebecca puts her in a panic. The bastard looks like he owns the place, stretched out on the swinging couch next to her, holding a beer, while Rebecca listens intently to whatever he's saying. What should she do? He knows he's not welcome. But if she makes a scene, Rebecca will wonder why, and Mimi doesn't want her asking questions. Climbing up the front stairs, she states in a carefully measured tone, "I wasn't expecting you, Gary."

"Oh, I just stopped by because I have a proposition for Rebecca."

She tries to hide her alarm. "And what's that?" she asks, putting down her briefcase.

"I'd like to have her apprentice with me this summer. I need help in the studio, and I can teach her a lot of skills. And it's a paid position too."

"I'm sorry," Mimi replies sternly, "but there's already a paid position for Rebecca in the company showroom."

"Pottery's a lot more fun. You're interested, aren't you, Rebecca?"

She smiles sweetly, falsely. "I'm not sure. I need to talk to my parents."

"I've already spoken to your dad and he thinks it's a great idea."

Mimi detects a plea for help in her daughter's eyes. "Rebecca and I will talk it over," she remarks, "but I really do need her help this summer."

Rebecca smiles again, then stands up, telling them a friend is picking her up soon and she needs to get ready. "Donnie and I are working on an English project, so I won't be home for dinner," she says to Mimi. "Nice to see you, Gary," she adds as she disappears into the house.

Gary gestures to the place Rebecca just vacated and tells Mimi to take a seat—there are things they need to discuss. As she remains standing, he holds her firmly in his gaze. He's always been onto her, she thinks, even when she was a little girl. During family gatherings he found ways to include her in the older cousins' mischief. She could squeeze through small spaces like pet doors, and her cherubic face came in handy when they were hauled up for stealing things like the coins in Grandma's purse. He bought her silence with candy, treated her like a puppy he could bribe with biscuits. But she's older now and can tell him to piss off.

"You seem tense, Mimi," he says calmly.

"Of course I'm tense," she retorts. "You're not supposed to be here. I thought I made that clear."

"I came with a proposition."

"Rebecca's not working for you, if that's what you mean."

"I'm willing to offer something in exchange."

"And what's that?" she asks sharply.

"Sit down and I'll tell you about it." She hesitates a moment before perching on a wicker chair facing him. "I'll tell Glendale Properties the deal's off," he begins, rocking the swing slightly with a foot. "Then you can buy me out for a hundred thousand and do what you want with the land. I know how much your reputation means to you."

She wants to come back at him for the snide way he says "reputation" but forces herself to stay cool. "All that just to have Rebecca work with you?" she responds. "Why, Gary?"

"You know why."

"No, I don't."

"Bullshit. Don't tell me you haven't figured out I'm her biological father." He leans forward to put his empty beer bottle on the table. "Seriously, Mimi, I'm offering you a good deal and you know it."

"I don't want her anywhere near you."

"It doesn't matter what you want. The ace is up my sleeve, not yours."

Her face starts to color from remorse or rage, who knows which—how can she tell the difference anymore? Does he really know the truth she's been hiding from him, or is he just bluffing? She studies his expression, but his face is a mask of cool indifference. Behind his back, the cousins used to call him Ghost, not only because of his pale coloring but his lack of emotion. Gary the Scary, Gary the Ghost. "Are you threatening me?" she finally asks.

He lets out a long sigh. "You were a bossy little girl, Mimi, a goodie-goodie, but I taught you about another side of yourself. You can't tell me you didn't like the trouble we got up to. And I always protected you in the end, didn't I? When it got serious, I took the rap. I'm offering to protect your reputation again. I'll protect Rebecca too, keep her safe, because you and David are doing such a piss-poor job of it. It's a mean world out there, in case you haven't noticed."

"Don't play the white knight with me, Gary."

Ignoring the comment, he rolls up his left shirtsleeve to show her a small black **R** tattooed on his shoulder. "Just got it," he says. "Like it?" Without waiting for a response, he informs her she has until Sunday to make the decision. If it's yes, she has the following week to put together a hundred-thousand-dollar buyout. "And I want Rebecca to start working with me right away, after school. I'll keep her out of trouble."

REBECCA WATCHES AS DONNIE pulls down the shades and dims the light. Dinner's over and his mom just left for her boyfriend's house. Donnie sits down beside her on the bed, putting his arm around her shoulder. Next he'll gently push her down, kiss her, unbutton her shirt. She's already bored with the routine. With Ricky each time and place they had sex was different and they had more fun. Even when he's really stoned, Donnie is too serious.

"I want to have sex somewhere else tonight," she says.

"Where?"

"I'm not sure—let's drive around and see what we feel like."

In the car she sits as far away from him as possible, up against the door, with the window wide open and her arm outstretched. She opens her palm as if waiting to catch something falling from the sky. "Let's get out of town," she decides, so he heads north. He'll do anything she wants.

A couple of miles on is an old logging road where she used to park with Ricky, but she can't quite remember where the turnoff is. Besides, it would be too weird having sex in the same place. Sometimes she wishes they were one person with Donnie's sweetness and Ricky's wildness, DonnieRicky, RickyDonnie, RicketyDicketyDon. "Wouldn't it be cool to have our own house, Donnie?" she suggests. "Maybe we could break into a vacant one." She did that once with Ricky, but junkies had been there first, leaving used needles and garbage on the floor. The mattresses were filthy. She refused to lie down, so they made love standing up, pressed against the kitchen counter. Then they fled across the overgrown lawn to the car, holding hands like Hansel and Gretel escaping the wicked old woman they pushed into the oven. That story had spooked her when she was a little girl. How mean did you have to be before it was okay to burn you alive?

Donnie tells her he has an idea. "Close your eyes. Where I'm taking you is a surprise."

With her eyes shut she drifts into a light sleep. She's been tired all day. Her parents had a fight late last night that woke her up. In the morning her mom said nothing about it, but she never does. She acts like Rebecca's deaf. Blind too. As if she doesn't know her dad's sleeping in the den.

The sound of tires crunching on gravel rouses her. As Donnie turns off the ignition, he says to open her eyes but wait in the car while he checks out the place. She watches through the windshield as he approaches a dark farmhouse using his cell to light the way. She finds the location on Google Maps: Sugar Hill Road. When he doesn't return after ten minutes, she starts to worry and texts him. I'm inside, he texts back. No alarm system. Just coming to get you.

On the way to the house, he holds her hand as if guiding her over a difficult trail. Proudly he opens the back door. The kitchen window was unlocked, he tells her, and he climbed through without breaking anything. The house belongs to people his mom knows who are away for a while. He leads her upstairs into the master bedroom, shining the cell light on the queen bed with its quilted spread and matching pillow covers. "Is this okay?"

What will he do if she says no? she wonders. Because really she doesn't want to have sex tonight at all, not with him, not with Ricky, not with anyone. But she owes Donnie and doesn't want to hurt him. "Take off your clothes," she whispers, "lie down." After he complies, she climbs on the bed and kneels over him. "Where are you ticklish?"

"I'm not going to tell you."

"I'm going to find out." She starts tickling his armpits.

"Don't, Rebecca," he pleads. As he thrashes around and giggles, she bends down farther and runs her tongue down his chest to the softness of his belly and then the hardness of him. Her fingertips are still tickling him, but more gently. He stops moving. She likes it when she makes him still.

"I've got cramps," she lies, "so let me give you this."

Afterward, as they curl up next to each other, two cats jump on the bed. One's a fat, fluffy tabby, the other short-haired and black, and both purr loudly as they stroke them. "I like this," Rebecca says. "Let's come back tomorrow."

They return three nights in a row. On the first two she lets him make love to her, though it's getting harder to pretend she's into it. What she likes is cuddling afterward with the cats beside them. They've named the tabby Caramel, the black one Night Sky. Donnie noticed a note on the counter that the owners are coming home on Monday—not much time left.

On the third night she takes her last Percocet before they lie down. He must sense something's off because he asks what's wrong. He pushes her to tell him what's happening with her parents, but she's floating by then and doesn't want to come down. He's insistent, he won't shut up. That's something she doesn't like about him—he wants to help too much, wants to know everything about her, even why she cut her arms. He tells her way too much about himself too. Last night he even showed her videos of his dad before he died. It freaked her out—she didn't know what he expected her to say or do.

To avoid talking, she spreads her legs passively, letting him make love to her, faking an orgasm so he won't go down on her. When he falls asleep afterward, she rolls over to look at him, propping herself up on an elbow. There's a little moonlight coming through the window, the glow of the digital clock. He looks so young, too young, though he's the same age as her. When he comes, he closes his eyes and whimpers. She's tired of her power over him. His sweetness should be enough for her, but it isn't. Nothing is enough except for nothingness. The pills are teaching her that.

She sneaks out of the room and texts Ricky that the plan's on—she'll meet him at the playground near her house. Donnie doesn't know she told her mom she's sleeping over at Michelle's; he thinks she needs to get back by ten. Shortly before nine thirty, she wakes him up, and they straighten up the bed. Caramel and Night Sky follow them downstairs, meowing for the cat treats Donnie carries in his pocket. When Night Sky rubs against her leg, she reaches down to stroke its head, not knowing if they're coming back another time or not.

After Donnie drops her at the playground, she starts off in the direction of home and then circles back once his car's out of sight. Drowsy, she lies down on the slide, staring up at a few faint stars in the bruised black-and-blue sky. She used to play here when she was little—the equipment seemed big and intimidating then, and climbing to the top of the jungle gym or hanging off the monkey bars was scary. She liked the swings the best, still does.

She checks the time on her cell—Ricky's ten minutes late. He wasn't happy when she asked him to score more pills for her, probably because of how she freaked out that night. Those were uppers though, not downers. Donnie still doesn't know what happened, how it wasn't Ricky's fault. He told her to go back to Donnie's car, but she didn't want to. She wanted to get high, super high, and have sex with Ricky one more time.

A car pulls up by the curb, the lights go off. She watches as Ricky crosses the playground to find her. "Jesus, Rebecca," he reprimands, "you shouldn't be sitting out here alone in the dark. It's not safe."

"You shouldn't have been late."

"I had to wait for a ride from some guys—they're in the car, I can't stay long."

"Who are they?"

"You don't know them."

"Did you bring the pills?" He reaches into his pocket and hands her a baggie with only a few inside. "That's all? I told you I wanted more."

"That's all I could get. The supply of real ones is drying up, and they're super expensive. The cheap ones are fake and dangerous."

"I can give you more money."

"It's not the money. That's really all I could get. You shouldn't do that shit anyway."

"I'll quit after these." She pauses, then tells him it's not working with Donnie, and she wants to get back together with him.

"So I can get you pills?"

"How can you say that, Ricky?"

"Because it's true. And we're not getting back together—I can't do that to Donnie."

His response pisses her off. What is it about Rickety-DicketyDon that keeps them so tied together? They should get over it, move on, like she's moving on from Michelle. Loyalty is overrated. She can see that from her parents sticking together too long. "I don't need to go home yet," she says. "My mom thinks I'm sleeping over at Michelle's. Can we drive around for a while? And then you can drop me home—I'll tell her I got sick."

"I don't like the guys I came with."

"So? All I want is to ride around a little bit. Please, Ricky, I've been so cooped up lately."

Two older guys are in the car smoking pot. One speaks with a heavy Boston accent; the other's accent she can't make out, maybe he's from the South. No introductions are made, though the driver hands her the joint before they take off. "Is there nowhere to hang out in this fucking town on a Friday night?" he asks.

"I know a place," she says.

11

SOMETHING'S NOT RIGHT, LAURA senses. Donnie got up earlier than usual for a Saturday morning, emerged briefly for breakfast, clutching his cell like a lifeline, then shut himself in his room. Eavesdropping once or twice, she heard muffled sobs. So soon to be so hurt, but then she remembers what it was like in high school, the rapid-fire heartbreaks and gut-wrenching pain. Naive of her to expect it would be different between Donnie and Rebecca, especially since she knows from Mimi how troubled her daughter is. Maybe it was wrong to facilitate their intimacy—feeding Rebecca dinner night after night, leaving them alone in the house afterward. Too much, too fast.

Too much, too fast. Can the same be said about her and Nate?

She ponders that question as she arrives at his house after lunch. Last night for the first time, neither of them had the energy for sex and instead watched a film on TV. But maybe that's to be expected, she thinks, even welcomed, a sign they're settling in for the long haul.

She finds him cleaning out the chicken coop, so covered in muck they can't embrace. She offers to help, but he says he's almost done and to wait inside. In the living room his family photo catches her eye again, and she picks it up, exploring the faces up close. She knows a little about his sister, Alana, now, but Nate's told her nothing about his brother except that his name is Rob. Cute kid back then, but he must be well into his thirties now. "So what's Rob do?" she asks when Nate comes in.

He frowns, seemingly displeased by the question. "He works as a ranch hand sometimes," he says, "but mainly bums around. Alana and I hear from him about once a year when he demands money from the business. The deadbeat doesn't deserve a cent in my estimation, but Alana is too nice to cut him off." A shadow passes over his face. "I don't want to talk about it right now, Laura. Another time."

Reluctantly, she agrees, though it irks her that he knows more about her family than she does about his. When he goes up for a shower, she studies the photo again. Rob looks so alive and full of possibility in the picture, as if he's ready to leap out of the frame and start running and jumping like Donnie used to do at that age. Hard to believe he's a deadbeat now.

On the hike they take that afternoon, Nate is withdrawn, hiding behind his binoculars. When he speaks, the tone he takes with her is of nature guide, not lover. He's overly pedantic too, lacking his usual spirited way with words. She falls back, wanting to be quiet, alone, free to hear birdsong without specifying the singers. Sometimes she tires of birding's taxonomizing of sound; it's like going to a choral concert to pick apart the separate sections rather than to hear the harmony of the whole.

Is she tiring of Nate too? she wonders. Or he of her? She reminds herself that this is to be expected. Sooner or later, the first glow of sex always fades, and you need to stoke the fire of intimacy with other kinds of fuel. The sharing of stories, for instance. You tell yours, I'll tell mine. And if there's too much reluctance or refusal, it can snuff the whole thing out. Why won't he tell her more about his family?

She's glad he's attending an Audubon fundraiser tonight that she begged out of. The birding group is meeting tomorrow morning for a walk near the Quabbin Reservoir, and afterward,

Nate and she plan to spend another afternoon together. Hopefully, he'll open up then.

AFTER DONNIE BAGS FIVE BOXES of cornflakes for an old lady on food stamps, there's a lull in customers, and his thoughts return to Rebecca. The text she sent this morning crushed him. She doesn't want to see him for a while, she wrote, needs some time by herself to figure things out. No heart emoji at the end. He called several times, but she didn't pick up. Desperate, he phoned Michelle for advice. "Rebecca hasn't told me anything," she said, "but she retreats sometimes, even from her best friends. It's happened to me; you just have to wait it out." He phoned Ricky too, who claimed to know nothing, though something in his voice made Donnie suspicious that they're back together.

In his mind's eye he sees her naked, coming on to Ricky, and it makes him feel like throwing up. It doesn't help that the next customer is buying a ton of slimy ground beef leaking red juice from the package. He bags it in plastic, and when the guy's gone, he squirts some hand sanitizer on his fingers. "You've gone all white," Patty tells him. "Need a break?"

He nods. "I'll be back in five."

He goes outside for some fresh air. He's working until nine tonight, doing an extra shift so another bagger can go to a Red Sox game. He walks around to the bushes in back of the store, leans over, and tries to retch, but nothing comes out.

He makes it through the next few hours on autopilot, barely looking at the customers he's serving. A few minutes after nine, when he's on his way to the car, he gets a call from Michelle. "I just picked up a voice mail from Rebecca, and she's in trouble," she practically shouts into the phone. "I could hardly hear her because of the noise, but she said something about a party on Sugar Hill Road that's out of control, and it's her fault. It was about an hour ago when she left the message. She wanted me to pick her up, but I'm in New Hampshire visiting my grandparents. She didn't want you to know, but someone's got to pick her up, Donnie. I just tried calling and texting her, but her cell must be turned off. Do you know where the party is?"

He pauses, his heart sinking. How could Rebecca do this to him? "I think so."

"Can you go get her?"

"I'll try."

"Thanks *so* much. Please let me know what happens, okay? I'm really worried about her."

He drives the dark roads out of town way too fast, taking thirty-mile-an-hour curves at over fifty. When he swerves into the opposite lane, an oncoming car blasts its horn, and he makes himself slow down. The worst thing would be getting pulled over by the cops. At least he's sober, stone-cold sober. He didn't even smoke a joint before work. Enough adrenaline is pumping through his veins to keep him awake for a week. He swears out loud at Rebecca. But the truth is he's more worried than angry.

The Addisons' driveway is full up with cars, so he parks on the roadside. As he approaches the house, he notices the shades are drawn, but light is leaking around the window edges, including from the master bedroom upstairs. Kids are hanging around outside, and he passes a guy pissing on the bushes, a girl barfing, a bunch of people smoking pot. He texts Ricky: I know what's going on. Are you here? Ricky texts back to meet him behind the garage.

Donnie stands there waiting in the dark. This time bile rises in his throat for real, but he forces it back down when he spies Ricky approaching. Ricky's agitated, jittery, turning his head this way and that to check if anyone's coming. He warns Donnie to leave right away.

"I can't—I've come to pick up Rebecca."

"Too late. She's with some guys you don't want to mess with. I tried to stop them taking her upstairs, but she said she wanted to go with them and to leave her alone."

"Why did she ask Michelle to get her out of here then?" Donnie challenges.

"That was before."

"Before what?"

"Before they offered to get her high."

"They could be raping her up there," Donnie protests, but Ricky shakes his head, claiming it's not their thing. "What is their thing then?"

"You don't want to know."

"Yes, I do."

Ricky grabs his arm. "You don't want to be here, bro. Like I said, just go home, pretend you were never here." Breaking free of his grip, Donnie shoves past him and heads for the back door. "I'm coming with you," Ricky insists.

Winding their way through the drunken party, Donnie recognizes a few kids from the high school, but most people are strangers, older than the usual crowd. The floors are slippery and sticky from spilled booze and it smells like a bar. He glances into the living room, where the couch is turned over and paintings are ripped from the wall. Loud music is playing, but no one's dancing. He wonders where the cats are and hopes they're okay.

At the top of the stairs, Donnie pushes open the door to the bedroom and Ricky follows. The first thing he notices is that Rebecca has her clothes on. One of her sleeves is rolled up though. She's sitting on the edge of the bed while a guy beside her unties a strip of rubber tubing above her elbow. An empty syringe lies on the quilt.

"What the fuck, didn't I tell you to stay out of here, Ricky?" the guy shouts. He's short, wiry, mean looking. His buddy stands silently in the corner, smoking a cigarette. He's taller, paunchy, with a shaved head. "And who's this other joker you're with?"

"That's my boyfriend, Donnie," Rebecca says in a high, childlike pitch.

"Well, boyfriend, you need to get the fuck out of here too."

Rebecca nods dozily. "Don't worry, Donnie, I'm fine, really. They just gave me a little bit. The cats are fine too."

"Carl, escort these two boys out, would you," the guy on the bed orders.

"Yeah sure, Andy," he replies, stubbing his cigarette out on the windowsill.

Downstairs Carl orders Ricky to stay inside while he takes Donnie back to the car. To buy time, Donnie fumbles for the keys, looking first in one pocket, then the other. He'll drive off but then come back with a tire iron, he thinks. He'll drag Rebecca down the stairs if he has to. Anything to get her out of there.

"Speed it up!" Carl yells in his ear. As Donnie unlocks the car, Carl shoves him into the side and puts him in an armlock. "You tell anyone about what you saw," he threatens, "and I'm not only going to mess you up, I'll slash your girlfriend so bad she won't have that pretty face anymore." He pulls back Donnie's arms so hard that pain shoots through his right shoulder. "I'd find another girlfriend if I was you. We didn't force her to shoot up—it was her idea. First time's a charm, but she has junkie written all over her." He tightens his hold again. "Now get the fuck out of here and keep your mouth shut."

12

ON SUNDAY MORNING WAITING at the reservoir for the other birders, Laura pretends to busy herself with her cell while Nate leafs through his old Forbush volume to select a reading. The warm, humid weather is making her groggy, and she wishes she'd brought along a mug of coffee. She slept through her alarm this morning and was late getting to Nate's. He wasn't happy about it, but they're the first ones here, so what does it matter? What matters more is that his aloofness has carried over from yesterday.

Twenty minutes later, when everyone is finally assembled, Nate gives his customary introduction to the trip. "I'm going to read to you about one of my favorite species of waterfowl, the hooded merganser," he begins, opening the volume like a Sunday preacher his Bible. "They've been spotted here several times recently, but I have yet to see them this spring. Hopefully, we'll find them." The congregation falls silent as he reads about how the returning spring "*kindles anew in their breasts the glowing fires of reproduction. The males, in all the splendor of their elegant spring plumage, seek and pay court to their prospective mates.... The ardent males chase the females, pursuing them on the surface and even under water.*"

Laura closely follows the movement of his lips, hoping to discern some hidden language meant only for her. She needs a signal, a reminder that he, like the mating merganser, is still an ardent male pursuing her, despite the tension between them. Periodically he lifts his eyes to look at the group. He smiles at Cora, his dimples showing through the stubble on his chin. His hair is unwashed, greasy—he hasn't had time to shower. She tries to catch his eye, but he looks over her, then down at the book. She fights an old childhood feeling of being excluded, shunned on the playground by a best friend turned traitor. He raises the book to show an illustrated plate. "See how the female has a darker breast," he says, "and the male has that crested head—fan-shaped almost, with a patch of white. Look out for that."

As they set off down the wooded trail to the water, Laura takes up the rear to help Cora. The older woman is remarkably agile with her cane, but her bad vision sometimes makes her stumble. She's wearing an incongruous assortment of clothing today, an embroidered cardigan with pearl buttons, denim carpenter's pants, and red sneakers with white rubber-enforced toes. Laura offers her arm, and as Cora takes it, she whispers conspiratorially, "I just think it's so nice you and Nate are seeing each other."

"So you know?" Laura responds.

"I may be old, my dear, but I'm not totally blind. Besides, I always thought you'd make a nice couple."

"You did?"

"I've always been good at spotting these things before they happen."

"You'd make a good matchmaker."

Cora shakes her head vigorously. "Only for other people, I'm afraid. My own marriages were both disasters. Do you know I'm the oldest person in Stanton to get divorced? I signed the papers on my eightieth birthday."

"How old are you now?"

"Eighty-three. Best three years of my life too. What a relief—getting rid of that oaf. There was nothing wrong with his health, but he wanted me to wait on him hand and foot. I told him to check into a nursing home if that's what he wanted. Terminal case of laziness, if you ask me. But Nate's not like that. Count your blessings, my dear."

"It's just the beginning of our relationship. . . ."

"It's never too early to count your blessings. Unfortunately, most people don't realize that until they have one foot in the grave."

Laura scouts the path ahead, steering them clear of a patch of shiny poison ivy. Nearby is a cluster of trillium, but their bloom is past and the crinkled petals are a dull rust color. She slaps a mosquito on her arm. No blood. The clammy air makes her shirt cling to her skin. She wonders how Cora can stand to wear a sweater.

Nate turns and stops, waiting for them to catch up. Five feet away, he finally meets her eye. A hint of intimacy, but beyond that something else. Resignation? Maybe he doesn't want to be here, she considers. Maybe he's losing his enthusiasm for birding with amateurs. As he points out a killdeer, a veery, and two eastern wood pewees in the brushy foliage, he acts almost too patient and upbeat, like he's following a script, performing the good teacher. He identifies the songs of the hermit and wood thrush and whistles back to them with perfect pitch. The group tries too, but none of them come close except young Jeff, who then can't stop whistling. She finds herself missing crusty Keith Addison, who would put a stop to it with one angry glare. Every bird group needs an enforcer.

At the water's edge, Nate sets up a scope along with Jeff's dad, Bill. Bill's is new, teched up with an adapter for his camera so he can shoot photos and video footage. A birthday present from his wife, Stacy, he proudly announces. People take turns viewing the waterfowl: mallard and wood ducks, a great blue heron, even a couple of white egrets, but no hooded mergansers. Laura separates from the group, crossing some rocks to another little inlet where she hopes to find Nate his mergansers.

She scans the water, but the only object of interest is a fishing boat. She thinks about her dad, how he never took her fishing here because he didn't like the idea of floating on top of the drowned ghost towns. To her, the reservoir's islands seem eerie too—the tops of submerged hills, they look like disembodied breasts, the carnage of a lost battle. She focuses her binoculars on the boat, watching the fisherman reel in his rod, take some grass off the line, and then cast again. The line curls and shimmers in the sunlight, which has just broken through. A split second of grace.

Nate calls her name as he rounds the bend. "It's time to go—the natives are getting restless."

"I wanted to find you a hooded merganser."

He shrugs. "I'm afraid it's not to be."

Back in the truck he tells her he has to drop by the Addisons' house before they go out for brunch. The couple is due home tomorrow, so he needs to feed the cats one last time and switch on the hot water. She notices his face is broody, tight around the eyes. When she asks if he feels all right, he claims he has a headache but won't accept the Tylenol she offers.

On the drive she gazes out the window, but the landscape she usually appreciates seems monotonous today, just trees and more trees leafing out and hemming her in. She yearns for a flat, wide-open landscape—ocean, prairie, desert—where you can see unhindered to the horizon and enjoy, if only for a few moments, a glimpse of eternity.

Instead what awaits them on Sugar Hill Road forces her brutally back to the present. First there is the smashed mailbox, then the driveway strewn with broken beer bottles, paper plates, pizza boxes, and fast food wrappers. Like a flag signaling enemy territory, a plastic bag on a tree branch flutters in the wind. The tires from invading vehicles have cut deep muddy ruts in the lawn. "What the hell!" Nate exclaims as he swerves around the debris and brings the truck to a sudden halt.

Hell indeed. Laura knows this kind of thing happens. At least once or twice a year a teenage party spins out of control. Usually, it's at a kid's house whose parents are away, but occasionally they break into a stranger's home. But how would kids know the Addisons are away? They're an unlikely target. She hopes she hasn't said anything to Donnie about their trip to Costa Rica. Why would she? Dread clutches at her stomach, her chest. No, please, she hasn't said anything—or has she?

Nate marches ahead of her through the open front door. She's wrong—this wasn't just a party. Something else has gone on here too, something beyond liquor on the floor and vomit in the bathrooms, something manic and crazy like the couch with multiple stab wounds; holes punched in walls; shattered mirrors, windows, lamps, and picture frames; broken chairs; burn marks on the carpet—a full-scale assault.

Worried about the cats, Nate asks her to search the upstairs for any sign of them while he looks around the bottom floor. She finds the first cat, a tabby, cowering in a corner of the master bedroom, his backside covered with his own shit. She kneels on the floor, trying to cajole him forward, but he refuses. "I found one," she shouts down to Nate, who joins her. They look in the other bedrooms for the black cat, but she isn't there. Laura suggests she might be outside.

"Emily told me she never goes out."

"Maybe she was freaked out by all the noise—the front door was open."

Nate goes downstairs to check. She's about to follow when the tabby emerges from the bedroom and stands by a hall closet. Laura opens the door and yanks the light chain.

Wedged between two dry cleaning bags, the black cat hangs from the rod, her neck snapped by a noose made from a necktie. There's something ghoulishly cartoonish about her bulging eyes and elongated body, and for a moment Laura allows herself the hope the vision isn't real. But then the tabby starts to meow high and sharp like the wail of a woman in a funeral march. She braces herself against the wall. "Nate," she screams. "Come here!"

Maybe it's too much to ask, but she wants him to offer some comfort first, place a hand on her shoulder, say a few words to calm her down, but instead he focuses only on the task at hand. He takes a penknife from his pocket and flicks open the blade. While he cuts the tie, she holds on to the cat's cold body and a chill seeps into her. "Who would do something like this?" he asks. "To a cat? It's evil." She nods, shivering so hard she begins to shake. He takes the cat from her arms and lays it on the floor. "I'm going to call the police."

"No, let me call," she replies quickly. "I'll see if my uncle's on duty."

In the time it takes Jack to arrive, they clean off the tabby in the bathtub. Nate holds him by the scruff of his neck while she washes him off. He doesn't put up resistance, and afterward, she wraps him in a towel and holds him in her arms like a baby.

She's still holding him when Jack pulls up in an unmarked squad car. "Jesus fucking Christ," he mutters as he comes inside.

Together the three of them walk from room to room as Jack takes a quick inventory of the damage. Keith's study seems relatively untouched, though the desk has been rifled through, and if he left his computer here, it's gone. "When was the last time you came over?" Jack asks Nate as they enter the trashed dining room.

"Yesterday morning. I fed the cats."

"Notice anything strange?"

"Well, kind of. I thought I smelled pot but convinced myself it was just the litter box. There were also a few cat nibbles on the kitchen floor. I figured there must be a bag of them somewhere the cats got into. Otherwise I didn't see any signs of a break-in. I should have been more suspicious."

When Jack's cell rings, he leaves the room to take the call. Nate tells Laura he's going outside to check the perimeter. Alone, she bends down to pick up a broken plate, turning it over to check the make. Limoges from France, a pattern of tiny gold-and-green leaves. The china cabinet's empty, every piece smashed. The dining table surface is covered with scratches with pools of hard liquor wearing off the finish. How will Emily take this? Laura wonders. She seemed a little fragile during that dinner at Nate's. This could break her, break anyone.

Jack rejoins her, a pained expression on his face. "It happened last night," he explains. "Tommy was on his way home and saw cars parked on the side of the road. There was no noise complaint, so he couldn't really do anything. But he did take down the license plates as a precautionary measure, and Donnie's car was here too."

"That doesn't mean . . . ," she jumps in defensively.

"Hold on, Laura, let me finish. This is still an investigation—no one's been arrested, but we're going to question everyone whose car was here, and that includes Donnie, I'm afraid."

"You know he wouldn't do this, Jack." She points to the smashed china on the floor. "And he loves animals. He'd never kill a cat."

"Who said he did?" He pauses, letting the words sink in. "You'd better get home. They'll be coming around looking for him."

"Can you interview him?" she appeals. "He'll respond better to you."

He shakes his head. "Conflict of interest. Just make sure he cooperates."

"My car's at Nate's house."

"Well, then get him to drive you there. He can come back if he wants. I'll still be here."

"Please don't say anything to him about Donnie being at the party."

"What the hell, Laura, you're going to keep that from him?"

"Until I know more."

"You should tell him now," he rebukes. "Out of respect, if nothing else."

She knows he's right, but during the ride to Nate's house she can't bring herself to do it. They hardly exchange a word, much less a goodbye hug or kiss. "I'll give you a call tonight" is all he says.

She arrives home to find Tommy interrogating a bleary-eyed Donnie in the kitchen. He's still in his pajamas with a tattered hoodie acting as a robe. The way he's slumped in his chair suggests he wants to slide under the table. "Your mother knows about the party," Tommy remarks as she takes a seat. "She's aware we have a record of your car parked nearby."

Donnie looks confused. "I just came from there," she explains. "Uncle Jack told me."

"Why don't you tell your mom your story," Tommy says, pronouncing *story* with derision. Then he sits back, folding his arms across his thick chest. A linebacker in high school, he still has a powerful physical presence, though his face has gone a bit flabby, his posture a little slack.

"Tell me what happened, Donnie," she urges. "I want to hear it from you. Were you there?"

"I heard there was a party so I stopped by," he answers with his eyes down. "I hung out on the driveway for a little while but didn't go inside." When Tommy asks why not, he shrugs and says he didn't see anyone he knew.

"No one was with you?"

"Like I said before, I was alone."

"Are you sure you didn't know *anyone* there?" Tommy presses.

"No one on the driveway—could have been some people I knew inside, I guess."

"Why didn't you go looking for them?"

"I wasn't in the mood."

"Is that right? How'd you hear about the party anyway?"

"The news was going around."

"Someone must have told you." He leans forward to get in Donnie's face. "Was it Ricky?"

"Don't remember."

"Maybe there's a text on your cell that will jog your memory. Want to check it for me?"

"I delete my messages every night."

"How convenient," Tommy retorts. "Listen, young man, if you help us with this investigation, we can help you. Think about it. I'm going to be interviewing other kids who were parked there. I hope you're not lying to me because if you are, I'll find out, and you'll be in trouble with the law. Not the slap on the wrist kind of trouble, but the real thing. Got that?" Donnie mutters something under his breath. "Was that a yes?"

"I get it, if that's what you mean."

When Tommy leaves a few minutes later, Laura's intuition tells her to follow him out to his car. She's known him since high school when he dated one of her friends for a while. He was shy back then, awkward, and she was nice to him when other girls in their group treated him like a dumb interloper. Maybe he remembers that.

On the driveway he asks what she wants but with less hostility. "I know you couldn't say much in front of Donnie," she begins, "so I wonder if there's more you can tell me."

He shakes his head. "Just putting the pieces together now. It's a slow process with kids—no one wants to talk."

"Was it just kids involved?"

"Don't know," he says too fast. "Look, I got to go. Keep me in the loop and I'll reciprocate as much as I can. Deal?" She nods noncommittally, and he turns away.

Any relief that Tommy has left dissolves as soon as she's back inside. It used to be so easy to figure out when Donnie was lying, but in the last few years he's improved on the art. He's tapping his fingers on the table, a clear sign he's anxious, but his face, half-hidden by his hoodie, is a practiced blank. She asks what really happened. "You can tell me—I'm not going to tell anyone."

"It's like I said."

"Really?"

"You don't believe me?" He acts hurt, but she senses he's putting her on.

She explains she doesn't know what to believe. "It was horrible—the way they trashed the house and hanged one of the cats. I had to help cut it down. And then we had to clean off the other one. It was covered with its own shit, totally freaked out."

His face goes pale. "They hanged a cat?"

"Yes."

"Which one?"

And so she catches him, at least for a moment. "How do you know about the cats?" she prods. "You did go inside, didn't you?"

"No, I saw the cats outside."

"In the dark?" He nods. "Really? Please tell me the truth, Donnie."

"That's the truth. Which one did they hang?"

"The black one," she answers, watching his reaction. He's trembling, holding back tears. She wants to hug him, or at least touch him on the shoulder, but she's afraid of a rebuff. He's already stiffening, putting on a brave face. "They hanged her from a rod in the hall closet, with a necktie."

"I didn't do it, Mom."

"Of course you didn't do it, but you need to tell me what happened. I have a feeling I told you the Addisons were going on a trip after I had dinner with them at Nate's. Were you the one who called the party? We may need to hire a lawyer, Donnie—I've got to know."

"I stopped by but didn't go in," he mumbles.

She lowers her voice almost to a whisper. "Did you let people know the house was empty? Did you tell Ricky or Rebecca?" He shakes his head. "Was Rebecca with you?"

"No one was with me, Mom."

"Was Ricky or Rebecca there?"

"I don't know."

She examines his face, trying to strip away the years. A little boy in his room accused of a little-boy crime—stealing a pack of gum from her purse. He was chewing it when she came in, so he parked the gum under his cheek and literally lied through his teeth. She never did get a real confession, though he had a hard time going to sleep that night. Lying wears on him still, she thinks, revealing itself eventually in dark circles under the eyes, a light rash around the nose. He doesn't have the right complexion for it. "I don't think you're telling me everything," she says.

"So now my own mom's calling me a liar."

"Well, you've lied to me before."

"Believe what you want to believe," he replies angrily. "I'm getting out of here, going to work."

"I thought you had the day off."

"They called me up. Someone's sick."

She doubts it but lets him go. The truth is she wants to be alone. She's convinced now she did tell Donnie that Keith and Emily were going away. And so that means she probably set the whole disaster in motion. Donnie probably took Rebecca to the house and then word leaked out. Empty house. Party time. Maybe Donnie even threw the party, though that's unlikely. He's too much of a loner. Could have been Ricky, but that's always her fallback position. Maybe it was whoever hanged the cat.

What's her obligation here? To confess her suspicions to the police? But she has no real proof, does she? There's a remote chance the break-in has nothing to do with her or Donnie. Keith's position on the conservation commission has made him a lot of local enemies. Maybe one of them orchestrated the assault. Improbable, though.

She takes a long shower to clear her head. When Nate calls this evening, she'll have to reveal that Donnie was at the party, she reflects, but beyond that? No doubt he'll ask a lot of questions. Easier to hide things from him on the phone, rather than in person where he'll see through her. She can't take that risk. Best if she claims she needs a little distance. He's been giving her that message himself, hasn't he? His withdrawal over the past couple of days provides an excuse for her to withdraw too.

DONNIE WAITS AT THE SECRET place for Ricky, sitting outside the shack on a log. He hasn't been here since that time they had sex with the girls from New Hampshire. He notices the roof is missing more shingles and there's broken glass where a window used to be. The bottom of the old rowboat tied to the dock is half-submerged in muck. When Ricky and he first discovered the place, they had a fantasy of restoring the boat and riding down the river like Huck Finn.

When Ricky shows up on his bicycle a half hour late, Donnie tells him he should have asked for a ride. "Better if we're not seen together," Ricky says as he removes his dark glasses to show Donnie a swollen black eye. "Carl punched me when I tried to go back upstairs."

"The fucker slammed me into my car."

"It gets worse. Look." He hands Donnie his cell. On the screen there's a photo of Rebecca holding Night Sky while someone else's hands put a noose around the cat's neck. "Carl sent me the picture this morning. Said if I don't keep quiet about last night, he'll spread it around. Jesus, Donnie, they hung the cat."

"I know. My mom found it this morning."

"Your *mom*?"

"She's friends with the people whose house it is. They're away, and she was over there with her boyfriend to feed the cats."

"Shit. Is that how Rebecca found out about the house—from you?"

Donnie nods. "We hung out there a couple of times."

"I'm so fucking stupid."

"What do you mean?"

Ricky bows his head, gazes down at the ground. Donnie doesn't push. Long ago he learned to be patient with his friend, to let him come clean on his own time. It takes a minute or so before Ricky lifts his head back up and tells him how a couple of days ago, Rebecca begged him to get her some pills. He refused at first, but she kept calling and texting, claiming she was desperate. He couldn't handle it, so he gave in. "Friday night I met her at the playground after you dropped her off," he reveals. "I copped a ride with Carl and Andy, who were waiting in the car. She wanted to go driving around afterward. I should have refused. Fucking disaster, man. Girl bragged to them she knew a place where we could all hang out and get high. We went to the Sugar Hill house and smoked a few numbers. Nothing else, but that's how it began."

Donnie doesn't want to believe him—how could Rebecca bring those jerks into the house? But he can see from Ricky's face that he's not making it up. And there's the way she was sitting on the bed, the same bed they made love on, letting Andy shoot her up. As if what they had together means nothing to her. She told Andy he was her boyfriend. Yeah, right. More like her fool. But he can't quite believe she'd hang Night Sky. She's smiling in that picture though. He asks Ricky what he thinks.

"She's smiling because she's totally out of it," Ricky says. "Carl and Andy staged the whole thing to get the photo."

"Why?"

"Can't tell you that."

"You have to." He delivers the words with authority—rare he has any power over Ricky, though there used to be times when he was the leader, Ricky the follower, because their friendship couldn't survive having it only one way around. *Today I get to be Batman*, Donnie would insist, *and you play Robin*. A tiny bird's hopping on the ground, coming nearer and nearer. Very slowly, Donnie reaches out a hand, and the bird brushes against his fingertips. He wants to be angry, but Ricky's hunched over now, starting to cry. What should he do? Touch him, comfort him? But will his friend consider that weird, weak, gay? But nothing's weirder than what's happened already. Night Sky's dead and Rebecca's shooting up. Donnie drapes his arm awkwardly around Ricky's shoulders. "You have to tell me what's going on, bro."

It takes a while for Ricky to calm down enough to speak. He can't take it, he says, Rebecca's driving him nuts. She comes on to him only to get drugs. He knows he hurt Donnie that night they went out on a date, and she ditched him. Ricky only wanted to talk to her for a few minutes, but she wouldn't go back to Donnie's car. "I wanted her to be with you, Donnie. I thought you could help her. She and I were bringing each other down. But she doesn't want to be helped, you know. I finally realized that, but I still keep doing what she wants because she has this control over me. Do you know what I mean? I mean she makes you want to save her or something."

"I don't feel like that anymore."

"Yeah, you say that now because you're pissed off she lied to you. But in a couple of days, she'll come back and have sex with you, and it all starts over again except it's not as fun as the first time, and it gets a whole lot less fun each time until it's no fun at all. Let her go while you still can."

"You can't?" Donnie asks, and Ricky shakes his head in response. "Because it's not just about her, is it? Tell me everything, Ricky, starting from the fight. Why'd you say I was gay anyway?"

"They told me to."

"Who's they?" He waits again, sensing his friend is hovering on the edge of telling him the truth. Their friendship hovers on that edge.

Finally, it spills out of him that the gang stuff is for real. The Blades are looking to recruit dealers here, trespassing on Jag territory. They tried to recruit Ricky. He went along for a while but, after the knife fight, told them he didn't want in. They started threatening they'd do something to his family and Rebecca. He was fucked. But then something else went down. Bigger guys moved in, like Gary, Rebecca's cousin. Carl and Andy work for him, Ricky explains, but they want a bigger cut of the action. And so there's this competition going on. Gary has a weird family thing about Rebecca, wants to protect her. Carl and Andy are trying to take her down so they have a way to get at Gary. They'll probably blackmail him with that picture.

"I work for Gary now," he admits. "I have to. The Blades won't touch me if I'm with him. Gary's their main supplier so they don't want to piss him off. He supplies the Jags too, tries to keep the peace between the two gangs." Ricky pauses. "Now Gary's trying to get Rebecca to work for him in his pottery studio. I'm in deep, deep shit, and so is she. That's why you got to stay out of this, okay? Forget you were ever involved with either of us. She's way beyond fucked up, Donnie. I'm going to try to get her and me out of this shit, but

I don't know how yet. You may need to help us escape. Until then you got to lie low. Play the good boy. Tell people we're not friends anymore. I'll only be in touch if it's an emergency."

"You could go to the police," Donnie advises half-heartedly.

"You know what happens to snitches. Promise me you won't tell anyone, Donnie."

They've sworn on secrets before but little-boy ones that didn't matter. Donnie gets up from the log and walks to the shore, where he picks up a rock and tries to skip it. It sinks with a plop. And so he finds a better one, thinner and flatter, that skips two times. Ricky joins him, and together they skip rocks long enough to make the promise hold.

13

THERE AT THE BOTTOM OF THE safety deposit box is her grandmother's brooch, a gold filigree wreath studded with tiny diamonds. It's worth at least $5,000, enough to pay Steve to expand his surveillance to Gary and gather information Mimi can use against him. Instead of him blackmailing her, she'll be able to blackmail him, or better yet get him put behind bars. If Rebecca has to work for him, it will only be for a little while. That's part one of the plan she devised over the weekend.

Still, it pains her to part with the brooch. Her grandma wore it on special occasions like Christmas. She was the real beauty of the family, tall like Rebecca and always stylishly dressed, able to turn eyes even into her eighties. Mimi still remembers their shopping trip to Boston before she went to college. "A girl needs to show her class," her grandma advised, "especially if she grows up in a small town like Stanton." At Filene's she selected a pleated wool skirt and matching cashmere sweater that Mimi wore once before donning the classless blue jeans and sweatshirts of her peers.

If only she could have gone to law school like she intended. The phone call had come in the middle of her senior year at Boston University. Her older brother, Benjamin, was hospitalized again, diagnosed with schizophrenia disorder. She was now heir apparent of Sullivan Lumber. While her best friends went off to explore the world after graduation, she had to return to Stanton to be groomed to take over the business.

After putting the brooch in her purse, Mimi summons the teller to return the box to the vault and then proceeds upstairs to Martin Snow's office to execute part two of her plan. She's known Martin since childhood, when their fathers dragged them along to boring Rotary Club events where Martin and she disappeared together to play cards. A whiz at poker, he patiently taught her strategy until she was able to beat him a couple of times. Through Facebook, she's aware that after his divorce he dated Laura Everett for a while. But now he's remarried to an IT expert the bank brought in for a consultation. Mimi went to the wedding but begged off the dinner.

Even before COVID, Martin had a thing about germs, so they don't shake hands. The office is warm—it faces east and morning sun is striking the windows—so she removes her linen jacket. "So, Mimi, what can I do for you today?" he asks as she takes a seat across from him.

She folds her hands in her lap and takes a deep breath. The supplicant position doesn't come naturally to her, though by now it's a familiar pattern with Martin. Except for the jewelry sales, he knows her finances in and out. "I need a hundred-thousand-dollar loan as soon as possible," she begins. "Believe it or not, my cousin Gary is finally ready to sell me his share of the Lake Amity property. It's worth about that."

Martin doesn't blink at the number, but then he never does. "Why the sudden change of heart? Has Glendale lost interest?"

"Apparently," she replies, though she's not sure. "Perhaps the conservation controversy put them off. Plus there's plenty of land for sale out here."

"Not much left with a nice lake view though."

She shrugs. "Still not worth the controversy, I guess."

He puts forward another explanation: Glendale could be bailing because of the opioid crisis. "The area's getting a bad name," he remarks, "and what senior citizens want above all is security. They're scared to death of crime. Most crime in these parts is petty—users doing a little shoplifting or dealing on the side to buy their next fix—but that March home invasion made news all over the state. The murder of an elderly couple doesn't exactly help the local real estate market. Maybe Glendale figures they won't be able to fill the units now. I saw it happen with another retirement project. We had a closing date, but the developer got cold feet after the murder."

"It was the couple's great-nephew who did it, right?"

"Yeah, hardly random, but you know the way it is—the media spooks you into thinking you're next in line, especially if you're old and have prescription painkillers in the house." He pauses, dons his optimistic face. "But you didn't really want to pursue the Glendale route, did you? This way you're free to do a deal with the conservation commission and the state. Is that what you want?"

"I think so," she replies, wishing she were smoking a cigarette and had the luxury of a little time to tap the ashes into an ashtray, the old glass kind, heavy as a paperweight. To get Martin on board, the logic of her decision needs to make sense to him. "It's not just because I'm playing nice, though," she explains. "I may need to sell more of our timberland in the future. So I reckon placating the conservationists now will give me more leeway later. Plus we depend on the loyalty of our local customer base, which is already dwindling, as you know. I can just see that horrid man Keith Addison organizing a boycott of Sullivan Lumber if I sell the Lake Amity property to a developer. He'll send people running to box stores as if they're somehow more politically correct than us."

Martin nods sympathetically. "Ironic, isn't it?"

"People like him love to talk about sustainability, but they just don't get how hard it is to sustain a local business. Sometimes I wonder if the struggle's worth it anymore."

"It is." He blinks a few times. He's a kind man, she knows, but nervous about showing emotion. "Really, I mean that, Mimi, though I'm sure it's easy to despair about the business. Remember you have a lot of other things on your plate too. Is David behaving better?"

"Thanks to you, he can't loot the accounts."

"But I mean. . . ."

When he hesitates, she asks the question for him. "Is he still gambling? If he is, I don't know," she lies. "In any case, he doesn't have much to gamble with."

"I only raise the issue because Carol and I went to dinner at the casino last week and saw him at the bar."

"He's drinking a lot—that's for sure."

"I'm sorry. I hoped his alcohol problem was under control."

"Afraid not."

Martin turns back to the business at hand—she's always liked that about him, he knows not to dwell too long on her personal problems—and says he'll try his best to arrange the loan as soon as possible. It shouldn't be difficult, since it will be a short-term loan that can be paid back once she sells the property. He'll help her complete the transaction with Gary and then negotiate the best price with the town and state. Her reasoning is sound, he assures her; any goodwill she generates now could pay off in the future. Besides, he reminds her, there's no more counting on interest from big real estate developers, at least not until the drug crisis is under control. "And who knows when that will be?" he concludes on a somber note.

She leaves with a sense of forward motion, allowing herself to believe that her plan will succeed. Her conviction lasts into her afternoon meetings with suppliers with whom she's characteristically cheerful but tough, striking hard bargains. She stays until six o'clock in the office to catch up on work she's missed. As soon as she turns off the computer, her mood crashes though. The idea of Rebecca working with

Gary, even if only for a few days, sends her into a tailspin. What if he shows the tattoo to her? Mimi needs the dirt on him immediately.

She calls Steve and leaves a message for him to proceed with a rush job on Gary—she's willing to pay the higher fee. And then she calls her jewelry dealer and tells him about the brooch, trying to keep the desperation out of her voice. He's interested but wants to see a photograph. She takes a closeup with her cell and emails it to him. The *whoosh* it makes entering cyberspace sounds like air being sucked out of her soul.

AFTER HOMEROOM, REBECCA ducks into a restroom stall and takes one of the pills Ricky got her. It's the only way she can make it through. What if kids know she was at the party? What if Carl or Andy posts that picture of her with Night Sky? Ricky showed it to her yesterday. She told him she was so out of it she didn't know what was happening, and it's true. Probably she thought Andy was just being silly and dressing up the cat. But really she doesn't know what she thought because she was incapable of thinking. Shooting up took her away like she hoped it would, but not far enough away, not for long enough.

Night Sky is dead. Donnie must hate her, though Ricky claims Donnie won't rat on her. Still, she can't face seeing him first period in English class.

The bell rings, but she doesn't move from the stall. Maybe Ms. Jenkins will let her lie down in the nurse's office. Maybe she'll even give her permission to go home. She'll say she has a bad headache and her stomach hurts, which isn't far from the truth. She wants her bed more than she wants anything else in the world except for Night Sky to be alive again.

14

AFTER PARKING ON THE ACCESS road, Laura takes a path toward Jack's fishing shack on the Diamond River. He called last night and asked her to meet him there this morning. In January a bad ice storm left behind a swath of cracked trees and broken limbs here, and although new seedlings are taking root, the forest still looks wounded and incomplete. As she nears the riverbank, a flash of orange catches her eye, and she recognizes the song of a Baltimore oriole. For a moment, she allows herself to think of Nate, wishing she could share the sighting with him. She hasn't seen him for a week. On the phone she told him she had family issues to deal with and needed some space. When he pressed her about it, she was cool, removed, kind of rude. He called a couple more times, but she didn't pick up.

She finishes a cigarette and grinds it out with her shoe. The butt looks so ugly on the path, like the larva of a giant grub. She hates herself for smoking again, but that's the point—to hate herself instead of Donnie for fucking up her life. Oh, there's plenty to hate him for, but a mother isn't allowed to hate her son. What a pipe dream to think things could work out with Nate. If she'd been home with Donnie those nights she was with Nate, maybe none of this would have happened. The Addisons' house would be intact, and their cat would still be alive.

As she turns a corner, the shack comes into view, the mossy roof making it seem like an extension of the forest. Jack's fishing on the dock, so she joins him there. Not bothering to get up, Roxie lets out one half-hearted bark and thumps her tail when Laura calls her name. The sun is warm enough that she sheds her sweater and drapes it over the back of a weathered Adirondack chair. Jack's wearing shorts and a Boston Celtics T-shirt—the team's in the playoffs this year. "Catch anything yet?" she asks as she sits down.

"Only a plastic bag." He gestures inside the shack. "There's beer and soda in the cooler if you want."

"No thanks, but do you mind if I have a cigarette?"

He gives her a disapproving look. "Don't tell me you're smoking again, Laura."

"Just a little," she says, bending the truth. Yesterday she smoked a pack.

"I can't stop you, but I sure wish I could."

She's careful to exhale away from him. He used to smoke too but quit after his heart problems began. She asks what he wants to discuss.

"What do you think?"

"The break-in. . . ."

"Yeah, we can start there, but there's not much new to report. None of the kids whose cars were parked on the road will tell us anything—Donnie included. They never do anymore. The honor code's stricter: keep your mouth shut no matter what. Better to serve time than to be a snitch scared shitless someone's going to pop you. They see it on TV. So no one talks, even in a Podunk place like Stanton."

"Is Tommy still working on the case?"

"Off and on, when he's not wasting his time in Snakehead meetings."

"Kids don't like him—that's probably why they're not talking."

"They won't talk to me either, and I'm a nice guy."

She shrugs. "I've tried, but Donnie won't tell me anything."

"Suppose he did, would you tell me?"

She takes another puff, gazes out at the river. A passing kayaker waves to them, and Jack waves back. "Honestly, I don't know," she admits.

"See, even parents won't come clean. Makes it hard to do my job. Neighborhood cops depend on little scraps of information they can piece together, and when it all dries up, you're stuck at square one. You find out something, anything, please tell me, Laura. You're my niece, goddammit."

Sheepishly, she meets his eye. He at least deserves to know she may have set the whole disaster in motion by telling Donnie that the Addisons were going away. She discloses that, quickly adding the caveat that her memory's fuzzy since it was late at night. Maybe she told Donnie, maybe she didn't.

"So that's what's eating you up?" He pauses, giving her a look halfway between pity and consternation. "Is that the reason you won't talk to Nate?"

"How do you know about that?"

"He called me."

"He did?"

"Yes, Laura, he's worried about you."

"Is that why you wanted to see me?" she asks, angry that Nate would go behind her back like that.

"It's not the only reason, but first let's lay this thing about Donnie and the party to rest. There's no evidence that he's to blame. It's your supposition, not ours. Plus no one on the force really cares about the party anymore, except for me. It's small potatoes."

"Hanging a cat is not small potatoes."

"I don't think so either, but the Snakehead task force couldn't care less about dead pets." A shift in the wind blows cigarette smoke in his face. "Will you put that damn thing out, Laura? And get me a beer while you're at it. Get one for yourself too."

She's never liked going into the shack with its smell of mildew and mouse droppings, but she obeys. Roxie gets up to accompany her, hoping for a treat. The dog moves slowly, one of her back legs dragging. Laura retrieves two Miller Lites from the cooler, then feeds Roxie a couple of pretzels. Back on the dock, Jack's pulling a fish off the line. "Trout," he announces, "but too small, under the limit." He thrusts its slippery body back into the water, then puts down the rod and snaps open the beer. "Shit," he says, and she's unclear whether he's cursing the size of the fish, the insipid beer, or her. "I don't know if I can take it anymore."

"Take what?"

"They're pushing me out, want me to retire next month. The chief called me into the office on Friday to offer me a severance package. He's just the messenger—I can tell he feels bad. They're not including me in meetings anymore. I guess I criticized Snakehead one too many times." When she asks what he'll do, he says he'll refuse the offer—he's retiring at the end of the year, and until then he'll just be a royal pain in their collective asses.

"Maybe you could write something for the paper about the war on drugs," she suggests. "Go out in glory. Frank doesn't know about it, but I'm planning on doing a whole series on the opioid crisis."

Jack laughs. "They'd shoot me first."

"No, really. . . ."

"I'm sworn to secrecy, Laura—remember that? I shouldn't have told you anything about what's going on."

"You could write something generic."

"Like what? Like it's a war without end—bust one network, and there's another to take its place that's usually worse. Like what happened with the Iraq War and ISIS. We're a country that doesn't know how to do wars anymore, so we should just stop, cut our losses. The drug supply will always be there; it's about cutting demand and getting people into treatment, real treatment. The harm-reduction people around here want to set up supervised consumption sites, and why not? They work well in Canada. I'll support anything that works. We were making so much progress here on these issues before Snakehead moved in."

"You could write that."

"Yeah, sure."

"I'd help you."

"You don't understand, do you? The only reason I'm not bolting out the door with their severance package is I need to stick around to help you and Donnie and Ricky and any other kids getting trapped in this bullshit. They may not invite me to meetings, but I keep my ear to the ground. If I start writing anything, I'll be totally cut out." While he swigs down some beer, she opens hers and drinks a few sips. It's tepid, even worse than usual, but she's thirsty, so she drinks some more. "You're not going to like this," he continues, "but I called your sister, Nina, this morning and told her Donnie's at risk. She agreed to take him as soon as school's out. And then I bought him an airplane ticket. I'm forwarding it to you."

How dare he call Nina without consulting her first? He knows their relationship is fraught. "What exactly did you tell her?" she demands, bristling.

"That you're too proud and embarrassed to ask for help," he responds calmly, "and that Donnie is in serious trouble and needs to get out of here this summer."

"I can't believe you did that."

"What else was I supposed to do, Laura? Sit around and watch you procrastinate when I know all that I know? I kept hearing your dad's voice in my ear: 'Laura's stubborn, she holds on too long, sometimes she needs a push. Push her for me when I'm gone, will you, Jack.'"

"He said that?"

"In so many words."

"He was stubborn too."

"That's why he understood you. You're holding on to an old idea of Donnie that you have to let go. You still see him as a little boy you can protect because you're his mom. It ends up being selfish because you don't let other people help him. I know this sounds harsh, but you're not enough for him anymore. It's going to take all of us who care about him."

Though deep down she knows he's right, it's painful to hear. It hurts too that her dad would say that about her. It's as if they're all conspiring together—her dad, Jack, even Nate—to push her from behind, budge her from the rootedness she has come to see as her only strength. But none of them knows Donnie as well as she does. He'll refuse to go. She tells Jack that.

He's already thought about it, he says, and lays out a plan. Donnie won't know he's going till the morning of the flight. Jack will come over, and she'll drive them both to the airport. "I'm going with him, you see. I could use a little vacation in Florida, and plus I'd like to see your mom. I'll get him settled in."

"But what if he says no—we can't just drag him into the car."

"By then he'll be scared enough to want to go. And I'm going to get Ricky out of town too, but I need your help convincing Angie. She must have friends or relatives somewhere who can take in Ricky. Find out for me."

"Angie and I aren't exactly close anymore."

"Doesn't matter. There's a long history there. Go see her, and while you're about it, you might give Nate a call too. And thank Nina for taking Donnie in. Be grateful for a change."

"I am grateful," she insists.

"Then show it. And I have one more piece of advice." Boldly he reaches across and grabs the pack of cigarettes from the arm of her chair. "Damn it, Laura, don't start that filthy habit again!" he admonishes as he hurls the pack into the river. It bobs on the surface until an eddy pulls it under and spits it out into a clump of reeds. Her dad did the same thing once, here at Jack's place, when he was trying to teach Donnie how to cast. She remembers how ashamed it made her feel, in front of her own son, but that was precisely his intention.

Chastened, she gets up and takes her leave, finding it difficult to reciprocate the hug Jack gives her. She walks along the riverbank for a while on the way out, trying to get her bearings again. She feels light-headed from the beer—probably she's hungry; the cigarettes suppress her appetite. All week she's kind of hollowed herself out, a familiar pattern, her response to grief. Holding that poor dead cat in her arms triggered it.

After Mike's death, she told a grief counselor she was borderline crazy. "No," the counselor refuted, "you're just crazy for borders. You put up walls and then get stuck behind them. You need to learn to leave a few gates open."

She wishes she were paddling her kayak now. About a mile downstream is a marshy inlet where she likes to float around looking at birds, dragonflies, even the occasional otter or beaver. It's peaceful there, too shallow for electric fishing boats. She'd lean back, stretch her legs on top of the kayak, and unlock a gate or two.

She takes one last look at the river before turning down another path to the access road. Swimming around the bend is a pair of ducks. As they come closer, she studies their markings—sure enough, they're hooded mergansers. Before she can talk herself out of it, she whips out her cell, takes a photo, and texts it to Nate. Within a minute or two he texts back: by any chance could he swing by and pick her up in half an hour or so—he needs her help on a purchase. She responds with a thumbs-up emoji.

He's already parked outside the house when she gets back, and she goes right over to his truck. "Climb in," he instructs through the open window. Strapping on her seatbelt, she asks where they're going. "It's a surprise," he answers without smiling.

The drive is tense with neither willing to break the ice. The last road Nate takes dead-ends on the far side of the dump at the Green Valley Trailer Park. An unlikely destination, Laura thinks. Her sister and brother-in-law lived out here before they moved down South. Back then it was well maintained—the grass was mowed, the playground kept clean, and the trailers were fixed up to look like respectable ranch houses. But five years ago the owners sold out to absentee landlords from Boston, and now it's the poorest housing in the county.

Nate brings the truck to a halt before a ramshackle trailer with peeling paint. Under a tattered awning are a couple of plastic chairs, a pot of fake sunflowers, and a patriotic pinwheel spinning in the wind. He turns off the ignition. "So what are we doing here?" she asks.

"You're going to pick out a new kitten for Keith and Emily, and then we're going to drive it over to their house."

"That's the surprise?"

"Yes, that's the surprise."

She takes a deep breath. "I'm sorry, Nate, but you should have warned me. I can't face them. Donnie was there at the party."

"You think they're not aware of that? Of course the police told them Donnie's car was parked out on the road. They went over all the license plates with them."

"I didn't know," she replies defensively. "Really, I didn't." She takes another deep breath. She could cry if she let herself but can't afford a show of weakness. "Donnie claims he never went inside the house. I don't know if it's the truth or not, but I have to believe him."

"Look, Laura," he says a little more gently, "I think Keith and Emily will accept that, but they need to hear it from you directly. They like you, you know."

He makes her get the kitten by herself. The owner is an elderly woman, so hard of hearing it takes her a while to respond to Laura's repeated knocking. She's wearing a cotton dress covered by a man's old sweater that hangs down almost as far as her knees. Inside, the smell of frying onions mixes with the reek of cat piss. Cats are everywhere, snoozing on the sofa, scratching the carpet, rubbing up against her legs. "The kittens are in the bedroom," she tells Laura. "Come on back."

Laura feels awkward sitting on the bed, invading the old woman's privacy. Hanging on the back of a chair are a bra, a pair of panties, and a floral nightie. A framed photograph of a man—maybe the old woman's husband or son—stares accusingly from the dresser. She hands each kitten to Laura like a religious offering.

Laura chooses the runt of the litter, a tuxedo cat, pure black except for white on the chest and paws. Despite being the smallest, she's the liveliest, batting at Laura's earrings. She's the old woman's favorite, and she's sad to see her taken away. Even though she hasn't asked for money, Laura hands her a twenty-dollar bill. The old woman hesitates but then accepts it, tucking it into a pocket.

On the way to Sugar Hill Road, Laura holds the kitten on her lap. Her little body trembles, and she has the tiniest meow she's ever heard. Nate takes a hand off the wheel to stroke the cat's head, and then his hand finds hers.

WHEN DONNIE GETS TO SCHOOL, Michelle's waiting by his locker to alert him that Rebecca's finally back. The story is she had the flu all last week, but he knows differently. She was in hiding, scared about the photo. As far as he knows, no one's seen it but Ricky and him. In English class he steals a look at her. Her face is puffy and pasty. Stay away from her, Ricky said. That's easy, since she won't even look at him.

During study hall Tuna Melt calls him into his office. Donnie expects the worst—another grilling about his tardiness—but instead the guidance counselor stands up as he enters and reaches across the desk to shake his hand. "Congratulations," he says, his face beaming. "You have the best SAT scores in the high school."

"I do?" Donnie replies in disbelief.

"You haven't checked them online yet? The College Board should have sent you an email link."

"I hardly ever check mail."

"Well, you should. You have a perfect score in math and your English score is very high too. If you can pull up your grade point average, you can apply to some good colleges, but you're going to have to work very hard to do that. All Cs so far this quarter, I see, though maybe you can raise those to Bs by turning in your homework and performing well on the finals. And next fall, excuse my language, you're going to have to work your butt off, young man. Get straight As. Think you can do that?"

Donnie stares at him. It's just too bizarre. Tuna Melt's always so fucking eager to turn him into someone he's not, but then, maybe he is kind of smart. The SATs weren't even that hard, and he didn't prepare for them. The nerds will be really pissed off he aced the tests. "I'll try," he responds. Maybe he will, maybe he won't, but the idea of going to college suddenly seems more appealing.

"You need to challenge yourself and be challenged, Donnie," Tuna Melt says. *Challenge* is his favorite word. "I'm here to help." *Help* is his second favorite. "Talk to your teachers about making up your homework and let me know how it goes. Let's check in before school ends."

After math class Donnie hovers by Mr. Robinson's desk as he finishes erasing the whiteboard. He's finicky about that, annoyed when the teacher before him hasn't done the job. "So what can I do for you, Donald?" he asks. He's a formal man, always wears a tie, and never calls them by their nicknames.

"I'd like to complete my missing homework."

"Ah, I see," Mr. Robinson replies, raising an eyebrow. "Better late than never, eh? You know my policy on homework. Points off for lateness."

"I know."

There's a lengthy pause as the teacher considers. He scratches his chin, smiles slightly. "But I suppose it could help, Donald. Assuming you do well on the final, you might be able to raise your grade to a B, B+ even. Then you could take calculus next year. Do you want to do that?" Donnie nods. "It'll help you get into college, and besides, I think you'll enjoy it."

Donnie thanks him and heads toward the doorway. He's a few steps into the hall when Mr. Robinson calls after him. He pivots around and returns. "I just want you to know I'm here if you want to talk to me about anything," the teacher says, blushing as he places a hand on Donnie's shoulder. "High school wasn't an easy time for me either."

Unsure of how to respond, Donnie mutters another thanks. It's embarrassing—Mr. H made the same offer after English class. It's like they all want to help him now because of his high SAT scores. Or maybe, he considers more charitably, he just didn't really notice their concern before. For the first time he walks down the hall not wanting to leave the security of the school. The lockers along the walls used to cage him in; now they're like a shield. Carl's attack on him at the party has left him fearful, like after the knife fight.

Outside he surveys the school parking lot. A group of kids with lacrosse sticks is milling around, so he charts a path near them, safety in numbers. Once inside his car, he locks all the doors. Checking his rearview mirror every few seconds, he drives to Stop & Shop on high alert.

For most of his shift he bags for Patty, grateful for the way her constant chatter takes the edge off things. After five the lines grow long with people coming home from work, and he has to concentrate hard to keep up with the endless flow of products. His eyes cast down, he doesn't notice who's in line until too late. A familiar voice tells Patty he doesn't give a shit whether the bags are paper or plastic. Donnie looks up quickly, then away. Carl's buying a bunch of groceries. He hopes it's just a coincidence.

But it's not. After Carl pays, he asks for help taking the cart out to his car. "Sprained my wrist," he explains to a skeptical Patty. Heart beating fast, Donnie pushes the cart to where Carl's car is parked at the end of an empty row. As Donnie leans over to put a bag in the trunk, Carl pushes him forward so the trunk's edge presses hard against his groin. "You didn't see anything at that party, right?" Carl threatens as Donnie doubles over in pain. "Your uncle's a cop. You tell him anything about us?"

"No."

"Tell anybody else?"

"No," Donnie repeats.

"Now come over here." He grabs Donnie's arm. "I want to show you something." He opens a back door and points to Rebecca lying on the seat, her eyes half-closed, her shirt pulled halfway up, exposing her midriff. "Your girlfriend came looking for us, wanting to shoot up again. We didn't go looking for her. What do you think I should do with her? I could fuck her, but I like my girls alert. Andy's not so fussy. Your choice—I could take her back home to him, or you could drive your car over here, and she can sleep it off inside."

PART THREE

Turtle Girl

15

ON A WARM DAY IN EARLY JUNE, Laura strolls down the street toward the Deerfield River in Shelburne Falls, stopping for a moment to look in the bookstore window where a calico cat is stretched out licking its paws. Must be a nice life hanging out around all those books, she thinks. She'd like to go inside and browse, but she's meeting Frank in fifteen minutes and wants to visit the glacial potholes first. She doesn't know what to make of her boss booking a nice restaurant for lunch out. Usually they meet at his golf club's café, where the tab is under $25. The paper's revenue is going down, not up, so his largesse must have to do with something else. She's both nervous and curious, feelings she associates with the last time she was in Shelburne Falls, on her first date with Martin.

She sifts through memories of that date from the view deck above the cascading river. Beyond the information on Martin's online profile, she didn't know what to expect. In the flesh, she found him attractive enough, if a touch didactic. He took little time debunking the myth that glaciers formed the scooped-out holes in the rocky riverbed. It's water pressure pure and simple, he pronounced, and instead what's amazing is the rock itself. He explained how it had been created three hundred million years ago when the continents collided to make one super continent, the Pangea.

Three hundred million years. Geological time puts everything in perspective, she reflects now, except it doesn't because humans mainly obsess about the present or lack the imagination to grasp that entire continents can merge and fall apart, inch by inch, eon by eon.

Chattering tourists break her reverie, so she moves on to the nearby Bridge of Flowers, an old trolley bridge spanning the river that the local women's club converted into a garden a century ago. Another memory of Martin comes—how he planted his first kiss on her there so their romance would blossom. She put up with his corniness in the hope that it would pass. It didn't. Nate's so unlike him, she thinks as she bends down to examine a patch of multicolored columbines, red and gold, purple, and a stunning pale white. Romantic gestures aren't his thing, and he's incapable of putting on an act. Mostly that's all right, but sometimes she'd like more overt reassurance. *Count your blessings*, Cora advised on their walk at the reservoir, but that doesn't come easily to her. Never too late though. If entire continents can shift, surely she can budge a little and appreciate Nate for who he is instead of some impossible ideal she wants him to be.

As she makes her way to the restaurant, she tries to shift gears from her love life to her work life. Any encounter with Frank requires strong defenses. The restaurant he's chosen, an upscale Mexican place, has a pleasant outside terrace, but he's sitting inside in a windowless corner. He waves her over without getting up to greet her. An order of chips, salsa, and guacamole is already on the table and he's halfway through a tall glass of iced tea. She notices the top of his bald head is sunburned the color of a ripening peach—probably he's come from a round of golf.

"Order whatever you want," he says. "I'm getting the steak tacos."

"I think I'll get the fish ones."

"I've heard they're good." He reaches a chip into the guacamole. "Help yourself."

The guacamole is fresh, and the salsa's homemade too. Both she and Frank dig in. After a few minutes, the waiter comes over to take her order, and then Frank leans back, wiping his mouth with a napkin, a sign that he's ready to talk business.

"I learned a few things about the Sullivan land deal I thought you might like to know," he begins. "Mimi's buying out her cousin, our resident *artiste*." He looks upward as if he's in the office and can see through the ceiling into Gary's studio. "Evidently, she's serious about doing a deal with the state and conservation commission. I think that interview you did with her helped make it happen. So congratulations."

"Thanks. Who told you about the deal?"

"Can't share my source yet." That's what he always says, she thinks, even though he demands she share hers. Spare with gratitude, he moves on quickly. "Something else I need to talk to you about, Laura," he says in his most honeyed falsetto, with his phoniest smile. "I've come to the decision that I need to sell the paper. I've put out some feelers but so far no interest, probably because advertising revenue's falling off. If I don't get a buyer by September, I'm going to shut it down."

"Shut it down?" she repeats incredulously. "Does that mean you're giving me notice?"

"Well, not exactly. If someone buys the paper, the new owners will probably keep you on. I mean, you *are* the paper, really. But maybe I'd be doing you a favor if I closed up shop. You've been stuck in a rut too long. You're talented, and you're still young. You'll get unemployment while you look for a better job with a bigger paper."

She stares at him, speechless. Deep down she's always known the *Gazette* might close, but not now, please, when it's the one anchor in her life that's holding steady. Frank doesn't understand newspaper jobs aren't so easy to find, and unemployment won't pay all the bills. She'll be forced to dip into Donnie's college account or take out a second mortgage. "Why so suddenly, Frank?" she finally summons in response. "I know the books are bad, but they've been worse before, and we pulled through. I have some ideas on how to make the paper more relevant. . . ."

"You can bring those to the new owners."

"But if there aren't new owners?"

He shrugs. "Market them somewhere else then. Look, Laura," he says, unable to disguise his impatience, "I know this is hard news for you to hear, but I'm sick up to here with the paper and ready to retire. If I don't find a buyer, I'm willing to negotiate some kind of severance with you. Let's wait and see what happens, but I advise you to start looking around. I can put you in touch with people I know." He starts listing names off the top of his head—he's always boasted about his many friends in local media circles. What he doesn't know is how they talk behind his back. It's an open secret he's been running the *Gazette* down ever since he bought it. Other reporters often ask how she can stand working for him.

The fish tacos arrive, but she's too upset to eat more than a bite or two. Apparently oblivious to her state of mind, Frank chows down his meal with gusto. She leaves as soon as she can, stumbling like a drunk through the restaurant's dark interior. Outside in the blinding sunlight she takes a few moments to steady herself. The car's only a few blocks away, but it seems like it takes forever to get there.

Back in the office, she spends the rest of the afternoon surfing the net for journalism jobs. Most are part-time, without benefits. She decides not to tell Donnie she might lose her job since it will make him anxious. Ever since Mike died, he's been concerned about having enough money.

At dinner she finds him uncharacteristically talkative, volunteering the information that he met with the Stop &

Shop manager today, and she promised him more hours in the summer. "I can start saving up for college," he says. She hasn't heard the word "college" from his lips in a long time and tries to conceal her pleasure as well as her worry that she won't be able to pay for it. "I haven't told you yet," he adds, "but I got the highest SAT scores in the high school. I'll show you online after dinner."

"Congratulations, honey," she replies, amazed. "That's incredible, I mean incredibly good news."

"I need to bring up my grades to get into a good college, but I think I can do it." His voice suddenly sounds like Mike's, serious and reasonable. A certain knitting of the brow. "And I'm going to stay out of trouble, Mom. I'm sick of it."

Is this change of character too swift? she wonders as she does the dishes, for what better way to weaken her defenses than by cleaning up his act. On the other hand, maybe she should give him the benefit of the doubt. Maybe he really is sick of trouble.

But trouble isn't sick of him. Just past midnight someone throws a brick through the bay window in the living room. The crash wakes her, and she rushes downstairs. Donnie's already standing there in the dark, barefoot amid the shattered glass. She turns on a light and warns him to step away carefully, then turns it off again, scared that the culprit might still be outside. Before she phones for help, Donnie and she cling to each other for a moment, the closest they've been in a long time.

Jack and Nate both come over, Nate bearing a large sheet of plywood that they nail over the window. It's not the way she intended for him to meet Donnie, but she's grateful for his offer to stay the night. She's seen him a few times since they gave the kitten to Emily, but they've lacked the courage to make love again. It won't happen now either, she thinks, as she lies down next to him in her bed. She's too rattled, speeding on adrenaline, worried about Donnie's safety. At least he agreed to sleep upstairs tonight, in the guest room across the hall.

Insomnia works in her and Nate's favor though—she can't fall asleep and neither can he. And so it happens as if by osmosis, slowly, gently, and quietly enough that Donnie won't hear. Lying in Nate's arms afterward, she allows herself a fleeting sense of safe harbor, but when she wakes at dawn, her heart is pounding. After easing out of bed, she tiptoes to the window and surveys the street like a sentry guarding a fortress under siege.

DONNIE WAKES AROUND THE same time and grabs his cell from the bedside table. He's using an encrypted app with Ricky now, one that Justin recommended. Before he went to bed, he messaged Ricky on it but got no response. There's a reply now: Happened to us too. Going to move out soon. Don't want any more shit happening to my mom. Check in with you later.

Later is not good enough, Donnie wants answers now. His groin still hurts from when Carl smashed him into the car in the Stop & Shop lot. Maybe it was Carl who threw the rock, or was it the Jags? Ricky needs to tell him so he can watch out for whoever's coming after him. Playing the good boy provides no protection.

16

THE BABY'S WAILING WHEN Mimi arrives at Steve's house on Friday morning. "Teething," he complains as he ushers her into his office. "I didn't get much sleep."

"I didn't either, but I have the opposite problem," she replies. "My daughter gives me the silent treatment." He nods sympathetically but doesn't probe. She wishes he would. It's hard to keep her fears about Rebecca all to herself. Her daughter's sick or moody most of the time. School ends in two weeks, so the countdown has begun. She's ready to buy Gary's share of the land now, but the other price he's exacting—Rebecca working for him all summer—is too steep. She needs something to nail him with. Hopefully, Steve's got it.

He's clutching a mug bearing the admonition KEEP CALM AND CARRY ON. There's a screaming contest going on upstairs now, and by the sound of it, the toddler's shrieks win over the baby's wails. Wincing at the noise, he suggests that they go outside to the gazebo. They walk to the end of the lawn, past a sandbox, slide, and kiddie pool inhabited by a rubber ducky and tyrannosaurus rex. She doesn't remember the gazebo being there before. "My office extension," he jokes as he holds the screen door for her. "Now that the weather's warmer, I work out here sometimes." The plushy cushioned patio set looks like something right off the floor of a home and garden store.

He sets some files on the coffee table but then engages in small talk. It's unlike him not to come straight to the point, and she senses a reluctance to start the briefing. Maybe he hasn't done the work, though he agreed to meet when she called and said he had something to tell her. To get the ball rolling, she asks if there's any new information. "Too much," he answers gravely, then reaches in the top file and pulls out her latest check, the one financed by the brooch sale. He tries to hand it to her, but she won't take it and asks what's going on. "I was warned off," he says.

"By who?"

"That's a good question. Turns out I'm not the only person surveilling David and your cousin. Last time I went to that highway truck stop, someone followed me home. They waited until I pulled into the driveway before speeding away. It was an unmarked car, but something about it smelled like law enforcement. I made some discreet inquiries and word came down that I should back off fast. My casino source gave me the same advice, but I managed to get some information out of him first."

She listens carefully as he tells her that David's been gambling with higher amounts, well above the $10,000 threshold that should spark the casino to file a report with the IRS. Not that all casinos or cashiers comply, of course. Black money fuels the system, and they want wealthy customers to keep returning. But the management here has been playing it straight so far—they're scared of negative publicity. "Why's David getting away with it then?" she asks bluntly.

Steve takes time to answer, his right hand cupping his chin and hiding his lips as he looks at her. He's probably debating what he can and can't tell her, she thinks. She meets his eye and holds her gaze steady as if they're playing the blinking game. She was good at that as a kid—friends usually caved first. "Could be a sting operation," he finally responds. "That's what my source suspects. Management could be cooperating with law enforcement. Maybe it's why I've been warned off the case. Do you know if your cousin has any history of drug dealing, Mimi?"

"In his midtwenties he was busted for selling pot in Boston."

"Why didn't you tell me that before?" he asks testily.

"I didn't think it mattered," she lies. The fact is she doesn't like to bring it up. She was busted along with him—it was the summer after her freshman year at college—but Gary took the rap, and her charges were dropped.

"Are you aware of anything bigger or badder he's done?"

"That's what I hired you to find out."

He takes a deep breath, peering down at the check on the table. She glances at it too, an image of the brooch flashing through her mind. It's gone, she'll never get it back. "Believe me, I want to find out, Mimi, but I can't. If this is a sting operation, my license will be pulled at the slightest provocation. So that's why I'm returning your check." As he slides it toward her, she notices her signature is less bold than on her business checks, scrawled tentatively like an old lady's.

"I won't take it," she insists, sliding it back while she ponders a countermove. She prides herself on reading other people's weaknesses—Steve's flaw is an excess of loyalty; the good soldier in him is still alive. "Don't abandon me, Steve," she pleads, the desperation in her voice part affected, part genuine. She needs the dirt on Gary. Now.

"I can't poke around here anymore, Mimi."

"My cousin used to live in Vermont. Can you poke around there?"

He considers a moment. "Only on one condition."

"What's that?"

"You file for divorce." He lets the words sink in. "I know I've been advising you to leave David for a long time, but I really mean it now. He's clearly involved in criminal activity, and you don't need to wait for me to discover exactly what it is. Stay married to him, and it's going to bring you down too. Think of the legal costs and the reputation of Sullivan Lumber. I'll give you the names of some kickass divorce lawyers. Throw David out of the house right away—his drinking's enough of a reason. And don't use your daughter for an excuse not to. If he's still living at home when the cops come to arrest him, it's not going to be a pretty scene for her to witness. You need to protect yourself and Rebecca. And make it known all around town that you've finally thrown the scumbag out. You do that and I'll go up to Vermont. Deal?"

"That's a tall order, Steve."

"Time's running out on this. Yes or no, you tell me."

"Give me those lawyers' names," she says.

REBECCA STRUGGLES TO MAKE IT through her world history exam on Monday morning. Usually she can trust her memory for dates and places, but they're all mixed up in her brain today. Besides, the battle of this or that is nothing compared to the battle on Jefferson Street yesterday. All morning she sat cross-legged on her bed listening to her parents shout at each other until finally her dad came upstairs and told her he was moving into a motel for a while until he found a place to rent. "Your mother wants a divorce," he said in a hoarse voice. He seemed sober, though he could have been faking.

"Do you want one?" she asked.

He went quiet for a moment before admitting he didn't really know. "Whatever happens we'll work out a way for you and me to see each other on a regular basis."

"Sure, Dad."

After he left, her mom sat her down at the dining room table to present the terms of the truce. "This will be better for all of us," she claimed coldly.

"Sure, Mom."

Sure, sure, sure. She isn't sure what she prefers, their fighting or the absence of it, the absence of him. He's a shit of a father, but at least when he was around, he distracted her mom. His drinking was the condition for her freedom. Now her mom will turn all her attention on her unless the divorce blows up in her face. Let it blow up in both her parents' faces, she thinks. Let the battle on Jefferson rage on until she figures out the safest path of retreat.

She weighs a retreat from the exam—getting up and walking out and telling Ms. Owen to stuff it—but she's never left any test unfinished. So she works her way down to the final essay question about the causes of World War I. She dredges up a few textbook answers before turning philosophical and writing about how you can never really know what caused something in the past because it's hard enough to figure out what's going on in the present. So much is hidden, even from those who think they know. We don't even understand our own motives, so how can we understand other people's? How can we see through the layers and layers of deceit and greed? The study of history peels off one or two at most. It's better than nothing, but nothing is where we started, and nothing is where we'll end.

Nothing is where she wants to be now. She looks at the clock. Five minutes left. Ever since she nodded out and woke up in Donnie's car, she hasn't been using drugs. She's desperate to do heroin again but scared to approach Carl and Andy. There's plenty on the street, but she doesn't know how to score stuff that's not cut with fentanyl.

After school, she wanders around town, scoping things out. She finds her angel in a park by the mill pond where users and dealers often hang out. A young woman sitting on a bench is feeding bits of bread to the ducks. She's older than Rebecca, dressed in blue medical scrubs, with a long French braid hanging down her back. She looks straight, but as Rebecca passes by, their eyes lock, and the woman gestures for her to take a seat. She introduces herself as Susana. "Want to feed the ducks?" she asks. Rebecca takes the bread she offers and casts it on the water's edge, where the ducks scramble for it. "They expect me now," Susana states proudly. "I come here every day after work." Rebecca nods, accepting more bread. Silently they feed the ducks until Susana asks if she's looking for something.

Rebecca isn't sure how to answer. Susana could be put here by the police or social services to report on people. "Just . . . you know," she replies.

"Yeah, I do know. Want to come back to my apartment and see what I've got? It's right around the corner."

Rebecca hesitates. What if it's a setup or Susana's crazy? But a sisterly kindness in her eyes suggests otherwise. And so Rebecca follows her, hoping no one she knows will see her. It's the bad part of town—her mom once warned her not to go here.

Susana lives on the top floor of a three-story clapboard house wedged between a warehouse and a couple of abandoned storefronts. The stairwell is smelly and dirty, but the apartment is clean enough, the walls painted a soft lavender. Rebecca waits on the couch while Susana goes into the bedroom to change out of her scrubs. On the way over she told Rebecca she works the early shift as a nursing home aide and manages her habit by shooting up only once a day in the late afternoon.

Reappearing in a T-shirt and pajama bottoms, she draws the curtains and then proceeds to lecture Rebecca on how she needs to use clean needles, buy only from people she trusts, stop herself when she wants to take too much. Susana will be her supplier if she wants, and they can shoot up together one at a time. Rebecca can go first. It's safer that way since if she overdoses, Susana will give her Narcan.

Susana puts on some slow music while she prepares the heroin in the kitchen, explaining each step. She has some nursing training and is meticulous about everything being sterile, from the water she mixes with the powder to the spoon she holds over a candle flame. On the refrigerator door, Rebecca notices a child's drawing of a butterfly, signed with crooked letters spelling Rosie. On the magnet holding it in place is a school photo of a little girl, maybe five or six, with short braids and a wide smile. She wants to ask Susana who Rosie is, but now isn't the time, since Susana is concentrating hard on filtering the liquid heroin to remove any lumps. Afterward, she draws half of it into a syringe. "Come," she says, "you can lie down on the couch." The soft way she says "sweet dreams" as she injects the drug reminds Rebecca of how her mom used to say it when she bent down and kissed her goodnight.

17

MAYBE IT'S THE MENTAL FOG of yet another restless night, but Laura has the illusion that the car is driving her instead of the other way around. It drives past her office, turning east until she finds herself at the trailhead to a rocky outcrop with a view of Stanton and the Diamond River Valley below. The parking lot's empty, and she relishes the solitude as she begins the climb to the top. She's already a few hours late for work—the window people finally came this morning to replace the broken glass—so what's an hour or two more? She needs to take stock of so many things.

Like Nate continuing to spend the night. She's grateful for the protection but uncertain whether she's ready to share her bed, her life, so fast. Last night after he fell asleep, she slipped across the room to the rocking chair in the alcove. It was strange to view him from that angle, the same angle from which she observed Mike as she nursed Donnie in the middle of the night when everything was still except for the cranky old radiator wheezing and steaming. At eighteen, she wasn't prepared for a man permanently in her bed, much less a baby at her breast. So much physical intimacy all at once for a girl who was used to living mainly in her head.

As if sensing her thoughts, Nate had turned over and kicked off the sheet, naked except for a pair of boxers, shy that way. At least he hadn't woken up. In the moonlight she must have looked like one of those ghostly maidens who wander at night, searching for lost dreams like the second child Mike and she planned to have after he got well. They kept the illusion alive until it was brutally clear there would be no recovery.

A second child. Her biological clock is ticking faster now. Is that what freaks her out about Nate—that unlike Martin and the few other men she's dated, she can imagine having a baby with him and nursing once again in the rocking chair?

A slippery patch on the trail forces an end to her ruminations, and she grabs hold of a sapling to keep her balance. She passes through a grove of blooming mountain laurel whose pointy pink-and-white flowers remind her of decorations on a birthday cake. Farther up she picks her way over the steep rocky ascent to the summit, where she sits down and rests, dangling her legs off the ledge.

In the hazy distance, Stanton appears like a charcoal smudge in an otherwise verdant landscape drawing. On the hillsides surrounding her, winter's stark separation between evergreens and barren hardwoods has given way to minor variations on the theme of green. New England is almost 90 percent forest now, all grown back from the days of farming and livestock raising that cleared the land. A moral there, she supposes: in this landscape, nature takes over in the end.

Perhaps that's why people work so hard to stake their claims—as gestures against inevitability, futile as they might be. The stone wall that stands triumphantly to mark a property line turns into a quaint crumbling relic encountered on a ramble through the woods. Down there in the smudge, so much useless gesturing is going on. And like all the others, she's flapping her arms in the wind. How much better to be like the pair of red-tailed hawks she spots now, riding the wind currents, diving down only to snatch some prey. They see the little picture within the big picture and soar effortlessly between them. For a brief time, painting gave her that perspective—even when her subject matter was close in, her vision came from far away.

She needs to rediscover that talent, she thinks, put it to strategic use. Of course, she doesn't have hawk eyes, but what she lacks she can make up for with imagination, speculation, anticipation. If she trains her eye correctly, she can see the whole picture in a way few others can.

"She sees too much, that child," she once overheard her mom complaining over the phone to her aunt. "I can't keep up with her questions. Nina's content to just play with her dolls. Laura's too smart for me, maybe too smart for her own good." At eight years old, she was more perplexed than hurt by her mom's comment. How could you be too smart? What was wrong with asking questions? And what was so great about being dumb?

Later she learned the benefits of playing dumb—more popularity, less responsibility—but it means turning the questions inward, becoming too self-critical, a habit of mind that's hard to shake. She's still fighting it, but the fight itself takes energy better spent elsewhere. She should be focusing her mind on the task at hand: how to prevent more violence. The knife fight, the sick, crazy party, the brick coming through her front window and Angie's too—these are nothing compared to what could be coming down the road if the situation escalates as Jack worries it will. She needs to take more risks but be smart about it, very smart, see the little picture within the big picture, the big within the little. Use the *Gazette* while it still exists, thumb her nose in Frank's face.

Taking risks will be easier after Donnie leaves for the summer, she reflects, but then there's still Ricky to attend to. Despite Jack's constant reminders, she's put off talking to Angie because their last meeting was so painful. But how long can you hold a grudge when there's a plague on both your houses? It's not only selfish but foolish of her not to reach out. She whips out her cell and texts Angie to see if she can meet today.

They arrange to rendezvous at the bowling alley at four o'clock when Angie gets off work. Laura arrives first and takes a table in the back of the empty snack bar. The decor has changed little since she was a kid—red vinyl chairs, gray Formica tabletops, a wall clock in the shape of a bowling ball, Stanton-style vintage chic. No service anymore, though, just a water cooler and a couple of soda and snack machines.

A few minutes later Angie marches in, still in work clothes with her hair tucked into a company baseball cap. She removes it after she sits down, shaking her blond hair free. Laura braces herself for harsh treatment, but instead Angie immediately launches into an apology about their last conversation. "I was in shock—I couldn't see clearly," she admits. "Now I can, but it's too late. Ricky's left home." She retrieves a piece of paper from her purse and hands it to Laura. "Read it, please."

The note is handwritten:

Dear Mom,
I'm moving out for a while because I don't want anything else bad to happen to you or the house. I'll be okay, don't worry, I got a job and a place to stay. I'll call you later. Sorry about everything.
Love, Ricky

"I should have seen it coming," Angie remarks as soon as Laura's finished. "Ricky's hardly been home lately; sometimes he's away two or three nights in a row. I hoped he was spending the night at your place, but didn't want to call you. That was stupid of me. Was he over at all?"

"Afraid not." She passes the note back to Angie, who confides she doesn't know where he goes or what he does. Laura asks about his job.

"He turned down a custodial job at the factory. The other day he said he found work with a potter. It's crazy—what does he know about ceramics?"

"Is it with the new guy in my building?"

"I think so."

"He's Mimi Sullivan's cousin, you know. His name's Gary Plant."

"Shit, I didn't know. That probably means Ricky's still seeing Rebecca."

"Donnie went out with her for a few weeks," Laura ventures, "but she broke up with him. She seemed nice. . . ."

"She's not nice, don't kid yourself. Don't let Donnie get back with her."

It's time for her to bring up sending Ricky out of town, Laura thinks, but what if Angie disagrees and they're back to conflict mode again? What she most likes about her friend is what she most dislikes about her too—the way she wears emotions on her sleeve. "Jack's worried things are going to get a lot worse this summer," Laura begins tentatively. "As soon as school's over, Donnie's going to stay with Nina in Florida. He doesn't know yet, so please don't tell anyone. Is there somewhere you could send Ricky? Jack's willing to help, and so am I."

"What do you mean by help?" Angie bristles. "I have enough money. I don't need charity from anyone, you know that."

Laura searches for the right response. Angie's always hated stereotypes of lazy poor people living off handouts, and who can blame her. As a skilled machinist, she makes a much higher salary than Laura. "I'm not talking about money," she responds calmly. "Jack helped me see I had to do something fast. He's the one who called my sister—we're still not getting along great, but family is family. And," she adds, "friends are friends."

"Okay, I get the point," Angie responds, "but it's not as easy as you think. I know people who would take him in, but he turned eighteen two weeks ago. I don't have legal control over him anymore." Ricky's a year older than Donnie, Laura remembers now. The school system made him repeat kindergarten because of behavioral issues, which only made his behavior worse. Angie's been pissed about it ever since. "Before I can do anything, I need to find him," Angie continues. "What did I do wrong with him, Laura?"

It's a question they've asked each other many times since the boys started getting in trouble. "You did nothing wrong," Laura reassures her. "You've always been an amazing mother."

"For Justin, maybe, but not for Ricky. You know how well Justin did in high school—I just assumed Ricky would follow in his brother's footsteps. That was foolish."

"But understandable. Justin was such a star. How's he doing anyway? Is he liking Peru?"

A smile passes over Angie's lips as she describes how much he loves the research and being in the high Andes. "I miss him, but I'm also glad he's far away so he doesn't have to feel responsible for his brother. If Ricky is in a gang, I don't want Justin involved. He doesn't know Ricky moved out. Sooner or later I'll have to tell him, but maybe things will be better by then."

Taking a deep breath, she leans back, resting her hands on her stomach, a familiar signal that she's figuring out what to say next. Laura gives her time, listening to the satisfactory smack of a bowling ball hitting the pins.

It turns out Angie wants to talk about Tommy, whom she ran into yesterday outside the factory. He was off duty, picking up his little sister, who now works on her floor. "He actually thanked me for showing her the ropes. First time he hasn't snarled at me, but it made me wonder if he's playing a double game. He asked how Ricky was doing like he knew he'd left home. Acted all concerned about him. I don't trust him, so I said nothing, but he gave me his personal cell number in case I want to be in touch. 'I'm not a cop all the time,' he said. It was weird, Laura. Maybe he was coming on to me, but I don't think so. How can you come on to someone you've hated for years?"

Laura describes her interchange with him after he questioned Donnie, how he seemed more sympathetic. "But I don't trust him either. Be careful."

Before they leave the bowling alley, Laura promises she'll see if Donnie knows where Ricky's staying and will keep an eye on Gary too. Angie gives her a hug, the first in a long time.

Back in the office, she can't bring herself to sit at the computer and paces the room. Gary's van is gone from the lot, and there's no noise coming from the studio either. She opens the top drawer of Frank's file cabinet. In case of emergency, the building manager entrusted him with a master key he hides in a file marked Miscellaneous Bills. After retrieving it, she goes upstairs. If Gary returns, she'll make the excuse that she heard a loud noise and worried about the kiln.

She unlocks the studio door and stands at the threshold, calling out to make sure no one's there. Silence, so she steps into the long and spacious main room outfitted with a sink, work table, two wheels, a large kiln, and shelves with bowls, dishes, and mugs ready to be fired. Two doors lead off the studio, one to a supply closet, the other to a small side room, which she enters.

On the floor is a mattress covered with a familiar-looking Batman sleeping bag—Ricky's. His backpack is in the corner, and his shirts are folded neatly on a shelf. Even as a little boy, Ricky took great care with his clothes, while Donnie threw them carelessly on the floor. She takes a photo with her cell and texts it to Angie.

AFTER SCHOOL DONNIE DRIVES to Pete's, a burger and soft-serve joint next to the mini golf, where Michelle asked him to meet. It's his day off, so he agreed. He's been keeping his head down after the brick incident, but Pete's should be safe enough.

He arrives first and orders a chocolate milkshake. Michelle comes a few minutes later and gets a soda. They find an empty picnic table, but a trash can nearby is surrounded by yellow jackets, so they walk farther away and sit on the lawn. This is his first time alone with Michelle, and it feels awkward. Usually she keeps her back super straight like she's riding upright on one of her show horses, but now her shoulders are slumped and she's bent over picking at the grass. Her dark curly hair hangs down, shielding her face. He's never really noticed her hair before. "I don't know what to do, Donnie," she says, then lifts her head and looks at him sadly. "All week I've been asking Rebecca to come with me to the stables to say goodbye to my old horse, Ruggles. He's dying, and the vet is going to put him to sleep soon. She says she'll come, but then she blows me off. It hurts, you know. She used to be my best friend. She used to love Ruggles. Do you know what's going on with her?"

"We're not seeing each other anymore."

"I know, but what happened at that party, Donnie? She hasn't been the same since."

She's not the same, he wishes he could tell her. Whether she's using or not, she's fucked up bad. "I don't know what went down at the party," he lies. "She was gone by the time I got there."

"She doesn't tell me anything. Her parents just split up—did you know that? Her mom called mine to tell her, but Rebecca said nothing about it to me."

"She didn't tell me either," he says, which is the truth.

"Can you find out what's happening from Ricky?" she pleads. Her brown eyes are intense, unwilling to let go. He always disliked her because he assumed she disliked him, but Rebecca ditching them both creates a bond between them. Spooks him a little. Strange how sometimes people reveal themselves suddenly, like *boom*, like a flash of light. Michelle's horse is dying. The sorrow on her face makes her softer, prettier. He tells her he's out of touch with Ricky. Picking at the grass again, she asks if he'll come with her to see Ruggles.

"Now?"

She nods. "You can leave your car here—I'll drive you back."

They find Ruggles lying down in his stall, seemingly asleep until he hears Michelle's voice. She kneels beside him and strokes his forehead. He's skin and bones with a milky cataract in one eye. "I've brought a friend to see you," she says gently. She pulls an apple from her pocket and gives it to Donnie. "Here, you feed him." Donnie extends his hand, but the horse isn't interested. "He's losing his appetite," Michelle explains. "He's got stomach cancer."

"That's terrible." The apple feels useless in Donnie's fingers, so he passes it back to Michelle. Ruggles accepts it from her. "That's the way," she coos, "eat it all up now."

Before they leave, she asks him to take a picture of her and Ruggles with her cell. Stroking his mane, she cocks her head and smiles faintly. "I'll text it to Rebecca," she says. "Maybe then she'll come to say goodbye to him."

On the way back to Pete's, she turns off on a dirt road and brings the car to an abrupt halt, collapsing in sobs over the steering wheel. A few moments later she reaches for him and he holds her, stroking her hair and kissing her lightly on the top of her head. Her hair smells nice. He can't tell whether she wants more from him than comfort, so he waits. He's not turned on, but he could be. There's a certain relief in being passive. Her call, not his.

18

MIMI GETS OFF THE ELEVATOR on the twenty-third floor of the UMass library in Amherst. It's the tallest library in the country and one of the ugliest too, its brick tower poking up like a middle finger mocking its bucolic surroundings. An unlikely place to find Steve, Mimi thinks, but he asked to meet here while he's attending a ROTC reunion.

With the students gone for the summer, the library is sparsely occupied, and she easily finds Steve waiting for her in the stacks. They walk over to a window with a view south to the gentle contours of the Holyoke Range. Even though no one else is around, he keeps his voice to a whisper as he thanks her for coming to the campus. "Maybe I'm paranoid, but I feel like my house is being watched, and I don't trust my phone or email either. This seemed as safe a place as any to meet." When she asks how the reunion's going, he shrugs resignedly and says it's sad. "One of the guys I trained with died in Afghanistan. Another had his legs blown off. We're raising money to help their families."

"I'm sorry."

"Yeah, puts my own problems in perspective." She wonders what those are but, not wanting to pry, instead asks if he found out anything in Vermont. He heard rumors, he says, but hasn't been able to substantiate any of them.

"Rumors are better than nothing."

"It depends. Look, Mimi," he remarks, drawing closer, "let's just say it's a good thing you're separated from David, and I think it's time you break off all contact with your cousin Gary too."

"I can't," she replies fast, feeling his breath on her face.

"Why not?"

"He's Rebecca's biological father." There, she finally declared it out loud, as much for her benefit as his. He's clearly shocked, but she continues, her voice surprisingly steady, matter-of-fact. "A couple of years ago I secretly collected cheek swabs from David and Rebecca when they were asleep and sent them off for DNA testing. Their genes don't match, so that leaves Gary. I slept with him at a family wedding on the Cape. David got drunk and went to bed early, so I hung out with Gary on the beach. He was doing drugs as usual, and I joined in. I got so zoned out I didn't realize until too late that we were having sex. One of those gray areas, you know—not rape exactly, but I didn't say yes."

"Why didn't you tell me this before?"

"I've never told anyone. I don't want Rebecca to face the stigma. Even if it's not legally incest, it's close enough. But now Gary's sure he's her father—I think he got tests done too, though how he managed it, I don't know—and he wants to spend more time with her. He even offered her a summer job. He threatened he'll reveal his paternity if I don't let her do it. I don't know what's worse, that he's my first cousin or a criminal. He is a drug dealer, isn't he, Steve?"

"It would be a lot easier for you if he was behind bars," he states candidly.

"Yes."

The judgmental expression on his face suggests he doesn't quite trust her anymore, thinks she's out for revenge for a sexual encounter that happened seventeen years ago. Or is it because he disapproves of her behavior that night on the beach, getting so high she allowed Gary to take advantage of her? Steve's a straight arrow, doesn't like drinking or drugs. Whatever the case, she senses his mind is recalculating, forming a revised image of her.

The elevator door pings and opens, followed by the sound of someone rolling out a book cart. Steve waits for it to pass before giving her an account of his trip to Vermont. He can't prove Gary's a dealer, he tells her, but a search warrant was served on his Burlington house and studio in December. Apparently, nothing was found. Steve emphasizes the word *apparently*. "I asked around and finally found a cop who was part of the bust who agreed to talk to me. Turns out things *were* found." She asks what kind of things. "Drugs, presumably—he wouldn't say exactly. The Feds swept in and took over, and some kind of deal was cut with Gary. The local cops were pissed since they'd finally caught a fish bigger than a street dealer, and they had to let him off the hook. So it looks like your cousin's cooperating."

"In a sting operation?"

"That's my guess. The situation is beyond dangerous, Mimi. Get yourself and Rebecca as far away from here as you can. I hear Paris is nice in July." He reaches for his wallet, pulls out her check, and returns it to her. "You can use the money for the trip."

"It's your payment, Steve."

"You need it more than me. And case closed as far as I'm concerned. I'm considering changing jobs. Father-in-law's been bugging me to take over his landscaping business, and I'm just about ready to say yes. I don't like being followed, never have. I don't like being bored either, but the idea of sitting in an office and ordering truckloads of mulch and manure sounds pretty good right now. And I got my kids to think about. I wish you all the best, Mimi, but no more contact, okay?" He reaches out to shake her hand, but she can't bring herself to reciprocate. Feeling dizzy suddenly, she leans against the wall. "Are you all right?" he asks worriedly.

"Of course I'm not all right."

"I'm sorry, it's way bigger than we both expected. I've reached my limit—sometimes you just have to stop."

"I can't afford to stop, Steve."

"Yeah, but now you've got enough to go on to do what you need to do. Me snooping around some more isn't going to help. You're tough, Mimi. Divorce David, protect your daughter, and refuse to be blackmailed by Gary's fatherhood thing. So what if he can prove he's Rebecca's biological father—David's still her legal one. Don't let Gary hold that over you. Call his bluff and don't be so worried about the stigma. We live in different times now. People will sympathize with you as the victim. You'll get over it, and so will Rebecca. In the long run, it's better if it's out in the open."

She read him wrong, she thinks; he doesn't judge her past behavior so harshly. Yet that doesn't prevent her from judging him. He makes the "fatherhood thing" sound easy to handle when he knows it's not. He's scared, weak—she expected more of him. A real warrior would stay the course. Steve's in retreat, fleeing back to his roots.

REBECCA WAITS FOR RICKY AT the corner of the football field. He texted that he wanted to see her right after school. Usually it's the time she shoots up with Susana, but her new friend is gone for the day and won't be home till seven. Yesterday she confided she has a five-year-old daughter, Rosie, who lives with her parents, and showed Rebecca some photos and videos of her. Susana visits her once a week on her day off. She wishes she could spend more time with Rosie, even get her back, but she needs to break her heroin habit first. She's thinking of going on suboxone if she can find a place nearby that distributes it. The last treatment center that offered it just closed down, so now you have to travel miles to get it, and she doesn't have a car.

Rebecca wants to shoot up now. The midafternoon schedule suits her because by evening she's come down enough to go home. Her mom's been working late, so Rebecca just grabs a bite to eat and shuts herself in her bedroom, supposedly to study. It will be harder when school's out and she has a job. Better to work for Gary than her mom, though. She'll arrange to start work early and leave by midafternoon. Getting high with Susana is the only thing that's good about her life. A lot of the time they just lie on the bed listening to music, watching the tropical fish mobile twirling above the bed. Sometimes they hold hands, swim off together.

For her tenth birthday, her parents took her to a resort in the Caribbean. While they drank and bickered by the pool, she hung out with a family that had kids around her age. Ellen, the mom, was super nice, including her in all their activities. Ellen taught her how to snorkel, and she fell in love with it, especially swimming alongside the sea turtles, watching them flap their legs like wings as they rose for a breath of air. From Ellen she learned that they're different from land turtles, unable to retract their head and legs into their shell.

She spent so much time swimming with the turtles that the family called her Turtle Girl, much nicer than the nickname Royalty. Susana makes her feel like Turtle Girl again. Maybe someday she'll take her and Rosie snorkeling and show them the incredible world underwater.

She's thinking about that when Ricky arrives a few minutes later in Gary's van. He seems uneasy, scowling as he relays the information that Gary wants to see her. "First you and me need to talk," he says, but instead he goes all quiet on her as he drives to the outskirts of town. She gazes out the window, but the glass is covered with a film of fine yellow pollen that makes everything look fuzzy and out of focus.

A mile or so past the last traffic light, he pulls into an abandoned used car dealership and parks by a rusty dumpster. All around are skeletons of dead cars. "What's up with this place?" she asks. Maybe he wants sex, but he's not giving off those vibes. They haven't touched each other for weeks. And why would he want to do it here?

He turns toward her, demanding to know if she's still shooting up.

"Of course not," she lies. He doesn't know about Susana and she intends to keep it that way.

"It freaked Donnie out, finding you passed out in the car like that. Carl and Andy could have raped you."

"Don't worry, I learned my lesson," she responds. And it's true—Turtle Girl will never shoot up with those men again, only with Susana. And she doesn't need Ricky to buy her pills anymore either. Susana's heroin is much safer and cheaper.

"Show me you're not using again," he orders. "Pull up your sleeves."

"What the hell, Ricky?" In the crook of her left arm are track marks she can't let him see. "I've been cutting my arms," she lies again. "Please don't make me show you."

"Jesus, Rebecca, I thought you were over that."

"I was until my parents split up."

"Doesn't mean you have to cut your arms."

"You have no idea how bad it's been, Ricky." He lets it drop, though she can tell he doesn't want to. It strikes her how much older he appears when he's serious. Uglier too. He'll probably have jowls like her father. "Can we leave now?" she asks. "This place spooks me."

"There's something else we need to discuss."

"And what's that?" she replies, irritation creeping into her voice. She's sick of his shit.

"We need to leave Stanton—soon. They're starting to fight over you."

"What are you talking about?"

He presents the case as if he's rehearsed it, putting all the facts in logical order. Fact one: Gary's a drug dealer. Fact two: Ricky works for him because he needs protection from a gang that tried to recruit him. Fact three: Carl and Andy are Gary's enforcers. They want a bigger cut of the action and are threatening to break away. Fact four: Last night Ricky overheard Carl and Gary having a fight in the studio. Carl showed Gary the picture of her with the cat and another one of her passed out in the car. "He said you're a junkie and next time they're going to have sex with you unless Gary gives them what they want. Gary pointed a gun at him and threatened to kill them if they mess with you. Carl left, but I don't know what's going down next. That's why we have to get out of here."

She looks at him in disbelief. Maybe he's putting her on, but that's not his style. Even if everything he says is true, she doesn't want to go. She tells him that.

"You think I want to go, Rebecca? Leave my mom all alone? But there's no choice. You're not safe." He pauses, grabs her hand tightly. "Listen, I have a plan. Sometimes Gary sends me down to Springfield to pick up cash. Next delivery should be in a couple of days. We'll split town with the money."

"That's crazy, Ricky."

"Crazier to stay here."

She removes her hand from his grip. What if he's right? she thinks, but she doesn't want to leave Susana. He says to have a bag packed ready to go, acting like she's already agreed.

19

THE CALL COMES SATURDAY ON Laura's way home from grocery shopping, a classic Nina tumble-jumble of excuses delivered breathlessly like the world is about to end. "Right," Laura says to conclude the conversation, then hangs up.

She was wrong to have trusted her sister. Of course Nina would pull out at the last moment and blame it on her husband, Doug: *He just got laid off from UPS. He's falling apart, Laura. He can't take the responsibility of one more kid in the house. He isn't getting along with Mom either. He thinks we should have left her in Massachusetts for you to deal with. She's driving us all nuts, even the kids. Maybe Doug will calm down in a couple of weeks when he finds another job, but now isn't a good time for Donnie to come. So sorry, but it would be a disaster. Push Doug over the edge. I wish he would go on meds for anxiety. Maybe I need to go on them too. . . .*

Doug always gets laid off from his seasonal UPS job in the summer when the snow birds migrate back north. Hardly unanticipated, but that's their marital modus operandi—manufacturing crises.

The crisis she faces is real. School ends next Friday. Donnie was supposed to fly to Florida the following Monday. How will she get him out of town now?

Before unloading the groceries, she calls Jack. He's out fishing on a friend's boat on the Connecticut River and didn't take his cell, Nancy tells her. "Give him a call this evening," she advises, and then reminds her of Jack's birthday barbecue next weekend. She would call Nate, but he's leading a bird walk in Brookfield and won't be back until dinnertime. Laura doesn't want to panic, but if she stays home alone, she will. She needs to go someplace she can think things through.

Even though showers are in the forecast, she decides to go kayaking on Lake Amity. By the time she reaches there, the afternoon haze has congealed into a heavy mist, and most people at the boat launch are leaving. She puts in and paddles along the shore. Past the camping ground, she enters a shallow inlet where she lets the kayak drift, listening to the soothing sound of reeds and water lilies brushing against the side. She swats a mosquito on her forearm. There's something satisfying about killing it before it draws blood.

She closes her eyes to quiet her mind and find the right questions to ask herself.

All her plans have been predicated on Jack taking Donnie out of Stanton and Nina taking him in. But she's his mother after all. Why has she been so reluctant to take him away herself?

Because of her job? Yes, but now that the paper's probably shutting down, she could leave and it wouldn't make much difference. Besides, she has over a month of unused vacation time. Use it or lose it.

Because of Nate? It's true she'd like to see how their relationship develops without Donnie around, but that's selfish of her.

Because of Donnie? It's hard enough living with him in the house, harder to imagine traveling with him, cooped up with each other day after day.

Yet these reasons alone don't quite account for her resistance. There's another explanation too, a more selfless one, having to do with her ability to see the big picture. As far as she knows, she's one of the few local people outside the police who know about Operation Snakehead. If she stays here, maybe she can do something to minimize its harm. But her duty as a mother comes first, she reminds herself. That much is clear.

So clear, so clear, so clear. She hears the words like the call of a black-capped chickadee.

As the shower begins, she paddles back to the main body of the lake. The rain falls harder, converting the water's surface into an energy field so alive that it seems an electric current might pass through the boat and into her body like the lightning strikes her father used to caution her about. *When you hear that first clap of thunder, head back immediately to shore*, he used to say. No risk of a thunderstorm today though. The shower's already receding, first over the far end of the lake, then over the middle, then over her. She wishes for a rainbow, but there's just a return to a lighter shade of gray. If her father were still alive, he would take Donnie away. She wonders how far his ashes have drifted from where she scattered them.

No other boats are visible, so she strips off her wet shirt down to her sports bra and starts paddling fast without any precise destination. She gives herself over to the movement, racing against the trees on the shoreline to see how quickly she can leave them behind. The water parts for her because her strength makes it part.

Speed is the answer, she realizes. Whatever decisions she makes, she has to act fast.

She's still in that mode when she grabs the last booth at Tony's and orders a pizza for Nate and her. It comes before he does, slim pickings of sausage and red pepper but lots of dough. Soon after, she spots him at the door and waves him over. He looks exhausted as he wends his way slowly between the tightly packed tables to join her. He rose at dawn to spend all day with a petulant group of novice birders. "Like two-year-olds with gray hair," he describes them. Letting him unwind, she listens to his account while they eat their pizza. Before long he picks up on her agitation and asks if anything's wrong. She tells him about Nina and how Donnie needs somewhere else to go. "How about Texas?" he suggests.

"Texas?"

Every summer he drives to Rockport to see his sister, he explains. This year his plan was to go in August, but her assistant just quit, so she can use his help until she finds a replacement. It's another peak tourist time. The cranes have all migrated, but people come to see the alligators and other birds in the wildlife refuge. "How about we take Donnie down there and get him settled in? He can stay with Alana—we have a big house—and help her on the boat. He'll like her. She's a lot cooler than me."

"That's a generous offer, Nate, but he won't want to stay."

"Don't be so sure about that. It's obvious he's scared shitless sticking around here."

She wants to believe him, but it doesn't seem possible Donnie would agree to living in a place he's never been, with a stranger no less. But at least the road trip would buy some time to figure out next steps. When she asks how long Nate's planning to stay in Texas, he tells her two weeks at most since he can't be away from the farm much longer than that. "And when would you go?"

"Got to line up someone to take care of the chickens and water the garden, but that shouldn't be too hard. We can leave whenever you want."

"Monday, the twentieth? That's when Donnie was supposed to fly to Florida."

"I don't see why not."

"Thanks so much, Nate."

He smiles slyly. "It's not just altruism, you know. I want you to meet my sister."

"I wish I could say the same about mine."

Back at home Nate falls asleep watching the news. She sends him up to bed early, then awaits Jack's arrival—he called when he got back from fishing to say he'd come over at nine. It's still light out when she greets him at the door, not long till the summer solstice. They sit in the kitchen, where she pours him a beer and puts out a bowl of pretzels. Uncharacteristically restrained, he only eats a couple before pushing the bowl away. He's furious with Nina. "She didn't even have the guts to call me," he fumes.

"She probably didn't want you to talk her out of it."

"I can just hear Doug barking in her ear. Why she married that jerk, I'll never know. Your dad didn't approve of him."

"Neither did I."

"But your mom did."

Laura nods. "Afraid so. She didn't think Nina could do any better."

"Still doesn't, I suppose."

"Well, she's so dependent on them now, she's hardly going to rock the boat."

Gradually she steers the conversation away from Nina to the Rockport plan, and he agrees it's worth a try. "I've spoken with Angie about getting Ricky out of here too," she tells him. "She wants to, but he's left home—did you know that? He's working for Gary, sleeping in his studio."

"Yeah, I know. Everyone knows."

"Who's everyone?" When he doesn't answer, she pushes further. "What's happening, Jack?"

Frowning, he eyes the pretzels, then reaches for the bowl and takes a few, washing them down with a slug of beer. "I'm totally out of the loop now," he finally responds. "All I know is what Tommy tells me."

"Tommy?"

"Yeah, Tommy. Believe it or not, he's getting disenchanted with the Snakehead jerks. They're bearing down hard, suspending normal procedures like wearing body cameras and relaxing the rules around lethal force too. Tommy told me he wants to bail, but I advised him to stay put so he can find out what's going on. He's starting to suspect a sting operation. Gary's involved somehow and maybe David Bentley. Tommy's worried about local kids getting swept up in it. Turns out he even has a soft spot for Ricky."

She mentions his approach to Angie, and how Angie doesn't trust him. "Are you sure he's not playing you, Jack? Maybe he wants to find out what you know."

"Could be, but I've got a pretty good bullshit detector. I think he's for real. I know he can be a real asshole, but he's a stickler for rules. He helped me come up with a Plan B for Ricky. Worse comes to worse, we bust him for something and put him in county jail. Safer there than on the streets. The Feds will go ballistic, but what the hell."

"Angie will post bail, or if not her, someone else. Gary for instance."

"Well, then maybe Ricky gets released on the condition that he wears an ankle monitor and stays at home because he's a flight risk. Those details can be figured out later."

"I hope it doesn't come down to that."

"Yeah, me too, but sometimes you do what you have to do."

After Jack departs, she goes to bed but can't fall asleep. Nate's snoring, but that's not the problem. The issue is Tommy coming over to Jack's side—his change of heart seems too abrupt. She looks at the clock. Donnie promised he'd be home by midnight. Another hour and a half to go. Lately he's been more forthcoming about his movements. Before he left, he said something about needing to support a friend whose horse was being put to sleep. Which friend? she should have asked. Where is he?

RISING NAKED FROM MICHELLE'S bed, Donnie tiptoes into the bathroom to take a pee, hoping the flush won't wake her. She's exhausted and needs to sleep. Her parents made a point to say they were coming home at eleven. Past ten now, time to leave. He doesn't want to, though. What happened between them was more than just sex—she shared her sadness and he shared his. First time he's cried like that in front of a girl. The way she liked him inside her, got on top so her breasts and hair dangled over him, kept going even after he came until he had to push her away playfully and go down on her until she begged him to stop, all that made him realize Rebecca never really desired him.

When he returns to her room, the nightlight's glow makes the horses on her trophies seem eerily alive, like they want to jump from the shelf and prance around the room. Everything is horse, not just in here but all over the house. Even the dining room wallpaper is a horse-and-buggy print. "Michelle wants to go to a college with a horseback riding program," her mom said during dinner. "Where do you want to go, Donnie?" Maybe Michelle told her parents about his SAT scores, because they treat him like he's smart.

He's so used to not fitting in that it's weird to feel included. "Thank you for being here for Michelle," her mom whispered as she left for the evening. All he'd done was stand in the corner of the barn and watch while the vet put Ruggles to sleep. It was kind of sweet really, the way Michelle hugged Ruggles, her mom sang a song, her dad said a prayer. Afterward, when the three of them made a small weeping huddle, he thought about his own dad—how three makes a better family huddle than two.

When he cried with Michelle, it was because he was missing his dad. She asked what he was like, but he could hardly remember. He needs to remember more, he tells himself as he pulls on his jeans, before the memories all disappear. Maybe he'll show her those old videos of him and his dad. Rebecca couldn't handle them, but Michelle probably can.

He lingers by the bed, gazing down at her. They talked about Rebecca too. "You know, in some ways I'm happy our friendship's over," Michelle admitted. "I don't owe her anything anymore. Do you feel the same way, Donnie?"

Instead of replying, he kissed her, but what would he have said? On the drive home he ponders that question. He wishes like Michelle he had a choice, but he doesn't. He might not owe Rebecca anything, but he owes Ricky, and Ricky wants to rescue her. His life would be so much easier if he and Ricky weren't tight anymore. He'd spend the summer hanging out with Michelle, having good sex. Maybe they'd be an item all senior year. Nothing to drag him down.

But he's in too deep. Suddenly anger at Ricky surges through him and he strikes a fist on the dashboard.

20

AFTER HER LAST MEETING ON Friday, Mimi searches the internet for summer programs in Europe that still have openings. She should have looked before, she knows, but it was a busy week and the last day of school caught her by surprise. Most programs are pricey, but if necessary, she'll sell all the family jewels to put Rebecca on a plane. She can't go with her—between business and the divorce, there's too much to do here. Besides, Rebecca would resist. This way she'll be with other kids the same age having fun. Mimi will present the trip as a surprise early birthday present.

The timing's excellent. Yesterday Gary signed the papers and got his buyout. Now the lake view property is hers alone. And if Gary's so pissed about Rebecca leaving that he plays the paternity card, she'll deal with it. She's come to see the wisdom in Steve's advice. People will take her side, especially when word spreads about Gary being a drug dealer. She'll make that happen somehow. Gossip travels fast in Stanton. Just about everyone in town now knows she kicked David out and filed for divorce. Wherever she goes, she gets sympathetic glances.

Things will get better. They have to. She can't take any more stress.

Lately she finds herself wishing sometimes that she could change places with her brother and be the weak one. So few expectations are placed on him that it's almost like he's a baby.

Ben is making a lot of progress with these new meds, relatives say. Now he's crawling, now he's walking, now he's speaking more coherently. No one bothers to praise her endurance.

She doesn't really want to be her brother, of course, but it would have been nice if he were competent and had taken over the family business, giving her the freedom to pursue a law career. But what's the use of feeling sorry for herself? And deep down, she knows Ben's mental illness is not his fault and he's doing the best he can.

Leaving the office, she lights a cigarette as she walks to the car. She swings by the grocery store to buy a precooked chicken for dinner and lights up again on the way home. The car stinks of tobacco, but so what? Rebecca used to bug her about it but doesn't anymore. Kind of sad really—how little her daughter notices or cares.

As she rounds the corner onto Jefferson, the lawn service truck parked outside the house screens her view of the driveway. Only as she pulls in does she notice Gary's van occupies David's spot by the garage. Muttering a few profanities under her breath, she gathers the shopping bags and trudges up the steps to the veranda, where he's waiting on the swing. No Rebecca beside him this time though. "Where is she?" he asks before she can say anything. "She was supposed to come to the studio today for her first lesson on the wheel."

"I don't know where she is," Mimi replies.

"Did you tell her not to come?"

"I didn't even know about the lesson." It's true—she didn't. "It's the last day of school. Probably she forgot and is out partying with friends."

"You're not worried about her?"

A lawn mower revs up across the street, so he can't hear her reply and asks her to speak more loudly. "I always worry about her, Gary!" she practically shouts. "She's been sick a lot lately. My separation from David hasn't been easy on her."

His expression is more distraught than menacing, throwing her off guard—she's rarely seen him with his defenses down. The mower is deafening now. "Can we go inside for a few minutes?" he asks. "I have something to show you." As if anticipating her refusal, he adds that he won't stay long. He has a kiln firing to do.

He grabs the shopping bags while she unlocks the door. "Leave the groceries in the kitchen," she instructs. "I'll put them away later."

In the living room he takes a seat beside her on the couch. He's in work clothes and it crosses her mind that clay dust might soil the upholstery. As if that matters. She doesn't like being so close to him, but he's got his cell out and he's tapping on the Photos icon. "I want to show you how our daughter parties, Mimi," he begins.

"My daughter."

"*Our* daughter." He doesn't wait for a response. "Take a look."

The first picture is of Rebecca holding a cat with a noose around its neck. Drug paraphernalia is on the bed beside her. In the second photo she's sprawled on what looks like the back seat of a car. Her eyes are shut and her midriff's bare. One of her shirtsleeves is rolled up. Gary zooms in on her arm. "See those marks," he says. "She's shooting up—that's why she's acting strange."

Mimi fights off panic. The pictures are probably fake, photoshopped, and he's messing with her again. What does he want this time—to smear her as a bad mother so he can pretend to be the good father? When the cell screen goes dark, he taps it again. "I don't believe it," she declares. "Where did you get those pictures anyway?"

"I can't tell you, but that doesn't matter. I didn't want to believe they were real either, but yesterday when Rebecca came to the studio, I made her show me her arms. That's probably why she didn't come today. We need to get her into treatment right away, Mimi. The drugs on the street are really dangerous now—not just cut with fentanyl but other horrible shit too. People are overdosing right and left. Check out her arms tonight when she's asleep. You'll see."

She still doesn't want to believe him, and why should she? He's a liar and a criminal with a dangerous obsession about Rebecca. Probably he wants to screw her, not save her—Mimi wouldn't put it past him. After all, he crossed the line with her, his first cousin.

As if reading her mind, he says there's something he's been meaning to say for a long time. "I'm sorry I took advantage of you that night," he begins haltingly, coughing to clear his throat. "You were really out of it, and I should have stopped. It was wrong of me, but we have a beautiful daughter as a result. I'm looking into treatment centers for her. Money's not a problem—I'll pay for it. I'll be in touch tomorrow after you've seen for yourself."

She doesn't respond, just watches him get up and go. Stunned and exhausted, she retreats upstairs, where she does a search of the bathroom. All the prescription painkillers are gone.

I KNOW YOU CAN DO BETTER THAN THIS. In some form or another all of Rebecca's teachers wrote that on her exams. She got a C+ in history—Ms. Owen didn't appreciate her digressions. But it's the last day of school, so who cares? Chances are she'll never set foot in the building again. She's already cleaned every last scrap out of her locker. Down the hall she can hear Michelle joking around with Donnie. Rumor is they're sleeping together. Let her have him, let her rule the whole school, let her be Royalty for a change. She's sick of it.

She slams the locker door, then hefts her backpack onto her shoulders and heads down the hall. Ricky's waiting by the football field to drive her to Gary's studio, but she doesn't want to go. Yesterday Gary practically forced her to pull up her sleeves. He's an asshole and a hypocrite. Puts stuff out on the streets and then acts all moralistic with her, as if he owns her. They all think they own her, that's the creepy thing.

Her cell dings. Ricky, again, wanting to know where she is. He's turning into such a control freak. She's a couple of minutes late, so what? Still cleaning out my locker, she texts back to buy some time. Turtle Girl wants to escape all this bullshit and hang with Susana. Susana's the only person who understands what she needs. And so, exiting the school, she turns left toward town instead of right toward the football field, winding her way through back lanes so Ricky won't find her. He still doesn't know about Susana; no one does. Maybe Susana will let her hide out for a couple of days until she figures out what to do. She'll shoot up with her this afternoon and then ask to stay over.

Nearing Susana's, she takes care to walk in the shadows cast by the shuttered warehouses. A few cars pass by, but she's alone on the sidewalk. Inside the house she tiptoes up the stairs. The first floor is uninhabited, but an old man who lives on the second floor sometimes pokes his head out if he hears her footsteps.

Susana's door is locked—probably she's still outside feeding the ducks or inside taking a shower. Rebecca retrieves the spare key from a magnetic case on the backside of the hall radiator. Opening the door, she spots Susana's purse and a Walmart bag on the coffee table. No one's in the bathroom, so Rebecca knocks lightly on the bedroom door. "Susana, I'm here," she calls. No response. She peeks inside the bag, where there's a can of spaghetti sauce, some pasta, and a stuffed unicorn for Rosie.

She knocks harder on the bedroom door. "Susana, I'm here," she repeats, but still no answer. She cracks open the door to check if her friend's taking a nap or has shot up already. She sees her sprawled diagonally on the bed, eyes open, no pillow under her head. Rebecca takes a few steps into the room. "Susana," she chirps. No word, no movement comes from the body on the mattress. When she draws closer, she sees a needle stuck in Susana's arm. She bends down to touch her forehead. It's cold and she's not breathing. Her cell lies a few inches from her hand.

A scream rises in Rebecca's throat, but she forces it back down and stands frozen at the bedside. How can Susana be dead? She's always so careful. "Susana, Susana, wake up!" she pleads as she touches her forehead again. "It's Rebecca, and I'm here to help."

No response. The body is rigid.

She forces down another scream as she reaches over to pick up Susana's cell. There's a text from the nursing home wanting to know why Susana didn't show up for work this morning. She calls 911 on the cell but is speechless when the operator answers. She hangs up and drops the cell back on the bed, then grabs her backpack and flees the apartment. She runs down the stairs and onto the street, where by instinct she turns in the direction of the park. As the ducks waddle toward her wanting to be fed, she calls Ricky and begs him to pick her up.

That night in bed, she runs through the plan Ricky hatched when she told him about Susana and how she needs to leave town right away. The timing works—he's picking up a cash delivery in Springfield tomorrow morning. He'll get Donnie to take her out to breakfast and then drive her to the Springfield amusement park when it opens. They should hang out there for a while, and she should find a way to get Donnie's keys without him knowing. Around two o'clock, she should slip out—Ricky will be waiting for her in the parking lot.

She closes her eyes but can't fall asleep. If she'd been with Susana, her friend would still be alive. Susana always made her shoot up first so she could give Rebecca Narcan in case she overdosed. And even if Susana couldn't have saved her, it would have been better if she were the one who died. Susana had Rosie to live for.

Lying there wanting to cry but unable to, she hears footsteps in the hall followed by the door opening. She pretends to be sound asleep as her mom gently pulls down the sheet and shines a light on her left arm. Later it's the sound of her mom's sobs that finally allows her to cry. It all mixes together—Susana, Rosie, running away, hurting her mom. The hate Rebecca usually feels for her has drained away.

21

AFTER LAURA WRAPS JACK'S present, a new tackle box Nancy recommended, she stands at the kitchen window for a few minutes gazing more inward than outward even though the weather's perfect—sunny, midseventies, low humidity. Since her dad's death, Jack's birthday barbecue has become an ordeal. Among the guests are other people her grandparents fostered who want to share memories of him. The glowing picture they paint of her dad makes him out to be a saint, diminishing the messy, lovable human being-ness of him. The only ones she looks forward to seeing are two former biker brothers, Ted and Charlie, who live in Worcester. They did enough drinking with her dad not to put him on a pedestal.

When she arrives at the picnic around noon, the brothers are over by the grill, so she makes her way there through the usual obstacles: kids darting in and out, relations to greet, Roxie sauntering through the crowd, angling for scraps. Spotting her, Ted waves her over. "Hey, where's your boyfriend?" he asks with a wink of his eye.

"Hope you didn't leave him at home," Charlie adds.

She glances at Jack, who's flipping a burger. "I told them about Nate," he admits.

"He's coming a little later," she says.

"We need to check if he's up to muster," Ted jibes. "And that boy of yours—where's he?"

"At a class party at the amusement park—end of school, you know."

Laura moves closer to the grill to give the brothers space to greet others coming to see them. The kielbasa sausages are spitting bursts of grease, staining Jack's apron. She notices CHEF JACQUES is embroidered on the top, probably Nancy's handiwork. When it's just the two of them, Jack drops his smile and asks if she's heard the bad news yet. She shakes her head. "Frank didn't call you?" he says.

"He's still on the Cape, coming back later today."

"Well, there's been another overdose death, only this time here in town. Susana Porter. She worked as an aide at the nursing home. She's been battling heroin addiction for five years and everyone hoped she finally had it beat. Her parents take care of her little girl. Nice young woman apparently—the patients at the nursing home all loved her."

"Fentanyl?"

"Probably. We have to wait for the lab results."

"Who found her?"

"Someone who called 911 on Susana's phone and fled before Tommy got there. She died the day before though. Tommy's pretty shook up—first overdose death he's dealt with on his own. An old man in the apartment below told him he's seen a young woman visitor going in and out lately. Yesterday around the time of the 911 call he saw her running down the stairs. We'd like to find out who she is." He pauses to turn a sausage. "I invited Tommy to come today. He needs to be around people. Try to be civil."

"I'm always civil with him."

"Cut him some slack is all I'm saying. We'll talk more later. Got to play the happy birthday boy now."

Laura tells him she'll go help Nancy in the kitchen. She's a nervous hostess, overprepared beforehand, underprepared in the moment. Nancy relegates her to carrying out the side dishes and arranging them on the buffet table on the patio. A breeze threatens to blow away the napkins, so Laura finds a rock to put on top. When she's done, she pours herself a glass of sangria. As unsettling as Jack's news is, it's also an opportunity for a story, but she'll have to move fast to research and write it before going to Texas.

Death as opportunity. How can she even think that way? she chastises herself.

A second glass of sangria allows her to make the requisite small talk as she awaits Nate's arrival. Around one thirty he texts that he can't come—one of the chickens is sick, and he needs to find out what's wrong in case it's contagious. A blessing in disguise, she thinks, since this means she can leave the party early.

On her way out, she spots Tommy at the end of the driveway carrying a six-pack of beer. Peeking out from beneath the sleeve of his Hawaiian shirt is the tattooed talon of a bird of prey, probably an eagle or hawk. "I'm late," he remarks as he approaches. "Is the party over?"

"Nope," she replies, "tons of food left. They haven't even done the cake."

Normally he would brush on by, but he stops instead, planting his feet right in front of her and setting the six-pack down on the asphalt. His usual expression of contempt has vanished, and he looks lost, like he's waiting for directions from her.

"Jack told me you had a hard day yesterday," she ventures.

"Yeah, I knew the young woman who overdosed. She looked after my grandma. Used to read to her and stuff."

"I'm so sorry."

"Yeah, it sucks." He moves closer, only an inch or two shy of violating her personal space, then asks where Donnie is this afternoon. When she tells him about the junior class party at the amusement park, he insists there is no such thing.

"Well, then he's probably meeting some friends there."

"Which friends?" Suspicion creeps into her voice as she asks why he wants to know. "If I tell you, you have to swear to keep it secret," he says.

"I will."

He inches forward again and in a lowered voice tells her he just came from Mimi Sullivan's house. "We think her daughter, Rebecca, knows something about Susana Porter's death," he continues. "A surveillance camera at one of the warehouses near her apartment shows Rebecca walking nearby. Mimi gave me a note Rebecca left her early this morning. She wrote that Donnie was taking her to the amusement park for the day." He pauses and tentatively touches her arm. "Do me a favor, Laura—just call me when Donnie gets home so I know they're safe." He glances toward the backyard, where the guests are now singing "Happy Birthday" wildly off-key. "I don't think I can handle a party right now," he remarks, stooping to retrieve the beer. "I'll walk you back to your car."

DONNIE'S PISSED OFF THAT Rebecca will hardly speak to him. She won't take off her sunglasses either, even kept them on all through breakfast and then at the Holyoke Mall, where they went to kill time before the amusement park opened. They're sitting on lounge chairs in the waterpark area now, near the line for the gigantic slide. He went on it once with Ricky, but the height freaked him out. Ricky always egged him on to try rides that scared the shit out of him. The one he hated most used centrifugal force to press you against the wall and lift you off your feet, spinning you so fast you thought you'd turn into a cardboard cutout of yourself. Ricky screamed because of the thrill of it. He screamed because he thought he was going to die.

"What time is it?" Rebecca asks. First words out of her mouth in over half an hour.

He checks his cell. "One forty-five."

"At two o'clock, you should get in the wave pool, and I'll go to the locker room to change."

"Why the pool?"

"Ricky said."

"Is that all you can say—'Ricky said'?"

"Yes." She pauses. "I'm sorry how everything turned out, Donnie. It's my fault. Will you tell Michelle I'm sorry about Ruggles? I wrote her a card, but I forgot to give it to her."

He wishes she'd take off her sunglasses so he could see her eyes. Is she really sorry? What does it matter anymore? What matters is what she's done to Ricky. Do they even know where they're going? He doesn't want to be part of their craziness. He knows he should call his mom and tell her they're running away, but he swore to Ricky he wouldn't.

At two o'clock, he follows orders, entering the crowded wave pool, where he finds a place in a corner. When the waves start up, kids riding them smash into him, and he scrapes his arm on the wall. He's just about to get out and look for Rebecca when four guys surround him. He recognizes his attacker from the knife fight, but it's too late to escape. "Where the fuck did that girl go?" the attacker demands. "And where's Ricky?"

"I don't know," Donnie responds feebly.

They push his head under and hold him there long enough that he's gasping for air when they let him up. "Remember now?" the attacker says.

"Honestly, I don't know."

They hold him under again, this time for real. As the world starts to go dark, he sees an image of his dad beckoning him. He lurches toward it, finding a leg instead. He grabs on to it and sinks his teeth into the hard flesh.

22

LAURA'S CELL RINGS FROM AN unknown number, probably spam. Usually she wouldn't answer, but Tommy's warning has her concerned. A woman asks for Mrs. Everett. "Yes, that's me," Laura responds briskly, anticipating a sales pitch. "What do you want?"

The woman identifies herself as Patricia Leonard from the security office at the amusement park. "I'm calling about your son, Donald," she says. "He's fine but quite distressed. There was an incident in the wave pool, and it appears his car has disappeared. Can you pick him up? We'll keep him here—we'd like to speak to you when you come."

"Can I talk to him, please?"

"Yes, of course."

It seems like an eternity before the phone is passed to Donnie. His voice is faint, shaky. She asks if he's okay.

"They took my car, Mom."

"Who's they?"

"I don't know."

"What happened in the pool?"

"It was crowded and I kind of got shoved under."

"On purpose?"

"I don't know—it happened fast."

"Is Rebecca with you?"

"I drove her here, but she left early with some friends."

He's probably not telling the truth, she surmises, but he's alive, that's all that matters. Her hands start trembling, but she can't afford to panic, so she collects herself and tells him she'll be there by four thirty.

She speeds down the highway until construction around Springfield forces her to slow down. Near the exit to the park, traffic grinds to a halt. She calls Nate and tells him what happened but can't bring herself to get in touch with Tommy yet. She'll do it when she gets home, when she knows more, when she's in better control of herself. Even though the car isn't moving, her hands grip the steering wheel as if it might defy gravity and fly away.

It's past five when she finally reaches the security office, where Donnie's waiting in the reception area, a huge stuffed dolphin with a ridiculous grin in the seat beside him. "You won that?" she finds herself asking stupidly as she points to the dolphin. He never wins anything.

"The security people gave it to me."

She notices his face and arms are beet red. As usual he didn't put on suntan lotion. *As usual.* As if there's anything usual about being here. Before she can give him a hug, they're joined by Ms. Leonard, a middle-aged woman with gray hair that she does nothing to hide. No makeup either. Her eyes appraise Laura but in a kindly way. "Why don't you and Donald come back to my office," she suggests. "It's quieter there."

In the office they sit at a round table with a small purple orchid in the center, fake or real Laura can't make out. "I'll tell you what we know so far," Ms. Leonard begins, "and then maybe Donald can help me fill in some of the blanks. His memory is fuzzy, which is understandable, of course." At a clipped pace Ms. Leonard proceeds to describe the "incident," a word she uses repeatedly. The incident began when a lifeguard spotted a huddle of young men in a corner of the pool surrounding someone. She blew her whistle and was walking toward them when they quickly dispersed in different directions. That's when she saw Donnie gasping for air. The lifeguard helped him out of the pool and called for medical assistance. After they determined there was no serious injury, and Donnie's breathing returned to normal, he retrieved his backpack and was escorted to the security office. She interviewed him personally about the incident, but like she said, his memory was fuzzy. "Is it clearer now, Donald?" she asks. "Do you know any of those young men? Did they push you underwater?"

"I didn't recognize any of them. A wave pushed me against them—maybe they were mad about that."

"Then they did hold you down?"

"Maybe. Like a prank, you know."

"A dangerous prank. We don't allow things like that to happen here." She explains to Laura how she asked Donnie to go through his backpack to see if anything was missing. Although it rarely happens, sometimes a group of thieves will divert someone in the pool while an accomplice steals their valuables. That's why management encourages people to use lockers. What's unusual about this case is that Donnie's wallet and phone weren't taken, only his car keys, and the car's no longer in the lot. "Are you sure a friend didn't borrow it?" she questions. "Thieves would be unlikely to know where your car was parked."

Laura watches his reaction. According to Tommy, Donnie came to the amusement park with Rebecca. Now she's no longer here. He could be lying that she left earlier with friends. It's more likely that Rebecca, not the attackers, took off with the car. There are easier ways to steal a car, and besides, Donnie's old tank is worth next to nothing. But then why did they go after him in the pool? She knows it's not a prank—she can read that much on his face. He's freaked out but adept like her at the art of composure.

"Donnie might want to check with his friends before you file a report with the police about the car," Ms. Leonard recommends. "And if Donnie remembers more about the pool incident, we'd of course be happy to assist the police with an investigation. We have cameras at strategic points." She casts a maternal glance at Donnie. "I know it must be very frightening. My youngest son is your age."

In the parking lot, Donnie lays the dolphin on the back seat of the car. As she starts the ignition, Laura asks whether he wants to go to the police now or check first with his friends. He'll check first, he responds, claiming there were a lot of kids from the high school there. She remembers what Tommy said—there is no class party—but now is not the time for an argument.

At home Donnie hardly touches his dinner and heads to bed early, saying he'd like to sleep in the guest room upstairs. "You're not going out, are you?" he asks anxiously. She assures him she's staying in.

When she checks on him an hour later, he's already asleep, an arm draped over the dolphin. He looks almost beatific, as if his brush with drowning has stirred some deeper region of the soul. She watches him for a few minutes, thinking about Mike again, how Donnie's body is slowly assuming his manly shape. Yet with his defenses down, he's still a scared little boy hugging a cuddly toy after a nightmare. Perhaps Jack's right and it won't be so hard to make him leave town. Nate told her he's ready to take off for Texas anytime, tomorrow if necessary. He'll finish packing tonight.

At nine Mimi Sullivan calls, distraught about Rebecca's whereabouts. Laura tells her what she knows—Donnie claimed Rebecca went off with friends, but maybe she took his car since the keys are missing. "Please try to find out more from him," Mimi begs. "Call me anytime—I'll be up all night."

Twenty minutes later, she hears from Angie. Does Donnie have any idea where Ricky is? Two men just came by the house demanding to see him. They were polite at first but then got ugly. She had to threaten to call the police to get rid of them.

Laura goes back upstairs to wake Donnie, gently shaking him after he fails to respond to words. Groggily, he opens his eyes and asks if it's morning yet. "No, no, it's nine thirty at night," she says as she sits down on the edge of the bed. "Rebecca's mom called and then Angie. They're worried, Donnie—do you know where Rebecca and Ricky are? Are they together?"

When he doesn't answer right away, she suspects he's weighing how much he can tell her. She's patient, very still. "I don't know where they are, Mom," he says at last. "Really, I don't. I don't know if they took my car or not, but they were thinking of running away."

"And you helped them do that this morning?"

"All I did was take Rebecca to the amusement park—she asked me to. I hoped maybe we could get back together."

The way he delivers the last sentence isn't convincing, but she lets it pass. "Who held you under, Donnie?"

"Like I said, I didn't recognize them. I bit one of the guy's legs and then they let go."

"That was brave of you."

"I thought I was going to die, Mom."

She wants to lie down next to him, hug him, assure him that everything's going to be all right even if it isn't. But that would be too much. So she just sits by him quietly until he falls back to sleep.

Afterward, she calls Tommy to let him know Rebecca and Ricky may have run away in Donnie's car. Then Mimi and Angie. Then Jack and Nate. She's exhausted by the time she fetches a suitcase from the basement and starts packing Donnie's things.

DONNIE WAKES IN THE MIDDLE of the night unsure where he is. A shadow cast by the moon turns the floor lamp into an attacker with a knife. On the verge of screaming, he bolts to full consciousness. He's in the guest room, but is he safe? The Jags must be pissed he sunk his teeth into one of their legs. They must know where he lives. They probably threw that brick through the window. He hopes his mother set the house alarm downstairs when she went to bed.

He props himself up with pillows and checks his messages. Delivered at 11:05 p.m. from Michelle: Won first place in dressage! Want to get together tomorrow night? Home by 8. Signed with three heart emoji.

Congrats!!! he texts back. Let me know when you're back.

She's invited him to go to her next show in New Hampshire, where her parents are renting a cottage on a lake for the weekend. They're cool with him staying there too. But it all seems impossible now, like a happy movie where everything comes out okay until you leave the theater and life sucks. What will he tell Michelle? When her parents find out that Rebecca ran away, that he drove her to the amusement park, that she took his car, they won't let their daughter see him anymore. So it's over.

Everything's fucking over.

Rebecca and Ricky should have told him about taking his car. They should have warned him the Jags would come after him. Probably Ricky stole money from the gang that he was supposed to give to Gary. Gary must be really pissed off too. Ricky's nuts to think he can get away with it. We'll all end up dead, Donnie thinks. And for what?

His dad died in this room. Donnie used to sleep in the bedroom next to it, but his mom moved him downstairs so he wouldn't hear his dad moaning at night. After school he'd go upstairs and sit with him. His dad mainly slept, but his mom said to speak to him anyway—he was listening even when you thought he wasn't. "He likes the sound of our voices," she said.

Maybe his dad's still listening, he thinks, waiting for him to reach out. The glimpse Donnie caught of him when he came close to drowning—had his dad come to save him or take him away? Closing his eyes, he tries to summon the image again but can't. Maybe he doesn't need to see him to hear him. It's his dad's voice he remembers most clearly, reading him stories, singing him to sleep.

He hears his dad laugh, like in one of the videos he just showed Michelle. And then he thinks about what his dad would say now. Probably he'd try to convince him to come clean about Ricky to his mom and Uncle Jack. And then he'd tell him to hold on to the strong people. He said that to Donnie a couple of weeks before he died: *It's going to be tough when I go, Donnie. Remember to hold on to the strong people.*

PART FOUR

Refuge

23

DAVID DOESN'T ANSWER HIS PHONE. Neither does Gary. Mimi's been calling them all night in case they know Rebecca's whereabouts. After pouring another coffee, she sits on the veranda in the early morning sun, hollowed out until the berating begins again, filling her with self-hatred. How could she have been so blind?

Susana Porter is dead. Her father's a contractor—he's been in and out of Sullivan Lumber hundreds of times. Decent guy. If Rebecca overdoses too, it will be Mimi's fault for not reading the signs.

Coffee finished, she goes inside to take a shower, turning the water up all the way and standing under longer than she needs to, wishing it would pound her even harder like a freak heavy downpour that clears the air. As she brushes her teeth, she looks at her haggard reflection in the mirror. She forces herself to put on makeup, though it seems a poor use of what little energy she has left.

Through empty streets she drives to the Ridge Motor Lodge on the edge of New Salem. In autumn it's a favorite spot for deer hunters, but the rest of the year the vacancy sign is out. The office is just opening and the woman at the desk looks half-asleep. Pinned askew on her shirt is a name badge—MARIE. David's in number twenty, she tells Mimi.

His car's not there, but she knocks on the door anyway. No answer. She shouts David's name until an older man in a bathrobe emerges from an adjoining room and asks her to be quiet—his wife's still sleeping.

"Haven't seen him for a couple of days," he adds.

"Any idea where he went?"

He shakes his head. "Keeps to himself."

Back in the office she presses Marie for more information. "Girls went in there to clean yesterday," she offers, "but it looked like he hadn't touched the bed or used any towels. His suitcase is in there, though, and he hasn't checked out."

"He's my husband."

Marie nods knowingly. "Having a little trouble?"

"You could say that."

"Lots of liquor bottles in his trash." She sighs. "I married one of those bums too."

Mimi writes down her cell number and hands it over. "Could you call me when he comes back?"

"Not supposed to do that kind of thing, but sure, I understand."

Back in the car, Mimi tries Gary again, but he still doesn't answer, so she decides to swing by the place he's renting. It's out past the trailer park, down a road with only one other house that looks abandoned, its lawn given over to high grasses and wildflowers. Bright pink once, Gary's ranch is now the color of faded lipstick. She's relieved to see his van in the driveway. To the right of the house, a dog pen is enclosed by a chain-link fence. The occupant, a mutt with a long German shepherd face and short legs, barks loudly as she approaches. Gary never said anything to her about having a dog.

She rings the doorbell, but he doesn't come. She checks her watch. It's almost eight o'clock, but he could still be asleep. After ringing a second time, she tries the door handle, which is unlocked. She takes a few steps inside and calls out his name, then a few more steps that bring her into the living room. It's surprisingly tidy with a brown leather sofa and matching chairs. On the wall is a painting of a covered bridge her grandma did. It unnerves her to see it, a reminder that Gary and she shared her in common. Where is he? She's reluctant to search further, worried what he'll do if she catches him off guard. No doubt he has a gun.

She shouts his name again. Silence. When she calls his cell, she can hear it ringing, so she follows the sound past the kitchen and down the hall toward the bedrooms. She knocks on the door where the ringing's coming from. Nothing. Methodically, her mind runs through the possibilities. He's dead, he's fled, he's drugged himself into a deep sleep, or perhaps he's just out for a walk. How much does she want or need to know? If it weren't for Rebecca, she'd just turn around and go. Her life has been too intertwined with his already, but maybe there's a clue in that room, a message on his phone, something that reveals where her daughter is. Slowly she opens the door.

Though thick blinds block the sunlight, she can make out the figure of a man sitting in a chair. His back is to her, his head slumps forward. The shape of his shoulders is familiar: David, not Gary. She switches on a lamp. There's blood on the carpet, his body is bound to the chair with rope. Cautiously, she circles around. He's stripped down to his boxers, and his bare chest is crisscrossed with slashes and stab wounds. As a wave of nausea hits, she runs into the bathroom and retches into the sink, then grips the vanity edge so she won't faint.

REBECCA WAKES TO A NOISY medley of screeching tires, angry honking, and sirens in the distance. For a moment she doesn't know where she is, but then she remembers how, from the amusement park, Ricky drove Donnie's car to New London, where they ended up in a dingy motel that accepts cash without asking questions.

Ricky's sitting in a chair staring at the mute TV. She can't recall his body next to hers at night. Maybe he never slept. He carries the duffel stuffed with cash everywhere he goes, even the bathroom. Now he's clutching it on his lap like a pet animal that might run away. He instructs her to get up, they need to get moving. After glancing at the clock—it's only five thirty—she asks where they're going.

They're taking the bus to New York, he answers. His plan is to abandon the car in a grocery store lot within walking distance of the bus station. He's got it all figured out, down to the fake IDs. She's Ashley Morgan, nineteen, a student at UConn with short dark hair and big glasses. Last night he told her they were going to cut and color her hair this morning so she matches the photo. The scissors are on the dresser.

As he chops away at her hair, she stoically watches large clumps fall on the floor, more parts of her disappearing. Tears come when she looks in the mirror. Her hair used to hide her ugly face, but now it stares back at her vengefully. Ricky hands her a tissue. "It will grow back," he states matter-of-factly. The black dye he applies makes her look Goth.

On the trek to the bus station, he follows at a slight distance, weighed down by the bags. For a moment she considers sprinting down a side street, losing him, scoring some drugs. He didn't bring any along, claiming it would add to their troubles if they got caught. But she knows it's to punish her for shooting up with Susana, and she resents him for it. Before she can make a break, he catches up with her, whispering in her ear to turn left at the next light.

At the station they buy tickets separately, and on the bus she sits in front, Ricky in back. She wants to listen to music on her cell, but he took it away from her. In New York they'll meet at a McDonald's a couple of blocks away from Times Square. He hasn't told her where they're staying because maybe he doesn't know. She doubts he's been to the city before.

When she was in middle school, her mom took her to Manhattan once to visit her college roommate, Eliza, and daughter, Simone, who lived in a famous apartment building across from Central Park, the Dakota, where John Lennon was shot. Even though Simone was a year younger, she acted like a sophisticated teenager. In Stanton Rebecca was used to being at the top, but in the space of a few hours, she realized compared to Simone she was a country hick. Simone went to a private girls' school and discussed books instead of boys. She was friendly enough—she didn't need to be a snob because she had everything, including amazing shoes.

They never went back. During the visit, her mom seemed depressed and subdued, and Rebecca overheard her confiding in Eliza about her unhappy marriage and life. Eliza's husband hardly ever appeared. "He's a senior partner in a big law firm," her mom explained with awe in her voice. "I wanted to be a lawyer, you know."

When a trim young man in a suit asks to sit next to her, she mumbles yes and turns toward the window, watching as the bus pulls onto the crowded highway, merging between two container trucks. She wishes their destination was Eliza's apartment, where her mom would be waiting to take her home.

24

AFTER NATE AND DONNIE DEPART, Laura moves the grinning dolphin downstairs to Donnie's room as if it's a spirit animal that offers protection. May her son be safe. Though he wasn't pleased this morning when she informed him he was leaving for Texas in a couple of hours, he was too stunned from the pool attack to put up much resistance. She waited until the last minute to tell him she wasn't going with them. "I'm flying down on Friday," she said. "I need to be here a couple more days to help search for Ricky and Rebecca."

Jack thinks she's foolish; there's nothing more she can do here, plus it's unsafe for her to stick around. "You're placing a huge burden on Nate," he chided. "Sorry to be so blunt, but Donnie won't exactly make good company on a long road trip." Nate wasn't happy with her decision either, and they argued about it late last night. She won, but at the cost of him being short with her this morning, not even hugging her goodbye.

At eleven o'clock, she leaves for work, hoping the routine of putting the paper together will calm her nerves. When she arrives, the mill lot is cordoned off by the police, forcing her to park on the road. Getting out of the car, she spots Frank pulling up in his Lexus. She waves and catches up with him, then asks what's going on with the building.

He hesitates as if weighing whether she's deserving of the truth or not, a power move she's all too familiar with. Then he puffs up his chest like a wild turkey—she's used to that too—before finally telling her he got a tip this morning that David Bentley had been murdered. Mimi found the body in her cousin Gary's house. He's the main suspect, so the police are searching his studio and the entire building. The office will probably be off-limits for a day or two. "The news isn't public yet," he remarks. "Breaking story, as they say." When she asks how David was murdered, Frank says he doesn't know the details. Grimacing, he tells her to go home—he'll call when they can get back in.

"I should be on the story, Frank."

"Look, Laura," he says patronizingly, "I know what you're thinking—good scoop could save the paper—but I don't want you involved in this. Too dangerous, and besides, reporters from all over the state will be flocking in. Leave it to me to cover the local angle."

His response is so predictable—even though Frank refuses to investigate anything, he loves appearing on TV as a seasoned local commentator. But she also recalls how David was a friend of his, so that could be part of his reasoning too. When she says she's sorry for his loss, he goes on to confide his worries about Mimi—first Rebecca running away, and then this. He knows about Donnie taking Rebecca to the amusement park. "Your job is to help Mimi find Rebecca; David's murder is mine."

As if they're not somehow connected, she reflects driving home. On the other hand, he has a point about not competing right now with all the reporters sniffing around. If David was indeed participating in the sting operation, his murder is the tip of the iceberg. The story she wants to investigate is a longer, deeper one about Snakehead and the war on drugs. Frank doesn't need to know that.

At home she calls Jack, who tells her to stay put, and he'll be over shortly. Ten minutes later he arrives. If he's still angry about the delay in her departure, he doesn't show it and is eager to talk. He has more details about David's murder—"gruesome" is how he describes it. The pattern of wounds seemed intentionally designed, maybe a kind of signature. She offers him lunch, but he only wants a glass of water. His usually ruddy face is sallow.

She takes him out to the deck for some fresh air. "I'm feeling fucking helpless," he admits as he settles into a chair. "At least we got Donnie out of here this morning, but word came down today to lay off the search for the other two kids and leave it to the so-called appropriate authorities. I asked Tommy why, and he passed on what a buddy of his on the inside told him. Tommy won't give me his name, but I think he's a state cop who got disenchanted with Snakehead about the same time as me. Kept his head down though, so he's still in the game. Smart of him." He pauses. "Off the record, right?"

"Of course."

"Turns out there's a crisis," he continues. "The sting the Feds set up had Gary running the drugs, David laundering the money. The casinos cooperated to get on the good side of law enforcement. David didn't know the whole story; he was just happy to play with Gary's funny money. The idea was that the operation would expand until Gary developed stronger ties with the higher-ups in the fentanyl trade. He'd point fingers, and the Feds would close in, make big arrests. Probably Gary was promised witness protection. But things got fucked up. Someone in Gary's network figured out he was an informer. Now the Feds need to cover their asses. According to Tommy's source, they've come up with a new scenario."

"And what's that?"

Before answering, he gazes across her overgrown lawn and weedy flower beds. In normal circumstances, he'd likely criticize her gardening skills, but instead he turns toward her and begins grimly sketching out the scenario. Since the big fish have eluded them, he explains, the Feds plan to go after the small fry, the gangs and low-level distributors. Ricky did them a favor by running off with a drug payment from the Jags. He's the bait. Once they find him, they'll wait for the right moment to stage a bust. "The really sick thing is they don't care who gets hurt," he says. "They've accomplished their main mission of beefing up border enforcement and dragging local and state police in so deep they're going to drown in this shit. The Feds will spin the bust to convince the public they're keeping us safe from drug dealers and dangerous immigrants. Handy that Ricky's dad killed a cop—'bad father, bad son' makes for a juicier story."

He takes a gulp of water, then wipes his sweaty brow. "But there are a couple of flaws in the plan. They don't know whether Gary's alive or dead. Dead he's useful—they might even pin David's murder on him. But what if he's alive and so sour on Snakehead he's ready to spill the beans?"

"Maybe he's in witness protection already," she suggests.

"Doubtful. Tommy's source says they're frantically searching for him."

She considers a moment, letting the information sink in. "So," she concludes, "we need to find the kids before the Feds do. How long do you think we have?"

Gary's disappearance might buy some time, he tells her, since they'll concentrate on finding him first. "But there's not much you or I can do. Your first responsibility is to Donnie, and he's going to need you when he gets down to Rockport. You have to put family ahead of everyone else—your dad taught me that."

"Of course, I know Donnie comes first, Jack, but my dad also taught me to help other people."

"After taking care of your own."

She shakes her head. "He lent friends money when my mother didn't want him to, when we were pretty broke ourselves."

"I'm not saying it's always an easy choice. Nothing is fucking easy about this." He looks at his watch. She knows he needs to leave soon, but wants a few more minutes with him. She asks him to stay put, lying that she needs to use the bathroom.

She goes into Donnie's room instead and sits on his bed, searching once again for the clarity she experienced that morning on the ridge when the gliding hawks taught her the value of seeing the big picture and little picture simultaneously. There's not much Jack or she can do to affect the big picture, at least for now, but how about the little one?

The kids are still kids, as much as they've been thrust, or thrust themselves, into the middle of a war waged by grown-ups, she reflects. What they understand is limited by their age and experience. Maybe if she shrinks her world to theirs, tries to see things through their eyes, she can anticipate their next moves.

Throughout childhood, Donnie and Ricky were obsessed with superheroes. Ricky typically played the commander, Donnie the loyal lieutenant. Now there's Rebecca, a real live damsel in distress. They're trying to save her from the evil villains, not realizing she mainly needs saving from herself.

That's one of their frames anyway, probably there are others. It comes to her then: she needs to put Mimi, Angie, and herself in the same room at the same time. A lesson she learned early in parenthood is that if the kids put their heads together, the mothers had better put theirs together too, and fast.

Back on the deck she tells Jack that, but he's skeptical. "Mimi just lost her husband, Laura—she'll be grieving."

"They were getting divorced."

"That doesn't mean she won't be in grief. And she found the body, for god's sake. That would be enough to traumatize anyone."

"If I know her, she'll put off mourning him until she finds Rebecca. She'll want to stay in touch."

"With you maybe, but Angie? Forget it. They'll be at each other's throats."

"Worth a try."

"Well, if you're going to do it, do it soon. I promised Nate I'd personally put you on that plane on Friday. Any word from him?"

She tells him Nate called an hour ago from a rest stop in southern Pennsylvania. He's planning to spend the night in the Blue Ridge Mountains. "He's not happy that Donnie's giving him the silent treatment," she admits. "And when I told him about David, he was even more anxious about me being here."

"Are you surprised? Stay with him, Laura—guy's a fucking saint."

DONNIE LIES AWAKE WITH ONLY a few feet between him and Birdman, who's snoring so loudly it hurts his ears. How could his mom do this to him? It's bad enough being pushed out of your own house, but then to be stuck all day in Birdman's truck and now in a tiny tent sleeping next to him.

His back and butt ache from the trip. They stopped a couple of times for gas and a pee but ate lunch in the truck, peanut butter sandwiches his mom made. Dry and chewy, not enough jam. Neither of them said more than a few words. That's fine with Donnie. What's there to say? Gee, thanks for kidnapping me? At the first rest stop, he considered bolting and hitching a ride, but Birdman kept close watch, even waiting outside the men's room until he came out. He hatched a plan to escape tonight when they got to a motel, but instead they're camping in the middle of fucking nowhere. No cell service even. He could steal the truck, but he doesn't know how to drive a stick. Tomorrow Birdman's going to teach him so he can help with the driving. They'll start out on back roads near here. "If you can drive these hills, you can drive anywhere," Birdman claimed.

If he steals the truck tomorrow, where will he go? Where are Ricky and Rebecca hiding out? All day he kept checking for a message from Ricky, but there was nothing. He wonders if they still have his car.

Tired but wired, he wishes he could step outside and light a joint, but he's scared to leave the tent. At the entrance to the campground there's a sign warning about bears. What if one comes around looking for food? Bears in Virginia could be meaner than the ones back home. He read somewhere about a little boy being mauled in a tent because of a candy bar he left in his pocket. What if Birdman has trail mix in his backpack? He munches the stuff all day long out of a baggie he holds in his lap. Donnie listens for rustling outside but hears only crickets chirping. The air's chilly, so he curls up tightly in the sleeping bag to get warm. Closing his eyes, he sees the highway stretching ahead.

The scrambled eggs and bacon Birdman cooks for breakfast taste good and so does the coffee. Though he can't bring himself to say thank you, Donnie dutifully helps fold the tent and pack up. To get the hang of the stick, Birdman makes him drive around the campground, then guides him onto the road. Terrified at the sight of an oncoming car, he swerves too far to the right, almost sending the pickup into a ditch. He pops the clutch a couple of times and stalls out changing gears going uphill. Birdman acts calm through it all until they see a deer by the roadside. He loses it then, shouting for Donnie to slow down, be careful. "Deer can burst out of nowhere," he warns.

Before they get back on the highway, Birdman takes the wheel, promising another lesson in the afternoon. "Look around you, Donnie," he says. "The Blue Ridge are beautiful."

Donnie glances out the window, mutters yes, and then checks his cell signal—finally decent reception. Three new messages have come in from Michelle. The first two are about missing him—she knows it isn't his fault Rebecca ran away.

The third says to call her right away, so he does. "Oh, Donnie, Rebecca's dad's been murdered," she blurts before he even has a chance to say hi. "Do you know where she is? Her cell's turned off and so is Ricky's. Her mom called to ask if I knew where she was, but I don't. She found a card Rebecca was writing to me about Ruggles." She starts to cry. "Please try to find her, Donnie."

After the call, he messages Ricky, but it's undelivered, and he puts the cell back in his pocket. "I know about the murder," Birdman says. "I spoke to your mom yesterday afternoon at the rest stop."

"Why didn't you tell me?" Donnie asks accusingly.

"Because she wanted to tell you herself. She's going to call you this morning."

He wants to be angry with Birdman, but he can just hear her voice saying to keep quiet for now, let me deal with my difficult son. He's noticed she's beginning to order Birdman around the same way she orders him. Birdman probably doesn't want to be on this trip any more than he does. All for her, always. She was probably like that with his dad too, but he can't afford to waste time thinking about that. Somehow, he's got to reach Ricky. And then the thought comes to him: maybe Justin knows where he is.

25

AT NINE IN THE MORNING, MIMI enters the garage through the kitchen and gets into the car. The street in front of the house is piling up with news vans, and a few cameramen are already wandering around shooting pictures. Last night she changed the message on her phones to say she's not yet prepared to give interviews to the press, but they keep calling relentlessly. After opening the automatic door, she backs out fast before reporters can swarm her. She alerted the police that she'd be gone for a couple of hours, lying that she was visiting relatives. Her real mission is to find Steve.

Though she's playing the grieving widow, in truth she hasn't shed any tears for David. Maybe she will later. For years she hardened herself against him. At the beginning she hoped he might make a good father, even if he wasn't a good husband, but he was a failure in both departments. Physical affection, including holding a baby, didn't come easily to him. His emotional life was like a model ship stuck inside a glass bottle. No wind to unfurl the sails. The best she can do is feel sorry for him, dying that horrible death. She's trying hard to keep the image at bay, but it keeps haunting her.

She drives to the entrance to Route 2 and heads west toward 91. Her mind is in obsessive overdrive, and she's looped through the same questions so many times she's beginning to feel demented. Who would do that to David? Was it Gary?

Whatever deal they made between them could have gone sour, but to commit murder in his own house? Overpower David and tie him up like that? Gary's strong but not that strong, mean but not that mean. Then there's the other possibility—that, as Steve suspects, Gary and David are informers. They got found out. Gary could be dead too, or maybe he managed to flee. What she fears most is that Ricky and Rebecca are somehow involved. Are they next? Is that why they ran off?

Heading south on 91, she keeps to the speed limit. Rush hour—if you can call it that around here—is almost over, and the traffic's thin. Usually she likes this stretch of road, the sense of flowing down over the hills to where the Connecticut River Valley broadens into fertile flatlands, but today nature is the last thing on her mind.

David's image returns. What if they plan to do the same thing to her daughter? Don't go there, she orders herself. She's spent most of her adult years trying to rein in her impulse for worst-case scenarios. Hopefully, David's death has nothing to do with Rebecca's disappearance. More likely, Susana Porter's overdose pushed Rebecca over the edge. That and her growing use of opioids. Running away is common for kids on hard drugs. Keep it simple, she tells herself, until there's evidence otherwise.

And if she keeps it simple, maybe she can convince Steve to assist her again. Two weeks back she got an automated message via email that he was closing his agency to take a senior management job with Bolton Landscaping. This morning when she called the company and asked for him, the secretary volunteered that he was at a job in Sunderland preparing the entrance to a new housing development.

She knows it's crazy to surprise him like this. He'll probably be furious and refuse to talk to her, but desperation frees her to try anything to bring Rebecca back. She exits the highway at Deerfield and a few miles beyond crosses the blue bridge over the river into Sunderland. She parks on a side street a block away from the construction site, remaining in the car a few minutes to calm herself down. Her heart's racing. If this doesn't work, then what will she do next?

From the sidewalk she spots Steve and two workers planting shrubs and flowers around a granite boulder inscribed with the name ORCHARD VIEW, ironic since all the trees, save one lonely apple, appear to have been chopped down. Spotting her, Steve says something to the workers before he hurries in her direction. "What are you doing here, Mimi?" he exclaims angrily from a few steps away. Then he goes quiet for a moment. "Look, I'm really sorry about David, but. . . ."

"Rebecca's run away," she states flatly.

"When?"

"Two days ago."

"I'm sorry about that too."

"Please find her for me, Steve."

He gestures toward the company truck. "This is what I do now."

She observes the dirt streaks on his arms, sweat patches on his shirt, heavy work boots on his feet. He used to wear nice leather shoes. She asks if he likes his new work and, when he doesn't answer, adds that she thought it was supposed to be a desk job.

"My father-in-law lost a couple of workers last month," he tells her, "so he needs me out in the field. I don't mind the physical labor. At least it's honest work."

"Your other work wasn't?"

"You know what I mean, Mimi," he replies testily. "Let's not play games here. I closed my agency because of you. The surveillance finally stopped, and I don't want it to restart. You should leave now."

"My daughter's missing, Steve. What if one of your own children went missing? Wouldn't you do something?"

"I'd rely on law enforcement."

"No, you wouldn't. With your skills, you'd go out and look for her."

"Rebecca's not my child."

"Just for a second, try to imagine that she is." Tears well up in her eyes. Real ones, not premeditated.

He stiffens his back, making no move to comfort her. "I'll walk you back to the car," he says coolly, "and then you drive away. This conversation never happened."

"It just started," she replies, holding back more tears.

"What do you mean?"

"I know you, Steve. How much longer can you go on working like this, under the thumb of your father-in-law? You told me he's a jerk. Name your price and I'll pay it. I've got money—David had a good life insurance policy. Lucky for me we hadn't signed divorce papers yet. I can buy you time to think about other job choices. All you have to do is look for Rebecca, nothing else."

"You know it's not as easy as that."

"At least think about it. You have a lunch break?"

"Yeah," he answers warily.

"I'll be waiting at the top of Mount Sugarloaf at noon. Sitting on a bench. If you come, you come. If you don't, you don't. I have to leave at twelve thirty for an appointment with my lawyer." Quickly turning away, she denies him the opportunity to reject her.

To kill time, she eats brunch at a café, surprised by the intensity of her hunger. Afterward, she drives to the top of Sugarloaf and finds a place to sit in the shade, away from the tourists climbing the view tower. Below her the river snakes through the fields; above a chain of clouds drifts slowly by. Even up high there's scarcely any breeze.

The last time she was here, Rebecca was a little girl, six or seven maybe. David and she still had some family rituals then, like making a pilgrimage to Sugarloaf to see the fall colors. On the way home, they'd stop at a farm stand to buy a pumpkin. Rebecca always took a long time picking one out, insisting that it be perfectly round with no unseemly spots. David helped her—before he began drinking so heavily, he was more patient with his daughter's eccentricities.

She looks at her watch: 12:05. Stupid of her to expect Steve to come. He wouldn't have closed his agency unless he felt truly threatened. No amount of money she offers will change his mind. He's not for sale.

A few minutes later Laura Everett calls to say Donnie's car has just been found in a parking lot in New London. She asks Mimi to come over to her place tonight. They need to talk. "If I can, I will," she replies.

Still no sign of Steve at twelve fifteen. She's desperate to tell him about the car, the first real break. A young Chinese couple approaches asking if she can take their photo, and she does. Despairing that he'll show up, she prepares to leave at twelve thirty, but as she walks toward the car park, she sees him taking long strides toward her across the grass.

AT THE ROOMING HOUSE ON a crowded street in Washington Heights, the pervert manager ogles Rebecca, but again no questions are asked when Ricky pulls out a wad of cash to pay. The lumpy bed takes up most of the room, and the bathroom is funky. In the cracked mirror above the sink, her face appears split in two.

Ricky goes out to buy some food, taking her cell with him. He's worried she'll be tempted to turn it on, and they'll track her. Without it, there's nothing to do. The TV's crap—no cable, just a couple of fuzzy channels. She's desperate to get high. The duffel with the cash is hidden behind the dresser. She could take some money and score, but where? The streets around here frighten her. She could take it all and run away from Ricky. Set herself up in a better place where she fits in, like where her mom's friend Eliza lives. She could nod out on a nice bed. That's what she wants the most—a nice, clean bed.

But these are all fantasies, she knows. She won't do anything because anything she does ends up bad. Like Susana dying. Like Rosie losing her mother. Like hurting her own mom. Like letting Carl and Andy shoot her up and then hang Night Sky. Everything she touches turns to shit.

She reaches for her razor, making a few shallow cuts on her right arm, watching the little droplets of blood bubble up. It doesn't really do it for her anymore, but for the sake of symmetry she cuts the left one too. Waiting for the bleeding to stop, she hears a key turn in the lock. "Oh, Rebecca," Ricky cries out when he sees her, "please don't do that." He sets down his shopping bags and brings some tissues to wipe the blood, then tries to draw her close, but she's stiff, unresponsive.

She tells him she's hungry, so they sit together on the bed eating bagels and cream cheese. Afterward, he shows her the burner phones he bought for emergencies. Then he takes her hands and holds them. She assumes he wants to talk about the cutting, but instead he tells her he used a computer at a public library to check if there was any news about them running away.

"Was there?" she asks.

"Not yet. There was something else though." He pauses, looks down at his lap. "It's about your dad."

"What about him?" Ricky's silent, so she repeats the question. When he still doesn't answer, she grabs his arms and shakes him. "What happened, Ricky?"

"He was murdered."

"What? You're making it up," she says in a panicked voice. "You want to scare me into staying here with you in this horrible place."

"I swear it's the truth."

"No, it's not. Give me back my phone. I want to see for myself."

Holding her wrists to restrain her, he confesses he threw it in the river. "Don't you see, Rebecca, we can't let anyone find out where you are."

26

SHORTLY BEFORE FIVE, A call from Nate catches Laura waiting nervously for Angie and Mimi to show up. Donnie and he are in Alabama now, planning to stop somewhere along the highway for the night. They should make Rockport by dinnertime tomorrow. "Donnie's driving, or I'd put him on. Natural with a stick. I'll call you later, and we can talk more."

Part of her wishes she were with them, driving away from Stanton instead of delving deeper into the heart of it. The other part perches on the chair like an expectant hostess, hands on knees, ready to jump up and greet the guests. She told Angie to come at five, Mimi a half hour later. The appetizer tray she prepared is more formally arranged than her usual hodgepodge—cheese cut in even slices, crackers arranged domino-style, olives in a dainty china dish. The fruit bowl next to it has the symmetry of a still life, a sign that she craves order.

Hearing a car pull up, she goes over to the window and peels back the curtain, watching Angie hurrying toward the house. They hug in the doorway before Laura ushers her into the living room. Angie has shed her work clothes for a billowy black shirt and white pants. Dressing up for Mimi, Laura suspects. She's done the same, wearing a beige linen dress she reserves for serious occasions. They talk about the news of Donnie's car and then about the threats Angie's receiving on social media. "I want to shut down my accounts," Angie says, "but what if Ricky tries to get hold of me that way? Even Justin's getting threats."

"You talked to Justin?"

"Once on FaceTime, when he had a good internet connection. He wants to come home, but I told him not to. I don't want him mixed up in this. The police suspect Ricky stole a drug payment. If he did, it's because of Rebecca. I hate that girl."

"Hate's a strong word."

"So?" Angie glowers. "It's how I feel."

"I get that," Laura placates her, "but is it all Rebecca's fault? The boys were so susceptible. They both wanted someone to rescue, you know, to prove their manhood."

"No, they both wanted a girl to have sex with. She was the first one who came along."

"I'm not so sure she was the first."

"C'mon, Laura, you know what I mean."

She shakes her head slowly. "Maybe at first it was just sex, but it got complicated fast. I'm trying to figure out why Ricky and she ran away. Why Donnie drove her to the amusement park and was almost drowned. I heard Rebecca was hanging out with Susana Porter, the young woman who just died of an overdose. Maybe Rebecca's using too and that's what the boys are trying to save her from. I invited Mimi over so we can each put our cards on the table and then maybe we'll see a pattern."

"Does Mimi know I'm going to be here?"

Laura's been waiting for the question. "I didn't tell her. I was afraid she wouldn't come."

"She'll walk out as soon as she sees me."

"Well, it's worth a try."

"You're always such an optimist, Laura, trying to put things right. Remember that time with the Cub Scouts, that mean den mother. . . ."

"Maureen Ridley?"

"Yeah, that's her name. I blocked it out. When the boys got lost on that hike, she blamed it all on Ricky, wanted to kick him out of the troop. She blamed him for a lot of other things too, complained he was disruptive. The three of us had a meeting where you tried to negotiate, but she had it in for Ricky. She wouldn't budge, so we pulled both boys out. Mimi reminds me of her."

Laura weighs her next words carefully. With Angie you can push a little but not too much. If she loses her temper, it's all over. "These are different circumstances," she begins.

"Exactly, Mimi will probably try to slit my throat."

"Well, I won't let her." She pushes the appetizer tray toward Angie and urges her to eat something.

"Not hungry," she replies, "but thanks anyway."

When Mimi arrives, she begs off the appetizers too, tucking herself into the opposite corner of the couch from Angie, where they exchange a few seconds of hostile eye contact. Mimi has dressed down for the occasion in jeans and a crinkled shirt, the smell of tobacco smoke overpowering whatever perfume she's wearing. Makeup can't disguise her drawn face and puffy eyes. As if to protect herself, she crosses her arms tightly across her chest.

Laura starts her take-charge overture with a plea for openness and honesty. The three of them need to share information that might help locate Ricky and Rebecca, she asserts. The goal is to find them before the gangs or police do because of the risk of violence in either case. Trying not to betray Jack's confidence, she hints the kids could be pawns in a larger drug operation. Neither woman contradicts her, but they're not forthcoming, and the tension is palpable. Just to do something, she takes a grape from the fruit bowl and pops it in her mouth. It's sour, but it would be uncouth to spit it out. She tries an olive next.

Mimi finally makes the first move. "It's impossible what you're asking," she confronts Laura. "And you lied to me. I wouldn't have come if I knew this woman was going to be here. How can I possibly trust her? Her son took my daughter away."

"Your daughter took my son away," Angie leaps in. "It all started. . . ."

"Wait a second," Laura interrupts. She anticipated such a clash, but how to defuse it? "It doesn't help to blame each other," she begins in her calmest voice. "Whatever our kids have done—and I say *our* because Donnie's implicated in this too—they're bit players in something much bigger than them. Something that's going to crush them if we don't work together. We may not like it, but there's no choice."

Mimi glares at her. "You can say that because you've sent Donnie away. It's not the same for you."

"I know that," Laura counters quickly. "The stakes are much higher for both of you, which is all the more reason to join forces."

"Frankly, I prefer handling this on my own."

"Fine with me," Angie retorts. "Nobody's keeping you here."

Grabbing her purse from the floor, Mimi gets up to leave. Angie's right about the limits of optimism, Laura thinks. Her plan is so naive. All the platitudes she has at the ready—*Even if you don't like each other, you can work together; Remember, it's not about you, it's about the kids; Why don't you just give it a try*—suddenly seem trite and ridiculous. Even the appetizer tray is such a lame gesture. She'd like to pick it up and throw it on the floor.

Why not? She's being too fucking nice, that's the problem. She lifts the tray and lets it crash on the floor. The dish breaks and olives go rolling. The two women look shocked. "Don't you get it?" Laura shouts. "Your kids could end up hurt or dead unless we do something right now!"

DONNIE STEPS OUT ON THE BALCONY of the Comfort Inn on the outskirts of Nowhere, Alabama. Ku Klux Klan territory probably, though the people who run the place are from India. It's only eight thirty, but Birdman is already asleep and snoring as usual. Down below, the pool's blue water beckons in the hot night air. Birdman took a dip before dinner, but Donnie couldn't bring himself to go in. The sensation of drowning visits him regularly, making him choke and cough. He might never swim again.

It was a long day of driving, and he did at least half of it. In the afternoon they made a detour to see some ancient Native American mounds Birdman was all excited about. Afterward, they walked down to the nearby river, where Birdman pulled out his dick and pissed on the bushes. "See that pretty blue bird over there?" He pointed as he was zipping up. "That's a male indigo bunting—you don't see many of those in Massachusetts anymore." Donnie acted impressed, hoping that Birdman would shut up after that, but back in the truck he talked birds nonstop for over an hour. He was especially excited about whooping cranes. "Wish it was the right season to see them in Rockport," he said. "You'd be amazed by them, Donnie. They're one of the oldest bird species on the planet, grow to almost seven feet tall. They're summering in northern Canada now. I'll have to bring you and your mom back in the winter to see them. They almost went extinct, you know."

On the balcony, Donnie checks his cell. He has texted Justin multiple times, but none of the messages are marked as delivered. He tries again before returning his gaze to the pool, where a tall man has just jumped in. With a few long strokes he swims the crawl back and forth, back and forth, so easily, without fear. A woman, probably his wife, sits on a chair watching him, drinking a can of something. Donnie realizes he's thirsty, so he gets a Coke from the soda machine in the stairwell, then returns to his observation post. The man's doing backstroke now. Donnie can't take his eyes off him; it's like he's still driving, hypnotized by the highway.

To break the spell, he checks his cell again. Nothing, not even from Michelle. He's been waiting to hear more about the murder from her. Feeling homesick, he calls his mom's number. "Is everything okay, Donnie?" she asks worriedly. He's fine, he reassures her, then describes the Native American mounds and the indigo bunting because he knows those will please her. He should be angry with her but isn't. He just wants to hear her voice.

Before he goes back inside, he takes one last look at the pool, where the man's climbing up the steps in the shallow end. Rising from her chair, the woman hands him a towel.

27

RATTLED BY THE MEETING, Mimi lies in bed unable to fall asleep. Laura's provocation shattered her defenses, which is how it was intended, of course. She broke down, sobbed messy tears. Like a love-starved child, she greedily accepted comfort, even from Angie.

In her weakness did she give too much away? She sifts through her disclosures. Yes, she admitted Rebecca's experimentation with drugs but without mentioning Susana Porter or the damning pictures Gary showed her. She told them she'd hired a private investigator to find Rebecca but said nothing about Steve's prior surveillance of David and Gary. And although Laura tried to pry more out of her, Mimi was tight-lipped when she needed to be. She senses Laura knows much more than she's letting on.

And then Angie, how to get a read on her? After Mimi's collapse she was all sweetness and light, nicer than she expected. But how far can she trust her? Necessity has forced them into a truce, but their children's interests could soon diverge. If Ricky stole a drug payment, he won't want to be found because he'll get arrested, sent to jail, maybe even hauled up for absconding with a minor. Unlike him, Rebecca hasn't done anything criminal. Sooner or later she'll want to come home—if she doesn't overdose first.

According to Angie, Ricky's worried about Rebecca's drug use. He told his brother, Justin, about it and Justin told her. It will be a small mercy if Ricky won't let her shoot up, she thinks, recalling Laura's parting words: *You have to understand, Mimi—the boys are trying to save her, not hurt her. Their motives aren't bad, but they're teenagers, and they don't know what they're doing.*

If only Rebecca had come to her for help and not to those two stupid boys, but it's been so long since they were close. She thinks back to their trip to the Caribbean seven years ago, remembering how she grew jealous of the family that befriended Rebecca, especially of the mother, Ellen. Once she watched her teaching Rebecca how to body surf. When Rebecca finally caught a wave, the pride and joy on her face was directed at Ellen, not her. They high-fived before they dove back into the water, swimming in tandem to where the waves were cresting.

Something changed between Rebecca and her then, but she was so unhappy with David that she let it pass.

She rolls over on her back and looks up at the ceiling. No more logic left in her brain, just sadness and sheer terror at her daughter's disappearance. Shivering, she pulls the blanket more tightly around her, sensing that an ugly truth is stalking her. This happens sometimes when she lets her defenses down. The first time was in college, and it was about her brother. Worries about him consumed her until she finally went to a few counseling sessions to come to grips with his mental illness. Eventually, the therapist turned the spotlight on her, making her see how much his illness had cost her, draining her parents' emotional bank account until only spare change was left for her. It was an ugly truth because it didn't do much good, instead heightening her resentment. So much for the truth setting you free.

Now, she realizes, the ugly truth is about Gary. That night on the beach—were her eyes open like this before he assaulted her? Had she been staring up at the sky when his head suddenly blocked her view and his weight pressed her into the sand? How frightened was she? She didn't hurt afterward, so she suspects she went limp, too high to fight back. Was that his plan beforehand? Drug and rape her? Or was it something that happened more in the moment? His apology a few days ago didn't make that clear. She wishes she'd pushed him further. Premeditation makes her more of a victim, excuses her passivity. But it also means Rebecca was conceived in violence.

No, no, Mimi, she rebukes herself. That's the easy way out. The ugly truth is that either way she was conceived in violence, without consent.

There were lots of stars that night, she remembers now. She was stoned and just wanted to keep looking at the sky, searching for constellations, but he wouldn't let her.

THE TAXI DROPS REBECCA OFF AT the corner of Seventy-Second Street and Central Park West, and she pays with cash from Ricky's duffel. After he left to buy food this morning, she slipped out of the boarding house, leaving a note saying she'd be back in a couple of hours, she just wanted time to think.

Her plan is to find Eliza and Simone in the Dakota. She'll tell them she wants to go home because of her dad's death. Maybe they know about his murder already. They'll call her mom to come get her. While she waits for her to turn up, she'll take a bath in their marble bathroom, and Simone will lend her clean clothes. They'll give her a nice warm lunch. She won't tell them where Ricky is. She'll say he abandoned her, not the other way around. She's convinced herself she's not betraying him—he'll be better off without her.

She stakes out the Dakota entrance. A tall guard standing in the archway where Lennon was shot is refusing to let tourists proceed farther. She observes how he lets a delivery man go in, then a woman with a dog on a leash who must live there. Summoning her courage, she walks up to him. He eyes her critically, probably because of her bad haircut and dirty clothes. To make up for her appearance, she tries a flirtatious smile. "I'm here to see Eliza and Simone," she announces perkily.

"What apartment?" he barks.

"I was hoping you could tell me."

"Got their last name?" When she says no, he rolls his eyes. "Look, young lady, there are ninety-three units in this building. I don't know everyone by their first name."

"Simone is my age," she offers. "We went to elementary school together."

He studies her face suspiciously. "Is she expecting you?"

"It's a surprise."

Rolling his eyes again, he instructs her to check with the deskman in the lobby. She thanks him, then makes her way there. She remembers the lobby from before—the elegant chandeliers, mahogany paneling, and old rotary phone just for show. She waits while the delivery guy signs in, then approaches the desk, her heart beating fast. This is her chance.

Her smile works better on the deskman, who's short and dumpy, too fat for his uniform. After she tells him she's looking for Eliza and Simone, he picks up a phone and punches in a number. "Hey, Tony," he says after a few seconds. "Got a young lady here in the lobby who wants to visit Eliza and Simone, but she doesn't know their last name or apartment number. Know who they are?" There's a pause while Tony answers. "Yeah, yeah, okay, I'll tell her." He hangs up the receiver. "Sorry, sweetheart, but they moved out a couple of years ago. Husband got a job in Philly." Her lip trembles as she thanks him. "You all right?" he asks with concern. "Got enough money for a taxi?" She nods. "Okay, I'll call you one."

28

ROXIE BARKS BUT DOESN'T GET up when Tommy stands at the threshold dressed in boating shorts and a tank top. Laura came by kayak too, instructed by Jack to leave her cell at home. No trackable devices, he insisted. "Come in," she urges. The dog lets out one more desultory bark, then thumps her tail as Tommy bends down to pat her. Laura notices the bird tattooed on his left upper arm is a bald eagle, and on the right is an incongruous multicolored mandala.

Hot from battling the current, she wishes they could sit on the dock in the breeze, but Jack advises against it. Too visible. Instead they're trapped inside with only a small battery-operated fan stirring the stale air. No beer this time, just a few cans of soda in the cooler. Tommy pops the lid off one and guzzles it down. When he's done, his eyes dart nervously around the shack. From the fanny pack around his waist, he removes a revolver that he puts in his pocket. She doesn't like the gun, but it's not worth making a scene. Sweat drips down her back, so she moves her face a little closer to the fan.

"There's new information," Jack begins, "so I thought it would be good for the three of us to meet, get on the same page. Tell Laura what you found out, Tommy."

Tommy recounts how the Feds have tracked Ricky and Rebecca to New York City. Surveillance cameras caught footage of them at the New London bus station and then near Times Square. Rebecca has short black hair now, big glasses. They've pressured the NYPD to put out a missing child photo of her, claiming she's a victim of sex trafficking. "If we want to find them first, time's running out," he says grimly. She then asks about Gary. "He's been taken care of, so now they feel free to move ahead."

"What happened to him?"

"Not sure—it's all hush-hush at the station. But the Snakehead guys are strutting around with big smirks on their faces like they're sharing a secret joke at our expense. The chief's pissed off they're leaving him in the dark, but he's still following orders. Gary's off-limits for us lowly local cops."

"And the search for David's murderer?"

"Not a priority, though that's never said out loud."

"All rings true to me," Jack offers in case she needs convincing. "Somehow they managed to get Gary out of the way."

"Did they kill him?" she asks bluntly.

"Anything's possible," Jack responds and then reveals Gary has two thugs working for him—Carl Renton and Andy Foster, assumed names it turns out. Maybe they found out Gary was an informer and did him in. They could have murdered David too. No one knows where they are. "I wouldn't be surprised if they turn up dead themselves. They know too much."

"The Feds would go that far?"

"Or one of the cartels. In the drug war, lines get blurred. Both sides end up doing dirty business that helps the other. Put a few informers into the mix plus this border control madness, and the body count rises. It's taken me a long time to understand this, but I finally get it now."

"Yeah," Tommy says. "Used to think it was good guys versus bad guys. Grew up on that shit. Now all that counts is finding the kids before they do."

The room falls silent except for the buzzing of the fan. They both look at her expectantly, as if she has solutions to offer. She's already shared with Jack what happened last night with Mimi and Angie. A first step toward cooperation but not much more. Although the private investigator Mimi hired could be helpful, it sounds like it might be too late. She takes a soda from the cooler, then cups her hands around it like a crystal ball. Perhaps there's a silver lining to the bust the Feds are staging, she reflects. Even if they find out where Ricky and Rebecca are hiding, they might not close in until all the other actors are in place, including the people who want their money back. After all, the bust needs to look big even if it isn't. She voices these thoughts to Jack and Tommy, who agree that might buy some time.

"Before you both arrived, I was mulling some things over," Jack remarks. "Tell me if you think I'm wrong, Laura, but Ricky's got to be getting pretty desperate. He pretends to be macho, but he's not. He's going to be looking for a way out. Who's the most likely person he'll go to for help?"

"His brother, Justin." She hesitates a moment. "And maybe Donnie too."

"Yeah, that's how I see it. That's why you need to fly down to Texas on Friday like you promised and hound Donnie for information. He's not macho either—he'll cave, but you need to be there to make it happen." Taking a deep breath, he continues, "There's one more thing. Before you leave, you need to convince Angie that if she finds out anything from Justin, she should let Tommy or me know immediately."

"She doesn't trust the police," Laura responds, omitting that of all the cops on the force, she trusts Tommy the least.

"Well, in that case, convince her to tell you and you tell us. Whatever it takes."

Like a naughty kid called out by the teacher, Tommy bows his head and shifts awkwardly in his seat. She wonders if his willingness to help Ricky is an attempt to make amends, or is he playing Jack and her, feeding info back to the Feds? Jack claims Tommy's incapable of that kind of duplicity, and that once he's come over to your side, he stays firmly rooted there. She hopes he's right.

Without looking her in the eye, Tommy tells her he's concerned for Angie's safety. "Let her know I'm going to be driving by her place at night whether I'm on duty or not. Off duty I'll be driving my red Cherokee. I'll be checking your place and Mimi's too."

So they won't be seen together on the river, Tommy leaves first and she follows twenty minutes later. The current is with her so she hardly needs to paddle. She pays little attention to the birds darting about until a great blue heron swoops over her, heading up the river as if to show her the route.

Back in the car she checks her messages. A voicemail from Frank informs her that the mill building is no longer off-limits, and there's a paper to get out. Calls from Mimi and Angie too—they've been alerted by the police that Ricky and Rebecca may be in New York. Does she know anything more? Yes, she thinks, but how much can she reveal without breaking her oath to Jack? How much longer can she stay silent about Snakehead?

No one else is at the mill building when she arrives later that afternoon. The emptiness unnerves her, and for a moment she longs for Gary's blasting music, some sign of life. In the office she locks the door behind her. How frightened should she be? she wonders. Is it safe to be here alone? She turns on the computer. No obit for David yet, just a death notice. There's a long obit for Susana Porter though, a brave one by her parents, acknowledging her struggles with addiction. It ends with: *In lieu of flowers, donations can be sent to the Opioid Response Coalition*. She thinks of Dr. Goldin and wonders how his own daughter is faring.

She finishes the layout work quickly, but as she prepares to leave, she feels the ghostly presence of the mill workers who once toiled here, their sweat if not their blood seeped into the floorboards. Has another ghost joined them? Don't be silly, just go home, she commands herself, and she almost does. Her hand is on the doorknob when she pivots back and retrieves the master key from its hiding place.

She walks upstairs, where she unlocks Gary's studio. Inside, what strikes her first is how everything is still in order, with no visible sign of a police search. The only apparent difference from her last visit is the absence of pots on the shelves. Perhaps Gary recently fired them in the kiln, she thinks. The kiln is industrial-size, taller than she is, its door bolted shut. The exterior is slightly warm to the touch. She unlatches the bolt, then pulls hard on the heavy door, only to discover that the kiln's shelves are empty.

On the bottom she notices a thick layer of ashes with something poking through. After finding a scoop, she goes back to the kiln and bends down, digging through the ashes until she uncovers what looks like bone fragments. In her fingers they turn to dust. She digs once more, this time bringing up something larger and harder that didn't burn all the way. It too has the shape of bone, human bone.

She closes her eyes and forces herself into a zone where she can remain functional enough to proceed with the task at hand. She learned that trick when Mike was dying. Closing her eyes, if only for a few seconds, helped stave off panic, allowing her to detach and stay calm. She summons that same willpower now. When her eyes open again, she methodically wraps the bone in a tissue and zips it into a compartment in her purse. She then bolts the kiln door, washes the scoop in the sink, and puts it back where she found it. Downstairs she returns the key to Frank's file drawer.

DONNIE WAKES FROM A SNOOZE on the outskirts of Houston where below the raised highway, suburbs stretch to the horizon. He suddenly longs for the forests and hills of home. Because of heavy traffic, it takes more than an hour to get past the sprawl. Finally, Birdman exits the highway onto a county road where houses become fewer and farther between until there's nothing much to see except barbed wire, scrub brush, and an occasional gate to a ranch. They're heading west and the evening sun streams through the windshield, making it hard to see. Birdman slows down and pulls into a lay-by. "I need a break," he says.

When they sit down at a picnic table, Donnie realizes he's hungry. Their snack supply is depleted. Birdman's sister, Alana, called about an hour ago to say there was lasagna waiting in the oven. He can almost taste it now. He offers to drive, but Birdman says he's fine—he always stops here for a little while.

"Know why?" he asks but doesn't wait for an answer. Instead he launches into the story of how he was driving along here with his brother, Rob, one evening when a deer came out of nowhere. He couldn't swerve in time to avoid it, so he hit it straight on. Totaled the car and killed the deer, but Rob and he got away with a few bruises. "Whenever I pass by, I take a moment to feel grateful." He pauses, fixes his eyes on Donnie. "There's something else I'd like to share with you."

Donnie mutters okay, though he's not sure he wants to hear it. The guy's too fucking intense.

"It's about Rob," he begins. "For some reason our relationship went downhill after that. He started getting into trouble, and that September I went away to college. Maybe the accident triggered something in him, I don't know. In any case I wasn't around to help. Eventually he dropped out of school. He talks big but hasn't done anything with his life. So I feel regret when I come here too. Not guilt, but regret. Know the difference?" Donnie shakes his head. "Well, it wasn't my fault hitting the deer and it wasn't my fault going away to college, but I regret not being home for my brother. Maybe I could have made a difference, but then again maybe not. I probably couldn't have changed him even if I tried—but I'd have liked to give it a shot. It's taken me a long time, way too long, to come to terms with that. I just wanted to tell you in case you're going through similar stuff."

This is supposed to be an opening, Donnie knows, but he doesn't respond except to say he's sorry to hear about Rob. He wants to be alone to take in the view. Sunset isn't far off now, and the huge sky is streaked with trippy purples, pinks, and blues, the clouds neon rimmed. Before getting back in the truck, he takes a few photos and texts them to Michelle.

29

MIMI SCANS THE CAVERN-LIKE insides of Murphy's Irish Pub until she locates Steve slumped in a back booth, a baseball cap pulled down over his forehead. Happy hour over, the place is starting to empty out. A Celtic harpist, a gaunt woman with long frizzy hair, is playing a mournful ballad while the rest of the band packs up. Hugging her purse to her chest, Mimi steers her way through the departing crowd. This is a part of Springfield she's never been to before. Even though the pub seems safe, best to be on guard.

She slips into the booth and faces Steve across the table. Between them is a bowl of unshelled peanuts, and he's nursing a mug of beer. "Anyone follow you?" he asks by way of a greeting.

"I don't think so."

"Good," he utters perfunctorily. He cracks open a peanut, shaking the nuts directly into his mouth.

"What did you find out in New London?"

Frowning, he reports it wasn't a very productive trip. No one was willing to talk to him except one ticket agent at the bus station who let on that federal drug enforcement agents have been snooping around—they requisitioned surveillance footage from the last few days. "Ordinary runaways don't usually rate this kind of attention," he remarks, then takes a sip of beer. "You didn't tell me the whole story, did you, Mimi?"

"I told you what I knew."

"But not what you suspected."

"I know more now," she says. Leaning closer in, she informs him that Ricky likely stole a drug payment, and he and Rebecca have recently been traced to New York. "It's Ricky the police want," she continues, "so all I ask is that you find Rebecca and get her away from him."

"That's all you're asking?" he replies sarcastically. "You're dragging me right back into the abyss. My interference won't be appreciated."

"You knew what you were getting into, Steve."

"No, I didn't."

"Yes, you did." She reaches into her purse and pulls out her checkbook. "Name your price."

"That's not the issue. We've been through this before."

"How about a high-paying job with Sullivan Lumber when this is over? I need a new senior manager. Wouldn't you rather work for us than your father-in-law?"

He looks at her curiously, as if considering the prospect. "What if I don't find her?"

"You still get the job."

"Jesus, you never give up, do you."

"I have an idea," she says swiftly before he can remount a defense, "a long shot but worth a try." She tells him how she took Rebecca to the city once, where they stayed with a rich college friend of hers near Central Park. Rebecca loved it. Mimi reckons she must be getting tired of being on the run—she likes her creature comforts too much. There's a chance she'll split from Ricky and go there. "My friend has moved to Philly, but she doesn't know that. We could start by checking out if she's been to the building. Then at least we'll know she wants to leave."

"She could just call and ask you to pick her up."

"I know, but she's probably confused about what to do. She's been using drugs, Steve, heroin even. She was fragile even before she started using, and she's probably worse off now."

"How long have you known about the drugs?"

"I found out the night before she ran away, from my cousin Gary, of all people. And then the next morning, the cops showed up at my door wanting to interview Rebecca, but she'd already left. They think she discovered the body of a young woman who overdosed. She called 911 on the woman's cell, then fled."

"You knew this when you came to see me in Sunderland?" he says, bristling. "Why didn't you tell me?"

"I didn't think it mattered."

"Oh, c'mon, don't lie to me. In an investigation, the reasons people run away always matter—you know that as well as me. You were ashamed, weren't you—afraid I wouldn't take the job if I knew your daughter was using?"

"Maybe. I'm not exactly in great shape myself." Anger creeps into her voice, a little adrenaline pulses through her veins. "As you may recall, my husband was just murdered. It's a miracle I'm functioning as well as I am."

He doesn't take the emotional bait. "And what's the story on your cousin?" he inquires coolly.

"He's disappeared." She hesitates, then comes clean about Ricky working for Gary.

"Well, that explains a lot, doesn't it? Even if we find out where Rebecca's hiding, extricating her won't be easy."

She takes a peanut from the bowl and rolls it in her fingers, considering her next move. She's already tried to bribe him with more money and a job offer. She could break down and beg, but the bar's too public for that. She thinks back to the early days of their relationship, their respect for each other's directness. She needs to get back to that place, be herself, no bullshit. "Please come with me to New York tomorrow," she requests, "as a friend more than anything else. If I have to, I'll go alone, but I want your company. The truth is I'm really lonely right now. I know it's just an intuition, but I think Rebecca went looking for my friend. I need to be closer to where she's been, where she may be now."

"You're clutching at straws," he responds, but in a comforting way.

"What else is there to hold on to? And I know how her mind works. It's worth a try."

"New York is a city of over eight million people, Mimi. You're not going to just run into her."

"Please, Steve, I'm desperate. Just this time—as a friend, and then I promise I won't bother you anymore." He takes some time to consider, finally asking if the senior management job is still on offer. "It's yours if you want it," she says.

"Okay, meet me in front of Costco at nine a.m. sharp."

The next morning he picks her up as planned. After they get on 91 South, he keeps checking his rearview mirror. "Don't look, but there's a blue Toyota tailing us," he warns as they enter Hartford. "Hold on—I'm going to lose him." Before she can say anything, he dodges dangerously across two lanes of traffic and turns right on an exit ramp. He checks the mirror again. "Close call." He tells her to fire up the GPS—he's laid out an alternative route to bypass the highway.

Ordering them to turn here, turn there, the harsh digital female voice grates on her nerves as they wind slowly through suburban Connecticut, adding several hours to the trip. It's past two o'clock when Steve finally pulls into a parking garage on Manhattan's Upper West Side. Emerging onto the sidewalk, Mimi suddenly feels deflated. Steve was right last night. How can she ever expect to find Rebecca here? In the distance a wailing siren punctuates her thoughts. Taking her arm, Steve asks if she's feeling all right. "You look pale."

"Just a little carsick," she replies.

"Long trip," he says, "but at least we lost whoever was tailing us. Now do you believe me about the surveillance?"

A blast of wind whips through the tunnel-like street, throwing her momentarily off balance. She clings to Steve for the rest of the way. Her heart skips a beat when they turn onto Seventy-Second Street, and she views Central Park ahead. A girl walking a few feet in front of them has long hair like Rebecca's, but she's shorter, hips too wide.

In the Dakota's entryway, Steve flashes his PI license at the guard, who lets them pass. Inside the lobby Mimi rummages in her purse for the envelope of photos she brought along. She spreads them in front of the deskman, explaining in a faltering voice that her daughter has run away to the city. "I used to have friends who lived in this building," she says, "Eliza and Ben Latimer—they have a daughter named Simone. My daughter might have come here looking for them. I just wondered. . . ."

He studies the photos and looks up at her, then at Steve. "You the father?" he asks gruffly.

"I'm a widow," Mimi answers. "He's a private investigator. We drove down today from Massachusetts."

"Just asking because so many kids get kidnapped by one of their own parents these days. A divorce goes sour. . . ."

"Her daughter ran away with a teenage boy," Steve interjects impatiently.

"Well, that happens too, doesn't it? Mind if I see your license?" After Steve shows it, the deskman discloses that a girl did come in yesterday looking for the Latimers. "In distress, I'd say. She had short black hair though, not like in these pictures."

"She cut and dyed it," Mimi says.

He studies the photos again. "Yeah, same face. She was upset when I told her the family moved to Philadelphia. I called a cab for her." When Steve requests the taxi company name, the deskman writes it down and says to ask for Rudy, the dispatcher he spoke to. He wishes them luck, adding that he had a niece who ran away once.

"Did they find her?" Mimi asks hopefully.

"Yeah, but you don't want to know the story. The sooner you get your daughter back, the better. It's a mean town for runaways, you know. Lots of pimps plying the streets and stations."

From a café a couple of blocks away, Steve has her make the call to Rudy. "He might think I'm a cop," he says, "clam up." At first Rudy's suspicious, but finally gives into her pleas. He checks his records and tells her the driver is Habib Khan. She arranges for Habib to pick them up at three thirty.

Habib proves eager to help. He's a father himself, he tells them; his first daughter just got married. He drives to where he dropped off Rebecca on the corner of Broadway and 169th Street. The light was red, he explains, so he watched her walk west on 169th. He apologizes that he doesn't know more.

Mimi has a photo of Ricky too, and Steve and she walk up and down the street, stopping in stores to ask people if they've seen either of the kids. Finally, a grocery cashier recognizes Ricky and escorts them out to the sidewalk, where he points to a building on the other side of the street. "I saw him go in there. Talk to Fred—he rents rooms."

Rebecca's close now. So close. That her intuition is correct gives Mimi a burst of energy. In a break in the traffic she sprints across the street. When she rings the doorbell of the boarding house, no one comes, so she knocks hard several times and then rings again, keeping her finger on the button. The man who opens the door has his shirt half-buttoned and belt buckle undone. His forehead shines with sweat. "What do you want?" he snarls.

"I'm looking for Fred."

"Yeah, I'm Fred, so what?"

She pushes the photos at him. "I'm looking for these two. She's my daughter."

He shakes his head slowly. "Sorry, but you're too late. They left early this morning before I was up. Paid in advance, so I don't care. A couple of hours later two assholes show up looking for them and push their way in here. Turn all the furniture upside down in their room and don't put it back. Demand to see the cash the boy gave me, but I already spent it." When Steve asks who they were, Fred snaps, "How the fuck would I know? Dealers, undercover cops, I don't ask questions."

"What did they look like?" Steve persists.

"A little younger than you, maybe. I don't look too close—the only way to survive in this business."

"Any idea where the kids went?"

Fred shakes his head again. "If it makes you feel any better, the boy wasn't pimping her. I don't allow that kind of thing to go on in here."

"Fred!" a woman's voice calls from upstairs.

"Coming," he shouts, then shuts the door.

REBECCA WAITS SEPARATELY FROM Ricky outside the East Hampton rail station. All the way from the city to the tip of Long Island, she was afraid someone would recognize them on the train. Ricky sat in one car, she in another. She buried herself in a book, looking up only when the conductor asked for her ticket.

With Justin at the wheel, a gray Audi sedan pulls up to the curb, and she climbs quickly into the back seat and bows her head again. A moment later Ricky walks out of the station to join them. All she knows is that Justin flew from Lima to JFK last night and is staying in a vacation home owned by parents of one of his hockey teammates. The car comes with the house. The understanding is that Justin got ill in Peru and needs a few days to recover before he heads home to Massachusetts. He's stayed in the house before, and the parents, who are hockey fanatics, trust him.

On the ride the brothers hardly speak to each other, not wanting her to overhear anything, she suspects. After a couple of miles, the car turns down a narrow lane that dead-ends at a wooded driveway. The trees along the side are smaller and scrubbier than the ones at home, but she finds their presence comforting. The house is modern, weird looking, a concrete box with big windows. Justin parks inside the garage, then takes them inside and down some stairs to the basement. They pass through an entertainment room with a pool table and big-screen TV into a guest room with an attached bath. "You both need to stay in the basement," he states more to Ricky than to her. "There are hardly any curtains on the windows upstairs and you never know when the landscapers are going to show up. The cleaners aren't coming until next week, so we're okay on that. I'll bring your meals down here—I stocked the refrigerator."

Disapprovingly, his eyes fasten on her. "I know you ran out on Ricky in Washington Heights. Don't even think about it here. It's not just your mom and the cops who are searching for you, you know. Until I fix things, you can't go anywhere. You could get us all killed." He pauses for effect. "Got that, Rebecca?" Then his voice softens a bit. "Ricky and I need to talk, so why don't you take a shower, rest for a while."

In the guest room she lies down on the bed, relieved at first to be somewhere so clean and comfortable. But as she looks around, she notices the pastel shell-themed wallpaper, the ceramic sculpture of a breaching whale, a bowl of sea glass on the dresser. They seem to mock her memories of lying next to Susana and nodding out as her eyes followed the fish spinning on the mobile.

How can she ever go home and face Susana's parents and Rosie? If she were brave, she'd sneak out in the middle of the night and find her way to the beach, since it must be close by. She's seen pictures of the Hamptons in movies—white sand, crashing surf. She'd swim into the waves as far as she could go and never turn back. Instead she's a coward. She wants to take a shower. She wants to wash her clothes. She wants Justin to fix things.

30

LAURA'S TIMING IS OFF. Only by a few hours, but that's enough. She went to sleep with that thought and now wakes with it too. Yesterday between the time she reached Jack and he returned with her to Gary's studio, the kiln floor had been scraped clean. Someone must have been watching her in the building, or a camera could be hidden somewhere. If they know she has the bone fragment and it belongs to Gary, she's in real danger.

That's why Jack insisted she stay the night. He hid the bone in his basement in a space above a ceiling tile. They agreed they wouldn't tell anyone else about it for now, not even Nancy. If Gary's out of the picture as Tommy says, the question of how he was taken out can wait until they find the kids.

After breakfast she drives home to pack for her trip to Texas tomorrow. Last night she worried her house might be ransacked, but as far she can make out, nothing has been touched. At nine thirty she gets a call from Mimi, who wants to see her but somewhere outside of town, so they agree on the Petersham café. Laura gets there first and takes a table on the back deck, where they met in the spring. It seems so long ago, their concerns so petty in comparison to what's happening now. Like then, there's no one else outside. The weather's clammy, rain in the forecast.

Mimi arrives looking like she just rolled out of bed. It's disconcerting to see her without makeup and with her hair parted lopsided, scarcely brushed. When Laura offers to get her coffee and a pastry, there's desperation in the way she says *please*. She attacks her croissant like someone who hasn't eaten in days. That and the caffeine seem to revive her.

It spills out of her nonstop—her hunch about Rebecca going to the Dakota, how close Steve and she came to finding her. "They just left the boarding house yesterday morning, can you believe it? The manager said two men came looking for them afterward, so it's good they weren't there, but if we'd found them the night before, they'd be safe. Rebecca would be home now." She casts an expectant glance at Laura. "Rebecca's coming home soon," she announces like it's an indelible fact. "I know you probably think I'm nuts and it's just wishful thinking, but I was right to go to the Dakota. I'm starting to get these strong intuitions. There's nothing much else to go on, so why not go with them? What's there to lose?" She takes Laura's hands in hers and squeezes them. "Really, they're coming home soon. We need to be prepared. Tell Angie, please."

As soon as she leaves the café, Laura texts Angie, but there's no response. On the drive back she wonders whether Mimi is going nuts, but who's she to judge? She's running on nervous energy and instinct too. *Running*, that's the word. Running every which way, no clear direction. She needs to gather her thoughts, but where to do that? Jack ordered her to stay out of the office and minimize time at her house. She's not ready to return to his place and face Nancy's scrutiny.

Reaching the outskirts of Stanton, she decides to keep driving east along River Road, passing fields sowed with strawberries, corn, and vegetables, spring's translucent greens turning into the darker, more solid shades of summer. Mike died in late June and it still strikes her as a bitter irony that the

Grim Reaper chose to take him away then, just as the season of abundance began.

She parks in a public access space by a wide spot in the river. A few people are fishing downstream, but otherwise no one's there. She sits on the bank, takes off her shoes, and dangles her feet in the water, giving herself over to more memories of Mike's death. Not just the grief, but the sense of inadequacy that continued to haunt all she did. Caring for a young boy and a dying husband at the same time stretched her too thin.

She inspects the back of her hands, where signs of aging—sunspots, freckles, prominent veins—are already making an appearance. She was all of twenty-six that summer. What if she were to look at that period differently, not as a record of her failings but rather as a heroic effort for someone so young? Her worst error wasn't inadequacy but failing to ask for enough help.

People did help her. Her parents and Mike's came over every day. They brought food, entertained Donnie. But after Mike died, their visits slowly declined, and eventually Mike's parents moved away. Donnie and she were left more and more on their own. That's when she needed help the most but was too proud to ask for it. Or maybe she just didn't know how. Of all the people closest to her, Angie understood her needs the best. Her notion of family didn't depend on having a father around. She helped her fill the long empty spaces by dragging her out to family nights at the bowling alley and Saturday matinees at the movies. She breathed life back into her, into Donnie too.

A kingbird settles on a branch overhead, then darts off to catch an insect, fluttering in midair. Mission accomplished, it returns to the same branch, its white-tipped tail twitching as it watches for another prey. If Nate were here, he would tell her some fact she didn't know about it, create a whole world around that single bird. A better world than the one she must return to now. As if by way of reminder, her cell dings with a text from Angie, who wants to meet during her lunch hour. She'll be waiting in her car in the back corner of the lot, she writes.

It's raining by the time Laura reaches the factory, where she hurries from her car into Angie's. The windows are steamed up, the upholstery damp. Angie closes her lunch box and throws it in back, then tells Laura she's worried about Justin. When she didn't hear from him for a few days, she emailed his professor, and he wrote back this morning that Justin had flown to New York for a family emergency. "I called and texted him, but there was no response. And then an hour ago, he phones me on a factory line. He says don't tell anyone yet, but he's probably coming home late tomorrow night. And then he hangs up. Why would he do that? Something's going on, Laura. Maybe he knows where Ricky is. What do you think?"

Laura describes Mimi's trip to New York. "She has this gut feeling that Rebecca's coming home, but she doesn't have any real evidence."

"Maybe she's right, maybe that's the reason Justin left Peru." Angie checks her watch. "I've got to get back on the floor soon. Call Donnie—maybe he knows something."

SITTING ON THE BED IN ROB'S old room, Donnie can smell Alana's roast chicken cooking in the oven. He's looking forward to it—last night her lasagna was great. He likes her so far. She dresses butch, but that's fine with him. She's a lot more relaxed than her weird brother. Today she took Donnie down to the harbor, showed him their boats, said if the weather's nice, she'll take him out on the Whaler tomorrow before his mom arrives.

He's about to check his cell again, hoping there might finally be a message from Ricky or Justin, when Birdman knocks on the door and asks to come in. "Sure," Donnie replies without enthusiasm.

Birdman comes in, grabs a chair, and sits across from him. "I just heard from your mom," he says. "I'm afraid she's not coming tomorrow."

"Why not?"

"Something's come up. She can use my help, so I'm taking an early morning flight back East." He pauses, puts his hands on his knees. "Look, Donnie, I need to trust that no matter what happens, you'll stay here with Alana. Your mom wants to talk to you about it. Give her a call."

31

THE FOLLOWING DAY, MIMI arrives at Sullivan Lumber shortly after dawn when the rising sun casts a glow on her realm. In her altered mental state, the stacks of bricks and boards, fencing spools, rock piles, and roofing along the driveway seem to announce themselves to her: *See what we can build. See what you have built.* It's strangely heartening.

She hasn't been here since David's death. There are papers to sign, and she decided to come early before the first warehouse shift arrives. That way she won't face any ingratiating hellos or, worse, expressions of false sympathy. No one at Sullivan Lumber liked David.

Once inside, she shuts her office door behind her and cranks the window wide. It's an open secret she smokes, though company rules forbid it. No one dares call her out—one of the privileges of being owner—but she does her best to cover her tracks. Although they taste bitter this morning, it doesn't prevent her from smoking two cigarettes in rapid succession. Afterward, she takes a seat at her desk and signs the papers perfunctorily. She wishes it were a normal day and she had nothing more to do than meet with clients, suppliers, and underlings. But the news about Justin's homecoming has convinced her Rebecca may soon return. She needs to hurry home just in case her daughter walks suddenly through the door.

She's imagining their first all-is-forgiven embrace as she leaves the building and approaches her car. She pulls on the door handle—it's locked, though she could swear she left it open. Her mind playing tricks no doubt. Fumbling in her purse for the keys, she hears someone behind her. "Hi, Mimi, you're back," an unfamiliar voice greets her. She swivels around to face the stranger. He's tall with a shaved head and wearing tinted glasses. No smile. He takes a few steps, then pushes her hard against the car, pressing a gun barrel to her chest. "Open it up and get in," he orders.

He climbs in back behind her and wraps an arm around her neck. "I know you were in New York," he says. "Where's Rebecca?"

"I don't know. I didn't find her."

As he pulls harder on her neck, she gasps for air and he lets up a little. "Where do you think she is?"

"I wish I knew." Harder again. She almost blacks out before he relaxes his grip again.

"Look, we want Ricky, not her. You tell me where they are, and we'll make sure she doesn't get hurt."

"I want to know too. . . ." This time it feels like he's going to crush her windpipe. But then he stops, starts, stops, and starts again as if it's a game. Her body wants to thrash and struggle, but she forces it to go limp, needing to conserve each little bit of oxygen he allows her. Stop, start, stop, start. Maybe he's the one who tortured David.

"Why did you go to New York, Mimi?"

"Because I found out she took a bus there. I thought if she wanted to come home, she might look up one of my friends who lives there."

"Did she?"

He's letting her breathe normally now. "She tried, but my friend has moved away."

"So she wants to come home?"

"I think so. Really, that's all I know."

Maybe he believes her or maybe he's worried about workers showing up, but she senses the game's coming to an end. A few seconds later she feels a sharp prick in her neck. "Sweet dreams," he says.

She wakes fifteen minutes later, though it feels like hours, when a cop she recognizes knocks on the window. Slowly his name comes to her—Tommy something. He introduced himself to her a couple of days ago when he started keeping an eye on the house. He's in plain clothes now. He wants to call 911 or take her to the hospital, but she refuses. "I'm okay," she insists. "Please call Laura Everett—I want to see her."

Tommy won't let her drive, so he takes her to where Laura's staying. Mimi knows Jack—everyone in town does—but she's never been inside the house. Laura and he insist she lie down on the living room couch. She feels drowsy from the drugging and her neck is painful and bruised, but she's grateful it's not worse. As they gather around her, Tommy explains how he passed by her house early this morning and noticed the garage door wasn't completely shut. He checked it out and, seeing her car was gone, drove to Sullivan Lumber. She was just coming to when he found her slumped over the steering wheel. He's off duty today and doesn't seem keen to file a police report right away. Neither does Jack.

Though she dozes, she intermittently wakes enough to catch snippets of their conversation. Tommy is speaking now. Something about not being able to go back to the station, warned to keep his mouth shut and take vacation time. Tell Jack that too, Chief said. Probably Carl who attacked Mimi. He and Andy after the cash too. Blades staying out of the whole thing. Planning to pick up the pieces when the Jags go down. Fucking dangerous mess.

She struggles to hold on to the names so she can form the right questions later. So much has been kept from her, but she's too sleepy now to confront them.

ALL REBECCA KNOWS IS they're leaving tonight after dark. Ricky won't say where they're going. She's spent all morning alone cooped up in the bedroom while he and Justin huddle in the game room. Periodically, Justin goes upstairs to make calls, and Ricky comes in to check on her. Last night in his sleep he twitched and moaned like he was having nightmares. He reached for her and they woke up snuggled tightly together but then separated quickly. Awake, they hardly touch.

Ricky should tell her what's going on. Shouldn't she have a voice in their decisions? Justin treats her like she's a stupid little girl, a ho, a junkie. Fuck him.

She pounds on the door lightly at first, then harder and harder until Ricky comes running. "Calm down, Rebecca!" he says as he opens the door. "You're not locked in, you know."

She can hear Justin's footsteps on the stairs. "Quiet, both of you," he warns as he approaches. "Do you want the lawn guy to hear you?" Glaring at him, she threatens to scream if he won't tell her where they're going. "Okay, okay," he responds swiftly. "I get it, Rebecca. We're driving to Stanton tonight. Tomorrow Ricky's going to give back the money, and then you can go home to your mom."

32

EARLY THE NEXT MORNING, Laura wakes next to Nate, wishing they were at her house or his instead of Jack's. She rolls away from him, letting him sleep a little while longer. His arrival yesterday coincided with the aftermath of Mimi's attack. On the way back from the airport, he insisted on swinging by his place to pick up a hunting rifle.

She sits up and fetches her cell on the bedside table, wondering if Justin came home last night. There's a message from Angie that arrived at one thirty in the morning, a simple yes in the shorthand they agreed on. She wishes she hadn't slept through it. She texts Angie back and a few minutes later receives a response: Please come over.

She gets up quietly and leaves before anyone else is up. Still in her pajamas, Angie is waiting by the door. In the kitchen they sit across from each other at the table for the first time since early May when they quarreled about the boys. Laura wishes she could acknowledge how their friendship has survived to come full circle, but that thought will have to wait. Instead she listens to Angie's account of how Justin arrived by car late last night. "Whose car?" she asks.

"A rental one, I guess," Angie replies. "I was so happy to see him I didn't ask. He gave me a big hug, said he loved me, and we'd talk first thing tomorrow. When I got up this morning, I checked on him before coming downstairs. His bed was empty, and the car was gone. I don't even know what make it was." She pulls a small felt pouch from her pocket, emptying the contents into the palm of her hand. "He left these turquoise earrings on the table with a note that he'd be back later, not to worry, and hoped I liked the gift from Peru. He signed it with a big heart. I'm worried, Laura—something's happening. He took a bunch of breakfast food from the kitchen, which makes me think that maybe Ricky and Rebecca are hiding out somewhere around here. I'm worried they have some stupid plan, like returning the money. It's the kind of thing Justin would think of—he always wants to fix things, make everything right."

"But why do the exchange in Stanton?" Laura pauses to consider her own question. Why would the Jags want to come here, if that's who's getting the money? Why not on their own turf in Springfield? It doesn't make sense unless . . . and then a reason comes to mind. If the Feds are organizing a bust, then they'll have an informer in the Jags too, maybe someone high up who can persuade the gang to do the exchange here. All along, Stanton has been Snakehead's preferred local stage: they'll play the bust as big news from small-town America. "Where would the handover be?" she asks Angie. "Where near here would Ricky and Rebecca hide out?"

"Call Donnie," she urges. "Maybe he knows."

HE KNOWS NOTHING, DONNIE tells his mom, just like he told her two nights ago. It's the truth—he hasn't received any messages from either Justin or Ricky. Their silence hurts. They should at least find some way to signal they're alive. It's like he doesn't matter to them anymore. He feels left out, useless.

Out on the Whaler, he tries to hide his feelings, but Alana senses something and asks what's wrong. She suggests he might be seasick.

"Don't think so."

"Dehydrated then? It's wicked hot today. Get a couple of bottles of water from the cooler, will you? I could use one too."

She calms the engine as they pass through the bay between the wildlife refuge on one side and the barrier island on the other, pointing out likely spots to see whooping cranes in the winter. "I can't wait to show them to you," she says. She chatters on, but he doesn't mind. Like the slow *put-put* of the engine, her voice is soothing. "I'll take you to South Padre Island too—it's got the best surf in Texas."

It strikes him that he's already part of her future: *We'll go here, we'll go there.*

On the way back, closer to Rockport, she kills the engine and drops anchor. "I'm going to take a dip," she says. "Want to join me?"

"No thanks."

"It'll cool you off."

"No thanks," he repeats. He's too scared to swim but is ashamed to admit it to her. After she dives in, he takes his cell from the dry bag and checks again for messages. Nothing. By force of habit, he takes a selfie, Donnie in the Gulf of Mexico.

After Alana climbs back on board, she wraps herself with a towel, then sits and stretches her legs. Pointing to the cell, she asks if there's any news of his friends. "That's what you're worried about, isn't it, Donnie?"

He hangs his head. "Yeah."

"You'd be crazy if you weren't worried. You got attacked by a gang, right? That would scare the shit out of me. But it sounds like it's not just the gang who's after your friends."

Curious, he asks what she knows.

"My brother didn't give me many details—I don't think he knows them anyway—but he said something about bigger dealers, your friend Rebecca's dad getting murdered. Frankly, I'm worried about Nate and your mom too. It's hard for me to be here, doing nothing. Must be hard for you too. Hard to be out of contact with your friends. Tell me about them, Donnie. How did you first meet Ricky?"

She's fishing for information, put up to it by his mom, he suspects, but he feels an urge to talk—since leaving Stanton, he's been so shut down. He starts from the beginning, when Ricky and he were both outcasts in kindergarten and made funny faces at each other across the classroom. All through elementary school, other kids teased them a lot, but Ricky's older brother, Justin, provided protection. Mess with them on the playground and there were consequences. When Donnie's dad died, they got even tighter. So did their moms.

When they started getting in trouble, it was little stuff at first like running off from the Boy Scout troop, finding their secret place. Later it was the usual shit—cigarettes, booze, dope, nothing special, nothing that other kids weren't doing too. But then Rebecca came into the picture and screwed everything up. She's the reason Ricky ran away.

"Really?" Alana asks. "Sounds like he had a lot of his own reasons to split town too." She pauses, adjusting the towel around her shoulders. "Did you ever consider Ricky might have run away to protect you?"

"What do you mean?"

"Well, you mentioned Justin protected you growing up, so I just wondered if Ricky's trying to do the same thing. They're like your brothers, right? That's probably why they haven't been in touch—they don't want to draw you in. You're safe here and they know that. It's because they care about you, Donnie, they care a lot."

Donnie thinks back to their last meeting at the secret place, when Ricky finally came clean about what was going down. Already his plan was to escape with Rebecca. The role he gave Donnie was minor, playing the good boy. Driving Rebecca to the amusement park was the only serious favor Ricky asked of him, along with taking his car, though he didn't ask about that. Alana could be right that they're trying to protect him. But it doesn't make him feel any better since it means there's nothing he can do to help.

"Any idea where they could be?" his mom pleaded this morning. His mind came up blank.

The sea's calm enough that he could skip a stone. He wishes he were with Ricky now, skipping stones on the Diamond River, just the two of them, like the old times at their secret place. Suddenly, it comes to him, and he tells Alana he needs to call his mom.

33

THE TWO PIECES OF INFORMATION arrive about the same time: Donnie's tip about the secret place and a leak from the source in the state police that Snakehead is in high gear. An armored patrol boat has been trucked to an unspecified landing on the Diamond River. It's enough to go on. No time for doubts.

Nate, Jack, and Tommy all say no when Laura asks to accompany them. *No place for a woman*, she hears in their voices. "Stay with Nancy," Jack orders. They take his SUV, their guns hidden under fishing gear.

She can't stay here. Angie and Mimi deserve to know what's going on—their kids' lives are on the line. Because it's too risky to talk over the phone, she arranges to pick them up and sneaks out of the house while Nancy is upstairs. In the car she tells them what's happening, and both are adamant about going with her to Donnie and Ricky's secret place on the river.

"It's not so secret," Jack had told her right after Donnie called. "The local authorities have been trying to tear down the place for the last five years, but there's a dispute over who owns the land. Fish and Wildlife want to acquire it to expand the refuge." On the map he pointed to a spot a few miles downriver from his shack. He made the calculation that the safest approach would be to drive on the opposite side of the river for ten miles, crossing over on Miller Bridge, then backtrack from the west since others—whoever they might be—would probably take the more direct route through Stanton from the east.

Though it's frustrating to take such a long way around, she follows these directions, driving too fast and passing on double yellow lines until Angie warns her to slow down. After the bridge, they turn down the dirt access road along the river. The deep ruts are hard to navigate, so she crawls along. This stretch of the river is wilder and less populated than upstream, large parts of it already incorporated in the refuge.

There's no sign of other vehicles until they spy Jack's car in a brushy thicket—the men went by foot from here. She parks nearby, and the three of them get out, standing still for a moment to listen to the sounds around them. No human noises, only birdsong and insect buzz. Laura worries it's the wrong location and the rendezvous is elsewhere. Donnie was clear he was just making a guess.

They walk down the same trail the men must have taken toward the riverbank. Nearer the shack, they finally hear voices—Angie recognizes Justin's. To make sure it's safe, Laura wants to hold back and take cover behind a woodpile, but Angie refuses, rushing forward over an open patch of grass. "Justin! Ricky!" she calls out. "It's me, your mom, I'm here." Crouched down, Laura and Mimi watch through a gap between two logs.

Ricky emerges from the shack onto the rickety dock, yelling for his mother to run away, but she continues toward him. Then two figures, their faces obscured by balaclavas, spring from the woods. One grabs Angie from behind and puts a gun to her back while the other trains his automatic rifle on the dock. "Want your mama alive, little Ricky?" the man holding Angie threatens. "Hand over the fucking money then. Drop it right here, at her feet. Do something funny and we shoot her, understand?" Justin comes out of the shack holding a duffel he gives to Ricky, who climbs down the steps onto the grass.

"Kneel down," the other man commands after Ricky drops the bag. "Beg for mercy."

"I'm sorry, really, really sorry," Ricky pleads.

"Not fucking good enough." When the man kicks him in the side, Ricky screams out in pain. "Say your prayers, little Ricky. You steal from the Jags, you die. Tell your mama bye-bye." He presses the rifle barrel against Ricky's head.

From the cabin window two shots ring out simultaneously, the first hitting Ricky's captor, the other Angie's, his body acting as a shield as she falls beneath him. Ricky lies on the ground, dead or alive, Laura can't tell. Justin leaps off the dock and sprints toward them. The shooting from the cabin stops.

Maybe it's over, Laura thinks, rising slightly to get a better view. Mimi does too. But then a shot comes from the other side of the woods. A bullet hits Justin in the leg and he lurches forward, blood spurting from the wound. Suddenly, two more men appear on the lawn, one spraying bullets toward the shack window as the other grabs the duffel bag. "He's the one who attacked me," Mimi whispers.

Laura hears the patrol boat approaching. On deck she can make out a SWAT team in camouflage and body armor, pointing their weapons toward shore. Tommy bursts out of the shack and runs to the end of the dock, shouting for them to hold fire. "The mother and her boys are lying on the ground!"

A barrage of bullets mows down the man with the duffel bag first, his accomplice next. Then the target shifts. A sniper from the SWAT team lifts his rifle and shoots Tommy in the head and chest. When Nate runs to help, he's hit too. From inside the shack Rebecca screams.

EPILOGUE

IT'S TIME TO BREAK THE SILENCE.

Laura has had to wait, be patient, devote herself to Nate's recuperation. Shattered left shoulder and hip, punctured lung, nerve pain that pushed him to his limits. As soon as he was stabilized, she flew with him to Texas, where Alana, Donnie, and she could all take turns caring for him. He's better now, able to walk a little farther each day along the waterfront. Donnie has surprised her with his physical strength and the doggedness with which he pushes Nate to get up and go despite the pain.

Justin is recovering too, graduated from a walker to a cane, and back at college. The prognosis is he'll walk almost normally again, with a slight limp. No more hockey though. Angie put a brave face on it yesterday when Laura stopped by the house. "He's more interested in premed anyway," she said. "And he's planning to spend January in Peru to finish up his research." She put a brave face on Ricky's departure too. The Feds cut a deal with him—no prosecution if he kept his mouth shut and enlisted in the army. "Maybe the structure will be good for him," she remarked hopefully. "He's in basic training at Fort Moore in Georgia now." Laura didn't express her concern that he'd be sent to a war zone where it could be arranged for him to die from so-called friendly fire.

That's what the Feds claim about Tommy's death: friendly fire. Mimi and she both made sworn statements that they saw a SWAT team sniper purposefully take aim, but they were ignored. The cover-up was swift and efficient, though one thing the Snakehead team didn't get to do was boast about their grand slam bust. A local cop in a three-month coma generated too much public sympathy, threw a wrench in the works. For a few weeks Stanton was famous as a background battlefield in the war on drugs, but not a single journalist really pursued the story. The town was left alone to nurse its wounds.

She thinks about that as she stands in the cemetery for Tommy's burial. He was shot at the end of June, now it's early October. How much the family must have suffered to have him in a coma so long. According to Jack, they refused the pomp and circumstance of a police burial, knowing enough about the circumstances of Tommy's death to distrust the motives of his superiors. No bagpipers today, no winding lines of cop cars holding up traffic, no sugarcoated hypocrisy.

She watches as his mother and sister bend down to place flowers on the grave. Except for the difference in age, they look like twins with their wide faces, narrow noses, and short brown hair. Their synchrony has a noble air. The priest asks them all to bow their heads. *May his soul and the soul of all the faithful departed, through the mercy of God, rest in peace.*

Instead of looking down, Laura gazes at the red maples nearby, which are in their full autumn glory, the yellow ones not far behind. It's a crisp fall day, the kind of weather she misses in humid Rockport. She's grateful to be in the middle of a line of friends, Angie and Justin on one side—he was brave to come, she thinks—Jack and Nancy on the other. Mimi is a few rows behind, without Rebecca.

The tears she finally sheds aren't only for Tommy but for her hometown too. Tommy tried to protect it, but he's not the only one. All the people standing here or buried here hopefully provide gravity enough to withstand the powerful centrifugal forces threatening to rip Stanton apart, sending its little bits and pieces spinning off into an alien and hostile universe. Angie puts her arm around her. "It's all right, Laura. It's all right."

Leaving the cemetery, she tries to pull herself together. She's promised to help at the reception Jack and Nancy are hosting—Tommy's parents' house is too small. When she reaches the parking lot, she notices a man standing by her car with his back to her, his hands in his pockets. As he turns toward her, she recognizes Bill from the birding group. "Hi, Laura," he greets her. "Can I speak to you a moment?"

"Sure, Bill," she replies. "How's the family?"

"Good, good," he responds hurriedly. "We miss the group though. How's Nate doing?"

"Much better. We're moving back soon. Not sure when he'll be well enough to start up the group, but he's planning to."

"I want to give you and Nate something."

"How nice," she says, anticipating a gift of some sort. Instead he takes his hand from his pocket, his fingers in a fist, and reaches to shake her hand, passing her something in a small plastic bag. By the worried look on his face, she can tell she should hide it in her own pocket. "What is it?" she asks.

"A flash drive. Video shot from my scope."

"Of birds?"

He shakes his head. "I was out birding that day when I heard shots on the other side of the river. I scrambled down near shore, hid behind some bushes, and set up my scope to film. It's all there, Laura—Tommy running out on the dock, telling them to stop, and then the guy on the boat getting the order to shoot him, and then he shoots Nate too. I held on to it all this time because I was afraid of repercussions—that something could happen to me or Stacy or Jeff. And I told myself that if Tommy and Nate both recovered, then it didn't really matter anyway. When Tommy died last week, I knew I had to do something. I went to high school with him, you know; we played sports together. See what you think, Laura. I'm prepared to testify if I have to."

"Thank you, Bill. You don't know how much this could help."

"Won't bring Tommy back though."

"No," she says, feeling the full weight of his words less as a burden than a call to action.

MIMI WAITS FOR LAURA on the property overlooking Lake Amity that she once owned with Gary. Sullivan Hills Conservation Area is now its official designation. At the highest point are a sign to that effect and a wooden bench where visitors can rest and take in the view. Keith Addison and the conservation commission promise to provide more amenities next year.

It's a warm Indian summer day, a respite from the relentless march toward winter. Ordinarily Mimi mourns the change of season, but this fall the familiar signposts—purple aster along the roadside, birds migrating south, fewer hours of daylight—provide a certain relief. Time is moving on normally, not like it did last spring when she careened from one crisis to the next.

She lights a cigarette but stubs it out when she sees the car approaching on the logging road. She has mixed feelings about Laura returning to Stanton. The mere sight of Donnie could trigger her daughter's PTSD. On the other hand, she owes Laura for all she did. It could have played out much worse, she understands that now.

She rises from the bench to greet Laura as she gets out of the car. They hug awkwardly, but it's better than the brief handshake at Tommy's burial two days ago. The firefight forced them together, but that kind of closeness, Mimi realizes, doesn't translate so easily into everyday life.

Laura remarks on the beauty of the spot and how grateful she is that it wasn't developed. Perhaps she wants to be shown around, Mimi thinks, but there's no time to waste. "Shall we sit on the bench?" she suggests. "There's a lot to talk about." Laura nods and follows. After they take a seat, Mimi asks how Donnie's doing and if he's coming back to the high school.

"He could," Laura replies. "He'd just need to make up a month's work, but he's doing really well in Rockport. He's already made friends and he's studying hard, at least so far. He wants to establish state residency and go to the University of Texas. Nate's sister says he can stay with her after we move back. The truth is she has a better relationship with him than I do."

"Because you're his mom."

"Yeah, there's that, but I also think I remind him too much of what happened, and he can't face it yet. I don't blame him. And the fact is he doesn't want to live in Stanton anymore."

Music to Mimi's ears, but she tries not to show it. "What will you do?"

"I decided last night to let him stay in Rockport. Nate agrees. He's moving back with me, but we'll fly down to Texas periodically to see Donnie. Nate needs to help his sister with their business too. I keep telling myself that sometimes a little distance is the best thing." When Laura pauses, Mimi awaits the inevitable question. "And how's Rebecca doing?"

She has an answer ready, the same answer she gives other people who ask: *Thank you, she's doing better, off drugs, getting help, finishing up her high school degree at community college.* She repeats those words, but Laura's a better listener than most, and the expression on her face—not sympathy exactly, rather a deeper if unspoken understanding—propels Mimi to speak more candidly. "Rebecca's being treated for multiple traumas," she reveals, hearing the choked-up emotion in her own voice. "Drug use was just the tip of the iceberg. Her therapist thinks she has an underlying mental disorder, and we're waiting for a diagnosis. She's experienced so many deaths too—David's, Susana Porter's, what happened at the river. In the shack your uncle held her down, you know, so she couldn't move. He was trying to protect her, but it freaked her out. Her therapist told me it's going to take a long time for her to get over the fear, probably even longer to get over her guilt. I need to be patient. That's not my virtue, but I'm trying.

"Last week there were two breakthroughs—we drove over to Susana Porter's parents' house so Rebecca could apologize for fleeing after she called 911. They're kind people—they accepted her apology and told her it wasn't her fault. All they want for her is to recover fully. She didn't see Susana's daughter—it would have been too much—but she brought her a present, a children's book about the seashore. And then a few days later we went to see the Addisons so she could apologize about breaking into their house and what happened to their cat. Even Keith was gracious—I didn't think he was capable of that." She smiles slyly. "He's not quite so sanctimonious anymore."

She hesitates, unsure of how much more she should confide about Rebecca, but Laura still looks receptive, and it's been lonely dealing with this on her own. "I actually have the opposite problem from you," she continues. "In your case putting distance between yourself and Donnie makes sense, but my charge is to get closer to Rebecca. It helps that she stays at home most of the time. She's doing two of her courses online, and I make sure I'm home for dinner every night. We watch TV together after that. It works for now, but I worry what will happen when she finally goes back into the world."

"At least she has this time to heal," Laura says. "Donnie too. But not Ricky. I worry the most about him."

The mention of Ricky jars Mimi. She'll never forgive him; the best she can do is push him out of her mind. "He has the most to atone for," she remarks coolly.

"What do you mean by that?"

"For starters, he got involved with dealing drugs, stole

that money, took Rebecca away." Her voice rises. "Oh yes, and got his brother shot. He could have got us all killed."

"Your cousin pressured Ricky into working for him," Laura reminds her.

"He could have resisted."

"Maybe at the beginning, but then he stayed in because he wanted to protect Rebecca. Keep her from using. Donnie finally told me the whole story. Something worse could have happened to her if they hadn't run away."

Mimi considers whether to challenge her but decides against it. "We can discuss that another time," she says. "For now, I'm relieved Ricky's in the army and in basic training. He can't call and text her like he used to. I know it's uncharitable of me, but I hope he gets sent far, far away. That kind of love she can do without."

"So can he."

She lets that comment drop too, since there are other things besides Ricky she wants to discuss with Laura. She hates having outstanding obligations, whether they're financial or debts of gratitude. She already settled with Steve by giving him the position at Sullivan Lumber. It's a win-win—he's proved to be a very effective manager. Now it's time to repay Laura. "There's another reason I asked you to come here today," she begins. "Martin Snow told me you're trying to put together a group of investors to buy the *Gazette* from Frank. I'd like to join. I don't have a lot of money right now, but I might soon. It turns out Gary took out a million-dollar life insurance policy in Rebecca's name. If he's dead, and they find his body, I don't have to worry about paying for her college, or graduate school for that matter."

"Why would Gary take out such a large policy for Rebecca?"

Mimi delivers a prepared answer: "You'll be surprised to learn Gary had a soft side. He considered Rebecca the daughter he never had."

Laura pauses. "I think he's dead."

"Think or know?" Mimi presses.

"I don't know for sure, but I have a very good lead and should have more information soon." In a more professional tone, Laura alerts her that investing in the paper also means supporting a full investigation of the Snakehead operation. "I'm going to launch the paper with the results. We'll also have a biweekly special section on the opioid crisis and what's being done locally about it. Dr. Goldin has agreed to fund that. All this could land us in political and legal hot water—before you invest, you should know the risk."

"I'll make a deal with you, Laura. Prove Gary's dead, and I'll gladly take the risk. I'll even hire you a top lawyer."

DONNIE'S CELL RINGS WITH A call from Justin. He shuts his math textbook—it's late and the numbers and signs are all starting to blur together anyway. "What's up?" he asks.

"Just spoke with Ricky. They finally allowed him to make a call. I'm worried about him, Donnie. His drill sergeant is a pig who has it out for him. He started crying on the phone. It's brutal, and he hasn't made any friends. He told me he'd rather be in prison, and I tried to convince him no, that's even worse. He beats himself up about my leg, and now about Tommy dying." He pauses. "I went to Tommy's funeral a couple of days ago, saw your mom. She said you want to stay in Texas. Is it true?"

"Yeah, I like it here. Guys were hard on me at first, teased me for being a Yank and stuff, but then a couple of girls told them to shut up, and it's been cool ever since."

"Better than Stanton?"

"A lot better because there's no chance of running into Rebecca. I never want to see her again."

"I know what you mean. Look, Donnie, I'm calling for two reasons. Ricky wants you to know how much he appreciates your letters and please keep sending them. They're a lifeline. And then I have a favor to ask. I don't know what you've written to him, but if you could tell him he needs to forgive himself for what happened, it might help. In a lot of ways, I'm the one to blame for what went down at the end, not him. I was crazy to think he could hand that money back and everything would be fine. Please don't write that—he'll want to defend me—but you're good with words. Maybe you can put it in a way that makes him understand he was being used all along. Other people were pulling the strings. His mistake was to get tangled up with them in the first place."

"Okay, I'll try," Donnie says, not telling Justin that almost every letter he writes to Ricky ends with the same words: *Forgive yourself, bro, it wasn't your fault.*

REBECCA SITS ON A BENCH IN the park throwing stale bread to Susana's ducks. The bag is almost empty when a guy asks if he can join her. She's seen him around before, panhandling outside the diner or bowling alley. He smells bad, but she doesn't refuse. "Ten bucks," he offers. "Safe stuff. I've used it myself." All she has is a twenty, so she buys two.

Notes

Quote by Anne Lamott in Chapter Four from her book *Traveling Mercies: Some Thoughts on Faith* (New York: Anchor Books, 2000).

Quote by Robert Frost in Chapter Eight from "Birches" in Edward Connery Lathem, ed., *The Poetry of Robert Frost: The Collected Poems, Complete and Unabridged* (New York: Henry Holt and Company, 1979), 122.

Quote by Edward Forbush in Chapter Twelve from Edward Howe Forbush and John Bichard May, *A Natural History of American Birds of Eastern and Central North America* (New York: Bramhall House, 1939), 90.

Acknowledgments

THE OPIOID CRISIS IS A PAINFUL TOPIC, and at times I found it hard to confront its stark reality even in a fictional world. I am deeply grateful to all the people who helped and encouraged me to stay the course.

Special thanks to Jerry Lund, who generously shared his experience and wisdom and informed me about the inspiring harm-reduction efforts in northern and western Massachusetts. Rosalind Pollan's keen architectural eye helped me to see New England mill towns in a new light.

Thanks to my nonfiction agents, Rick Balkin and Anthony Arnove, for providing publishing advice, and to all those at She Writes Press who brought this project to fruition. In April 2018, a writing residency at Mesa Refuge in Point Reyes, California, provided valuable time and space to reconceive the book.

Many friends, fellow writers, and family members gave me much appreciated feedback on successive drafts. They include Suzanne Boyce, Anne and Michael De Pompolo, Lynn Duggan, Joyce Duncan, Rosette Gault, the late Mordicai Gerstein, Sam Gladstone, Frank Holmquist, Mary Hoyer, Joann Kobin, the late Zane Kotker, Katherine Pfister, Artemis Roerhig, Felice Swados, and my late aunt, Laura Tracy.

Darcy Hartmann gave me not only insightful comments on the manuscript but an abundance of sisterly love and emotional support. My husband, Jim Boyce, was with me every step of the way. In addition to his fine editing skills, he taught me about the joys of birding, and our kayaking trips on local rivers inspired some key scenes in the book.

Finally, I am grateful to live in a beautiful region where people are working together to find effective and just solutions to the opioid crisis.

—Betsy Hartmann, Amherst, Massachusetts

About the Author

Author, scholar, and activist **BETSY HARTMANN** addresses critical national and global challenges in her books, articles, and public appearances. She is the author of the feminist classic *Reproductive Rights and Wrong: The Global Politics of Population Control* and most recently of *The America Syndrome: Apocalypse, War and Our Call to Greatness*. Eerily prescient, her two political thrillers, *The Truth about Fire* and *Deadly Election*, explore the threat the Far Right poses to American democracy. Betsy did her undergraduate degree at Yale University and her PhD at the London School of Economics and Political Science. She is professor emerita of development studies at Hampshire College, where she taught for twenty-eight years. She lives in Amherst, Massachusetts. For more on Betsy, visit https://betsyhartmann.com.

SELECTED TITLES FROM SHE WRITES PRESS

She Writes Press is an independent publishing company founded to serve women writers everywhere. Visit us at www.shewritespress.com.

Del Rio by Jane Rosenthal. $16.95, 978-1-64742-055-0. District Attorney Callie McCall is on a mission to solve the murder of a migrant teen, but what is she to do when her search for the killer leads her straight to the most powerful family in town—her own?

Five Days in Bogotá by Linda Moore. $17.95, 978-1-64742-612-5. Desperate to save her gallery and her family from bankruptcy, Allison Blake travels to Bogotá to an art fair to meet wealthy collectors. She discovers paintings worth millions were added to her crates in a scheme to launder money. Caught between warring cartels, U.S. mercenaries, and shady characters from her past, she fights to save her gallery and protect her children.

Match by Amy S. Peele. $16.95, 978-1-64742-018-5. How does a San Francisco transplant nurse who never takes drugs die of an opioid overdose in Miami? How does an eight-year-old boy avoid the ravages of dialysis and get a kidney transplant fast, and what does a high-ranking politician have to do with it? Best friends and nurses Sarah Golden and Jackie Larsen are determined to find out.

The Third Way by Aimee Hoben. $16.95, 978-1-64742-095-6. A college student with a fear of public speaking finds herself leading a movement to abolish corporations, pushed to the forefront by a mysterious law student with a past.

A Matter of Chance by Julie Maloney. $16.95, 978-1-63152-369-4. When eight-year-old Vinni Stewart disappears from a Jersey shore town, Maddy, her distraught single mother, begins a desperate search for her daughter. Maddy's five-year journey leads her to a bakery in Brooklyn, where she stumbles upon something terrifying. Ultimately, her artist neighbor Evelyn reconnects Maddy to her passion for painting and guides her to a life transformed through art. Detective John D'Orfini sees more than a kidnapping in the plot-thickening twists of chance surrounding Vinni's disappearance, but his warnings to stay away from the investigation do not deter Maddy, even when her search puts her in danger. When the Russian Mafia warns her to stop sniffing into their business, Maddy must make a choice whether to save one child—even if it might jeopardize saving her own.

How to Grow an Addict by J.A. Wright. $16.95, 978-1-63152-991-7. Raised by an abusive father, a detached mother, and a loving aunt and uncle, Randall Grange is built for addiction. By twenty-three, she knows that together, pills and booze have the power to cure just about any problem she could possibly have . . . right?